$P.$

T
You

—

(

DREAMS OF HOME

Megan Oliphant was a schoolgirl when the war started. After her brother's death she continued writing to his best friend, Steven Caraford. Now the war is over and she is about to go to college and embark on a promising career of her own.

Steven has longed for the day when he can return to Scotland and continue the life he loves, farming at Willowburn, with his family. He is dismayed to find he is no longer welcome there. Although it will mean long days, little money, and no security his heart's desire is to have a farm of his own. He is surprised when he meets Megan again and discovers she has grown into a lovely young woman with a promising future and admirers who can give her far more than he could. He considers pursuing a lucrative career himself and sacrificing his lifelong ambition to farm but a crisis almost tears his world apart.

DREAMS OF HOME

Gwen Kirkwood

Severn House Large Print
London & New York

This first large print edition published 2011
in Great Britain and the USA by
SEVERN HOUSE PUBLISHERS LTD of
9-15 High Street, Sutton, Surrey, SM1 1DF.
First world regular print edition published 2009 by
Severn House Publishers Ltd., London and New York.

British Library Cataloguing in Publication Data

Kirkwood, Gwen.
  Dreams of home.
  1. Country life--Scotland--Fiction. 2. Agriculture--
Scotland--Fiction. 3. Scotland--Social life and customs--
20th century--Fiction. 4. Large type books.
  I. Title
  823.9'14-dc22

ISBN-13: 978-0-7278-7943-1

Severn House Publishers support The Forest Stewardship Council
[FSC], the leading international forest certification organisation. All
our titles that are printed on Greenpeace-approved FSC-certified paper
carry the FSC logo.

MIX
Paper from
responsible sources
FSC® C018575

Printed and bound in Great Britain by the
MPG Books Group, Bodmin, Cornwall.

All the characters and places (with the exception of town names) are entirely fictitious, but I try to check any facts which apply to the period in which my novels are set.

I would like to thank the friends and acquaintances with whom I have been privileged to discuss some aspects of this novel, especially Geoff Speed, who allowed me to see private documents and information, Ian Campbell, John Davidson and Mr and Mrs John Dirrom.

Homecoming
by Betty Tindal

Away too long

Now returning,
where my roots still grow,
around my feet,
longing for familiar landmarks,
homing, to the place I'd left behind.

On the tracks
wheels measure time, distance,
Carlisle to Gretna, to Annan to –

Excitement mounts.

Then looming up
a touch of heather here,
green flank lucent in evening light,
I see Criffel,
most significant of mountains,
A way-marker, in whose shadow
Nith meets Solway.

One

'They're making a party in Dornielea village hall for the local children, Mum,' Megan Oliphant said as she helped her mother to peel vegetables for a large pot of broth. The kitchen of the old Scottish farmhouse was warm and pleasant with the August sunshine streaming through the windows and glinting on the burnished steel hinges of the blackleaded range. 'It's to celebrate VJ Day. Isn't it a relief to know Japan has surrendered and the war is over at last?'

'Aye it is, but the effects of the atomic bomb sound terrible. There will be a lot of innocent people affected by it. Surely we shall all welcome peace in the world now,' Chrissie agreed.

She was as relieved as everyone else to know that 1945 had brought an end to the fighting in Europe, and in the Far East too, but her smile belied the ache in her heart. It was a pain she and her husband, John, shared with thousands of parents who had sacrificed their sons in the name of freedom. Never again would Sam return to the Scottish hills and glens he had loved so well.

'Providing food for everyone will not be easy with the rationing,' Megan remarked with

9

surprising maturity considering her age. 'I wonder how it...'

'I think most people will be glad to do what they can to make it a real victory celebration,' Chrissie reassured her. 'I think there's to be a bonfire and fireworks. I've promised to make sandwiches and the strawberry table jelly I've been keeping for a special occasion.' She smiled at her daughter's pensive face. 'Mrs Turner asked if you would lend a hand with the wee ones.'

'Yes, of course I will.' The Turners were her parents' employers, so Megan felt she would have needed a good excuse before she could refuse, but she loved children and she would enjoy organizing games for the younger ones. 'It should be fun.' She caught her mother's eye and her green eyes gleamed wickedly. 'Does "everyone" mean "our Natalie" will be helping too?' she asked with feigned innocence.

Natalie was the Turners' only child. She had always been rather spoiled and now that she was a teenager she considered herself superior to ordinary mortals such as Megan Oliphant and her parents.

'I shouldn't think Natalie will be seen near the village,' Chrissie responded drily. 'But the Turners have only themselves to blame for her snooty ways. After all, they sent her to that private school until she was eleven, and they would have sent her away to boarding school after that if it hadn't been for the war.'

'I suppose they didn't want her to mix with us village children,' Megan said, pulling a monkey face.

10

Chrissie couldn't hide a smile. 'She's the same age as you, so you would have been in the same class. I reckon they were afraid their herdsman's wee lassie might show her up. You were always a bright wee thing even then, and you have shown Natalie a thing or two ever since you both ended up at the academy,' Chrissie added, unable to hide a note of pride.

'Natalie never wanted to play with Sam and me even when we weren't at school,' Megan said. 'She used to watch us over the garden wall, but when we asked if she wanted to join us she always turned up her nose and turned away.'

'I don't suppose Sam cared. He and Steven Caraford were inseparable from the day they started school until the day Sam died.'

'And I tagged along with them,' Megan said, chuckling, 'whether they wanted me or not.'

'I don't think they minded having you most of the time.' Chrissie sighed reminiscently. 'Steven was always a kind laddie and I always knew the pair o' them would look after you.'

'I know. I don't think any of us would have enjoyed having Natalie join us. She always gave the impression she considered her family superior to Steven's, as well as to ours, even though his father farms at Willowburn.'

'I expect that's because Martinwold is the largest farm in the parish and the Turners own it. The surrounding farms all belong to the estate and the Carafords and their neighbours are only tenant farmers.'

'I know,' Megan said, grinning, 'and as for Dad...'

11

'Being an employee? Aye, we Oliphants are even lower down Natalie's social scale,' Chrissie said, unperturbed. 'Thank goodness her father doesn't share her views. He has always treated your father fairly and with respect, and he pays us generously.'

'*If* he is generous it's only because he knows he'd never get another man as knowledgeable about cattle as Dad, or as reliable and conscientious,' Megan said heatedly. 'He knows Dad couldn't manage such a big dairy herd without you to help him too. I once heard him telling Dad what a good team you make together.'

'I suppose we do. We've always worked together since we married. It's our life and the way we were both brought up.'

As the Martinwold herdsman, John Oliphant was in charge of the Turners' pedigree Ayrshires. This entailed organizing the daily routine of milking, feeding and cleaning, as well as studying the breeding and caring for the health of the cows and their calves. Chrissie was in charge of the milk and she was scrupulous about hygiene in the dairy.

'Anyway, Dad needs to be well paid when he has to hire his own labour.'

'Aye, ye're right there, lassie,' Chrissie said. 'The dairy herd represents a good two-thirds of the Turners' income so it's a responsible job and John takes a pride in his work.'

'And not only Dad,' Megan said loyally. 'You've always had to provide board and lodging for a hired man, except when Sam left school and before he had to join the army. That means extra cooking and laundry, as well as helping with the milking yourself.'

'That's true, but we're happy enough so long as we have our health and strength, and we have a wee nest egg put by for our old age.'

'About the party, Mum, did you know every child in the parish is being presented with a victory teaspoon?' Megan asked, her thoughts returning to the local celebrations. She chuckled. 'That includes me, even though I'm not a child any more.'

'Officially you're still a schoolgirl until you go to college so why shouldn't you get one? It will be a keepsake.' Chrissie turned to look at her pretty daughter. 'Don't be too eager to be a woman, lassie. Seventeen is a lovely age to be. Enjoy your youth while you can.'

'I do enjoy it,' Megan said, a smile curving the corners of her mouth; her green eyes held a dreamy look.

Chrissie had seen that look several times recently, whenever there was a letter from Steven in fact. She liked him, they all did, but she didn't want Megan to get hurt. Steven would be twenty-three now, the same age as Sam would have been, but he would be more mature than she or John had been at that age. He had seen fighting and suffering, witnessed destruction and death, Sam's death. Would he still regard Megan as Sam's wee sister, the child who had to be watched over and protected, the little girl they had teased, and whose long auburn pleats they had tugged, making her green eyes sparkle with temper?

When the two boys were called up to join the army Megan had missed them dreadfully. She had written to Sam every week without fail. Fortunately the two friends had been drafted into the same unit and they shared Megan's letters as they shared most things, including writing the replies. Sam had never enjoyed writing. Even at school Steven had often helped him with his homework. It proved a good solution to share their correspondence and Steven wrote interesting accounts of their new life; his letters were often humorous, at least at first. After Sam's death Megan had continued to write and Steven always replied. They knew he missed Sam badly and he had certainly given the impression that he welcomed her letters more than ever. But five years had wrought many changes and all Chrissie's instincts warned her that Megan's feelings had moved on from childish hero worship to teenage fantasy, at least as far as Steven was concerned. Young love could be so wonderful and tender, but it could be painfully heartbreaking.

'So do you agree, Mum?' Megan's voice interrupted her reverie.

'Agree? What about?'

'Mum! You were miles away.' Her voice softened. 'Were you thinking about Sam?'

'No. No, as a matter of fact I was thinking about Steven...'

'So was I. That's what I was saying. All the soldiers will be coming home now and we can all get on with our lives. It said on the radio that a million soldiers will have been demobbed by

14

1946. There will be plenty of men returning to take up their jobs. So I don't think I ought to waste three years of my life at college training to be a teacher.'

'Oh, Meggie, we've been over all this before! You have such a promising future. Please don't throw it all away. You've done so well at school. You've been promised a place at college, even without the results of your recent examinations. The Rector thinks we should be encouraging you to go to university. He says you are one of the best students at the academy.'

'My education at the academy will help me to get a good job in an office, Mum, maybe with one of the solicitors,' Megan protested. 'I would be working and earning money straight away. I could be saving up, and you and Dad wouldn't have the expense of keeping me for another three years. You've done so much for me already what with school uniforms and everything on coupons, and me having to board in the hostel during the week.'

'You know we don't mind all that if it helps you to have a career and a better future. We're proud of you, Meggie. You passed the examinations to attend the academy. Mr Turner had to pay for Natalie to go there and even with all their money she hasna done half as well as you. You have the ability. Please don't waste it now. We want you to have an easier life than we've had. We want to give you every opportunity we can afford. You're all we have now.' Her mother's voice wobbled and Megan knew she was thinking of Sam and the future he would never have.

She regretted upsetting her. She knew her parents loved her dearly and wanted what was best for her, but what was best? What did her future hold?

In their letters she and Steven could discuss almost any topic under the sun, but whenever he mentioned the future it always concerned his dreams of returning to Willowburn and his ambition to be as good a farmer as his father. Did he ever think of her as part of his future or did he still regard her as Sam's young sister?

Chrissie sighed, her own thoughts following a similar path to her daughter's. Megan always used to leave Steven's letters for her and John to read, but over the past year she had begun keeping them to herself. Had they become more personal? Had Steven given her any reason to believe she was special to him, or was it Meggie's wishful thinking? They all knew about Steven's dreams for the future and his longing to get on with farming Willowburn with his father and Fred, his half-brother, but how secure was his future? There were all sorts of rumours going around about Fred Caraford and Willowburn Farm and none of them were reassuring.

She frowned, remembering the beginning of January 1940 when the call-up papers for the army had arrived for Sam. She could still picture Jim Brownlea's grave expression when he delivered the letter and she remembered the shock they all felt when Sam had opened it. As the local postman, Jim had delivered many such envelopes and he had known what they meant. They had all believed that agricultural workers

16

would be exempt, as miners were. They all knew the government had relied heavily on imported foods and that the country had no reserves and starving British people would be a sure way of gaining their submission. War had no sooner been declared than one of the liners had been sunk. British ships were finding it increasingly difficult to evade the German submarines and their lethal torpedoes. Consequently Chrissie and John, and many other country folks, had believed all available hands would be needed to produce food for the soldiers, and for the British people at home. Even now Chrissie remembered the sinking feeling when they were informed that a land girl was to be allocated to them to take Sam's place at Martinwold while he was drafted into the army.

The Oliphants had not been alone in their belief that farm workers would be exempt. There had been considerable gossip and supposition amongst the neighbouring farmers when they heard one of the Caraford brothers of Willow-burn had been called up to serve in the armed forces. The authorities had informed Eddy Cara-ford that he would only be allowed to keep one of his sons to work on his seventy-acre farm with him. The other could be replaced by a land girl. Everyone knew Eddy was proud of Steven's prowess with the ploughing and it was common knowedge that he had inherited Eddy's own qualities when it came to good stocksmanship. Fred was the elder of his two sons, but he had shown no particular interest in anything; he had refused to learn to plough and he objected to getting up early to milk the cows.

Steven longed to stay at Willowburn and continue with the work he loved and the challenges of improving the land and increasing production, but Fred had flown into rages at the mere mention that he should go. He seemed petrified at the prospect of joining the army and being asked to fight. He was adamant that he should not be the one to go.

'I'm the eldest. My place is here!' he yelled, stamping his foot as he had when he was a toddler in a tantrum. 'It's my birthright to work the farm as my grandfather and great-grandfather have done.' He chose to forget that Steven shared these paternal ancestors, and in spite of his fine words he had never made the slightest effort to pull his weight and follow their example.

There was genuine astonishment when the neighbours heard it was Steven who would be going to fight in the army.

''Twad dae Fred a power o' guid tae join the services and have a boss, so 'twad,' declared one neighbour.

'Shittin' his breeks at the thought o' leaving hame, I shouldna wonder,' announced Willy McKay viciously. He had no love for Fred's lazy arrogance and bullying ways.

'A guid day's work wad kill the young devil, if ye ask me,' an older neighbour prophesied. 'I pity Eddy being left wi' yon idle bugger at hame.'

Whatever the neighbours' views, it had been Steven and Sam who had gone to fight for their

18

country and Fred who had stayed at Willowburn.

Hannah Caraford was one of thousands of mothers who breathed sighs of relief now that peace had been declared. She looked out of the bedroom window at the fields of Willowburn stretching down the glen; she raised her eyes to the sparkle of the Solway Firth in the distance, the Galloway hills to the west and the Cumberland hills to the east. The past five years had seemed like a lifetime with Steven away in the army. She knew how he had yearned for the day when he could return to Willowburn and the way of life he loved. She was filled with joy at the prospect of having him home again, but Fred's outburst at breakfast time had certainly marred her happiness. If only Fred could have shown a little pleasure at the prospect of his half-brother's safe return. Instead he had shocked her when he'd delivered an ultimatum which could put an end to a future at Willowburn for them all, including himself.

'I tried so hard to be a good mother to him. Where did I go wrong?' she murmured aloud as she gave a final glance around the bedroom she had lovingly prepared for Steven. She was sure she had never favoured one little boy more than the other, even though Steven was her own flesh and blood. Fred's jealousy had reared its ugly head when he was only six years old, almost from the day Steven was born. He had believed she didn't love him because he had hated school and she had to make him go while the new baby stayed at home with her. His resentment seemed

19

to have grown and festered with the years.

This morning Jim Brownlea, the postman, had delivered a telegram from Steven with the news that he would be home today. Joyfully, she had read it aloud to Jim. Edna, their land girl, was still eating her bacon and egg so she had heard the news too. Eddy had already eaten and gone out to get on with the day's work and Fred had not yet appeared, being late for breakfast as usual. Edna had lost no time in telling Fred the news of his brother's return. As soon as he heard Steven was due home, he had flown into a rage and dropped his bombshell.

'If I can't have *all* of Willowburn, none o' ye will have any of it!' he stormed.

Two

Whatever the future might hold for them all, Hannah couldn't help feeling a surge of relief to know that Steven was alive and well; he had survived, he was coming home. The war was over at last. His childhood friend, Sam Oliphant, had not been so lucky, Hannah reflected sadly. Sam had been such a fine boy with his cheery smile and twinkling green eyes. Unfortunately there were thousands who shared his fate. She had prayed for Steven's safe return every day for the past five years and she would count her blessings whatever evil scheme Fred had in mind.

Even so, her agile brain considered the possibilities of foiling Fred's spite. Eddy was looking forward to his younger son's return too and she was reluctant to spoil his pleasure by telling him about Fred's threats. Yet she couldn't deny Fred was so insanely jealous he would do almost anything to prevent Steven returning to farm at Willowburn, even forcing all of them to sell up and leave, including his own father.

Hannah was already worried about her husband. Eddy seemed to have aged fifteen years instead of five since the outbreak of the war. At eighteen, Steven had willingly done more than his share of the work, but they had only realized how much more when he was no longer there. As a schoolboy he had been eager to learn everything about the animals and farming. He had learned to plough as soon as he could trudge behind the horses and hold the plough to the furrow. They had a tractor now, but Willowburn still needed him. His knowledge and his instinct could not be replaced by the land girls. None of them had stayed long enough to gain experience. Not that Hannah blamed them. One of them, a lovely girl named Ruth, had been particularly kind and considerate in the house and a hard worker, eager to learn all she could about the farm and the animals. Hannah's heart had warmed towards her from the day she arrived. She had been with them about six months, then one morning she had run into the house, sobbing as though her heart would break. Alarmed by her evident distress, Hannah had tried to comfort her.

'Whatever is wrong, dear child? Have you had an accident?'

'F-Fred...' she sobbed, and ran upstairs to her room. She had packed her few belongings and minutes later she left Willowburn, refusing all Hannah's offers of help, even a lift to the bus. Hannah had worried about her for weeks until a letter arrived, written from her home in Westmorland, where her father was a vicar. They still kept in touch occasionally and Hannah still felt some concern for Ruth.

She had confronted Fred, but he had denied that he had assaulted her.

Their present land girl, Edna Wright, appeared oblivious to Fred's idleness and she ignored his bullying tactics, but she was not a conscientious worker herself. The other girls had all found Fred's persistent advances unwelcome, but Hannah was beginning to think Edna encouraged them. She hoped Fred knew what he was about. He would not be the first man to be trapped into marriage by a scheming woman, although she had begun to think the two deserved each other.

Fred's sullen manner and his sly ways, coupled with his idleness, had proved a heavy burden to Eddy. When Steven started sending home his army pay Fred had been more jealous and disgruntled than ever, especially when she put the money into a bank account for Steven instead of adding it to the meagre income the farm was bringing in. She was glad now that she had insisted or Fred would have frittered it away. In an effort to appease Fred, and in the hope of encouraging him to be more conscientious about the care of the animals, Eddy had decided to make him a partner in the farm.

'That will surely give him a sense of pride and responsibility,' he had confided to Hannah, and she hadn't had the heart to voice her doubts. 'When he sees the results of our hard work he will feel the satisfaction of knowing he has had a share in it.'

His father's generosity had not worked any miracles with Fred. It was a thousand pities he had not been the one to go into the army, Hannah reflected as she had done many times before. The routine and the discipline might have benefited him. He might even have found a niche he enjoyed. Being a partner had only made him more arrogant and overbearing. The older he grew, the more he reminded Hannah of her cousin Eleanor's father, Fred's maternal grandfather. He had been a boorish, selfish man. He had used his authority to browbeat his wife and his daughter just as Fred was planning to use the partnership which his father had bestowed on him. His threats almost amounted to blackmail.

She was glad Eddy had left the house this morning before Fred's outburst. She could only hope he would calm down and see reason before Steven arrived home. She shook her head in despair. She had been responsible for his upbringing since Eleanor, his mother, had died a few weeks after giving birth. She had done her best, but his greed and his unreasoning jealousy made him unbearable. She had never looked for gratitude from Fred, but his latest outburst had dismayed her and left her in no doubt of his feelings towards both her and Steven.

'Aye, I hoped your "wee laddie" would never come back,' he had sneered. 'Him and his pal, Sammy Oliphant.' The callous words echoed in her head clouding her joy over Steven's return. 'Why did he have to be one of the survivors? This should all be mine! All of it, d'ye hear?' He had flung his arm wide, knocking the milk jug from the table. It smashed into pieces on the kitchen floor, a pool of milk swirling towards the hearthrug. Hannah snatched it up in time, but still Fred ranted on. 'Why should I get only a share in the farm because of him? It's mine.'

Hannah shook her head in despair. She had done her best to be a mother to him after Eleanor's death when she realized Eddy's need of her. She had asked herself thousands of times what more she could have done. Fred's greed, coupled with his insanely jealous nature, made him insufferable. She had tried to reason with him.

'But, Fred, you know...'

'Shut up! You should never have married my father. There's no place here for your bloody son. I've already told you, I shall demand my share of this place in cash. I shall force the old man to sell up to pay me out. I have a claim remember,' he gloated. 'There'll be no place for you or your precious Steven then.'

'You would force your father out of the only home he's ever known?' Hannah was aghast. 'You only own part of the stock because your father gifted it to you when he made you a partner,' she protested. 'He trusted you.'

'So what? I'll make damned sure there's no place for your brat. This is my birthright, I tell you.'

Hannah hated his mocking sneer. 'At least consider your father, Fred. He's worked hard all his life for all of us. It would break his heart to leave Willowburn after all these years and in such circumstances.'

'You know what to do then!' he jeered. 'Make sure your clever little soldier boy never comes back here to live.'

The words went round and round Hannah's head, spoiling her pleasure over Steven's homecoming. She pressed her lips together. Eddy didn't deserve this trouble. They were both his sons. If Steven still wanted to farm, and she was sure he thought of little else, then he deserved help too, especially after sacrificing five years of his young life fighting for his country.

Steven Caraford made his way to the front of the bus. He had travelled from the south by train to Annan and as he crossed the Solway Firth he felt his heart soar, as it always did when he reached the last leg of his journey and saw the familiar landscape.

'Willowburn Farm road end, please?' he requested. That was the good thing about local country buses: they stopped wherever their passengers needed to get on or off. He glanced curiously at the driver. 'Where is Mr Crosby today?' he enquired pleasantly. Old Mr Crosby had driven the local bus for as long as he could remember. The young driver looked up with a grin.

'He's my father. He said he would retire the minute I got demobbed, so here I am.' He looked at Steven's army uniform and raised his brows. 'You're not demobbed yet then?'

'I'd expected to be.' Steven grimaced. 'The world is not all peace and goodwill yet it seems. We're being drafted to Palestine.'

'Ach, that's bad luck, mate. This is Willowburn up ahead, isn't it? That's where you want?'

'Yes. Thanks.'

'What're you planning to do when you do get back to civvies then?'

'Help my parents run the farm.' Steven smiled. 'They're expecting me home for good, but I only had time to send a telegram. I havena had the chance to tell them we're being posted again.' He sighed. 'Getting back to Willowburn is all I've dreamed about for the last five years.'

'Aye, I know what you mean,' Billy Crosby said, nodding. 'I plan to build up my father's business, run trips to the seaside and up to the Highlands. I reckon folks will be ready for holidays and a bit o' pleasure now the war is over. I shall have to go slowly though...' He gave another infectious grin. 'My parents are cautious. We had to get used to taking chances and snatching opportunities in the services, but my folks have seen none o' that.'

'No, you're right there. I suppose we were lucky to survive, but now that I have, my dream begins here and I wish I could get on with it.' Steven jerked his head towards the fields and the track winding beside the burn, up the glen to Willowburn. 'Good luck.'

'Good luck to you too, mate. I hope they'll not keep you much longer. I reckon we've done our bit for king and country.'

Steven stood on the grass verge and watched the bus chug along the winding road until it was lost to sight. He breathed in deeply, revelling in the earthy scents of the countryside.

'"This is my own, my native land,"' he murmured the poet's words aloud and with feeling. The smell of freshly cut grass drifted on the summer breeze and behind him a blackbird sang in the thick thorn hedge. He slung his army pack

27

over his shoulder and turned his steps towards the farm track. His gaze took in the flowers as he passed: foxgloves and red campion, the clear blue of the harebells, the climbing vetch and white wood anemones. They were all familiar, he had passed them hundreds of time on his way to and from school, and yet it was as though he was seeing them for the first time.

Up at the house Hannah kept scanning the track, watching out for Steven, longing to see his familiar figure striding up the glen from the main road. Would he still be in uniform, or would he be wearing a demob suit? She knew better than anyone how eager he was to get back to farming at Willowburn. Her tension mounted again as she remembered Fred's threats. As soon as he knew Steven would be arriving home today he seemed to lose all sense of reason. Surely he must realize this was Steven's home as much as it was his. As for the work, a good man couldn't be replaced by a mechanical tractor.

Chrissie Oliphant took a deep breath as she considered the things she wanted to say to Megan before Steven returned.

'Has Steven mentioned when he'll be home?'

'No, he mentioned there were some kind of changes afoot, so he wasn't sure what was happening when he posted his last letter, but I know he's expecting to be home soon. He can't be much longer now.' Her eyes shone with anticipation.

Chrissie's heart sank. She had set her heart on her clever young daughter having a good career.

Even Mr Turner admired her intelligence and academic success. Megan had qualities no amount of money could buy for Natalie, however wealthy he might be.

'Megan dear, I ... er, I know you transferred your affections to Steven when Sam died, but-but does he still regard you as Sam's wee sister, do you think? Does he ever mention going out with girls in his letters?'

'No, of course not.' Megan frowned and her cheeks coloured. She had heard about some of the pleasures many of the servicemen enjoyed and she had wondered about Steven. He never mentioned such things in his letters to her, so recently she had begun to hope he might think of her as his special girl.

'Steven was always a sensible laddie,' Chrissie reflected. 'He's sacrificed five of the best years of his life fighting for his country and I expect he realizes it will be a long time before he can afford to be serious about any girl. Willowburn isn't such a big farm, and, if the rumours are true, Fred Caraford nearly got his family put out altogether. He was always idle and when he refused to plough any extra land for cereals the government officials threatened to take over Willowburn and send somebody in to plough the pasture.'

'I know all that, Mum,' Megan said. 'And Steven knows what Fred's like. He can't wait to get on with all the work that needs doing to bring the farm back to the way it used to be.'

'Oh, I'm sure the Carafords will make more progress once Steven is there to help, but his father isna so fit these days and it takes a long time to build things up in farming. There are no farm cottages attached to Willowburn either, so there'd be no place for Steven or Fred to live if they wanted to get married...' Chrissie broke off and looked at Megan, hoping for some response, something which would tell her how serious her friendship with Steven might be. Her daughter remained silent, her face pale now.

Chrissie sighed, looking at Megan's set young face. 'What I'm trying to say...'

'I know, Mum. You're trying to tell me I should forget about Steven and get on with my career, training to be a teacher. But you were only nineteen when you married Dad. You've both been happy, haven't you?'

'Yes, love, we have, but we were lucky. We've both had good health and we both came from dairy families. We were used to hard work and early mornings and living in a tied cottage and no holidays. But it was a struggle in the early days until we got our household together, especially when Sam came along and then wee Callum less than a year later. I had to take you all to the byre with me in the pram at five o' clock every morning. I've often wondered if Callum might have survived if I hadn't needed to help with the milking, if I'd been able to keep him warmer in the house...'

'Oh, Mum, don't say that. You told me yourself the doctor had never held out much hope for him reaching his first birthday because he was so small and had difficulty breathing.' She had been angry with her mother a few seconds

30

before, but now she felt a surge of love. Her parents had always done their best for her and Sam, and now she was all they had. All their hopes and dreams rested on her. They had made sacrifices for her to go to the academy and stay on at school until she was nearly eighteen instead of leaving school at fourteen as Sam and Steven had done. She couldn't let them down now by refusing to go to college, but three years seemed like an eternity. When she was being honest with herself she had to admit Steven had never hinted at a future together.

Steven frowned as he neared the boundary to Willowburn. There were puddles and wet patches in the low meadow. Obviously a drain needed repairing, maybe more than one. He had often helped his father dig around wet patches which suddenly appeared where there had been none before. They usually found a broken clay tile which was allowing water to spout to the surface and form a pool instead of being carried away to a major drain.

'Draining is like your mother and her mending basket, laddie,' his father had once told him. 'A stitch in time saves nine. Replacing a broken drainage tile now will save a lot more digging later.' Steven smiled at the memory. There was nothing he had loved better than following his father, whether he was working in the fields or with the animals. His father was fifty-nine but the last time Steven had been on leave he had thought he had looked much older, he'd seemed so worn and weary. The war had affected everybody in different ways.

His heart sank when he remembered that instead of being home to stay he would have only forty-eight hours leave. He must make time to call on the Oliphants. He knew they would have questions about Sam's death and he had always felt as welcome in their home as he was in his own. He wished Sam could have felt as welcome at Willowburn, but Fred was six years older than them and big for his age. He had resented their friendship and bullied them unmercifully. Thoughts of Fred brought his mind back to the farm and the rumours which Megan had mentioned so tactfully in one of her letters.

His mother had written regularly too, but she had avoided telling him of the trouble with the War Agricultural Executive Committee. This was a group of men selected to check on farms, ensuring they were producing the maximum amount of food. They were generally known as the War Ag and they had authority to replace inefficient farmers if they couldn't, or wouldn't, comply with the demands and needs of the nation.

He noticed other signs of neglect: hedges overgrown with gaping holes at the bottom, places where a ewe or a young stirk could squeeze through and go wandering off, maybe never to be seen again. There were all sorts of stories about animals being stolen and slaughtered for sale on the black market. He knew there was a scarcity of fencing wire, but there were other ways of making the boundaries proof against straying animals. The hedges needed to be cut and layered so that branches could be woven in and out of upright stems. The layered branches would sprout and grow upwards to fill the gaps and thicken the hedge.

Steven's hands clenched. He longed to test his own skills and have the satisfaction of seeing thick, neat hedges as a result of his labour. His father was skilled at such tasks, but they took time and energy, and he had too much to do already. Fred had always avoided anything involving physical effort. Steven often wondered why he had been so insistent on being the one to stay at the farm instead of joining the army. Knowing his half-brother as he did, he was sure Fred would have wheedled his way into driving a lorry or chauffeuring a brigadier around.

A low groan of pain interrupted his reverie. He paused, frowning. He heard rustling, then a long, low mooing. He peered through the hedge and saw a cow lying stretched out on her side. She was the only animal in the field, which was unusual for a start. Steven realized she was trying to give birth to her calf and finding it impossible. He moved further along the hedge until he came to a gap big enough for him to squeeze through. He saw at once that the young cow was exhausted and must have been calving for some time. He quickly realized the problem was because the calf was coming backwards, its hind legs already straight out, but no amount of pushing by the cow was enough to release the rear end of the calf. Swiftly he stripped off his battle dress and rolled up his sleeves.

'Steady then, old girl. Let's see what we can do...' Steven spoke soothingly, his voice low and deep. Gently he bent beside her and felt around, trying to ease the passage. It was dry. Another sign that the cow had been labouring too long. He could have done with some soapy water. The tail of the calf was facing the wrong way. Gradually Steven managed to manipulate the tail head and ease the skin around about. Then he grasped the hind legs, wishing he had ropes to help him grip and pull. He increased the pressure gently and waited for the cow to push again. Once he had eased the calf's rear out, the calf came away easier than he had dared to hope. Quickly he cleared the skin from the calf's nose and mouth, surprised and pleased to see it was still alive. He rubbed it vigorously along its side until it gave a cough and a tiny bellow of protest, then he dragged it round to the front of the cow with a feeling of immense satisfaction. The cow was too exhausted to get to her feet, but when she saw her calf she sniffed and raised her head enough to give it a lick. Evidently spurred on by this, she managed to sit up and lick her offspring. Even as Steven watched, the calf raised its head and shook it vigorously. Soon it would be on its feet, he thought with a smile. He wiped his hands as well as he could on the grass and hooked his jacket with his finger as he scrambled back through the hedge to retrieve his kitbag and go on his way. He knew if that cow had been left much longer the calf would certainly have been dead and possibly the cow too. Even Fred couldn't say he hadn't earned his keep during this visit.

As he rounded a bend in the track, the familiar farmstead came into view and his heartbeats quickened. More than ever now he longed to get back to Willowburn and the life he had loved. Judging by the signs of neglect he had already seen, they were badly in need of another pair of hands. His heart sank as he recalled the words of his commanding officer. Apparently they would be spending the next twelve months or more in Palestine. How was he going to break the news to his parents?

Outside the back door at Willowburn, the old pump was still working, so he set his kitbag beside the door while he washed the remaining mucus and bloodstains off his hands and fore-arms before he crept into the house. His mother was bending over the fire, stirring something in a cooking pot, when he entered the kitchen.

'Hello, Mum,' he greeted her softly, and reached behind the door for the roller towel to dry himself. There was a lilt of laughter in his voice. As he had anticipated, she swung round, spoon in hand, her face beaming in welcome, her eyes full of love. He was unaware of it, but he had inherited his mother's smiling blue eyes and expressive face, as well as her thick wavy hair, but he had his father's square, determined jaw.

'Oh, Stevie, it's good to see ye, laddie!' She hugged him tightly, then stood back to examine him. 'Surely ye canna be growing still! You must be head and shoulders taller than your father and Fred now.'

'I've been taller than them for a while,' he said. 'I expect I'm broadening out a bit more.'

'Aye, maybe that's it. The bus must have been on time for once. Mind you, Joe Crosby's son took over the driving this week. He's home frae the war too. He doesna gossip to the passengers as much as his father. He doesna know them all yet.'

'Mmm, I met him. He seems a pleasant fellow. There weren't many other passengers on the bus today.'

'There'll be plenty on the afternoon bus. Standing room only, I shouldn't wonder. Friday is market day in Annan, in case ye've forgotten. The women will be in for their shopping. Mind you, the rationing is getting worse instead o' better. We thought things would be easier once peace was declared, but I suppose it will take time to take effect.'

'It will take a long while before things are back to normal,' Steven said gravely. 'There's so much destruction everywhere.' He frowned, not wanting to spoil her pleasure yet with his news. 'Rations or not, something smells good.' He sniffed appreciatively.

'Mr Kerr saved me a nice wee piece o' lamb to welcome ye back. After all that travelling you'll be ready for a cup o' tea. I'll shove the kettle over the fire and it'll be ready in a jiffy.'

A few minutes later they sat opposite each other at the scrubbed kitchen table with Hannah plying him with questions and Steven eager to hear what was happening on the farm. He noticed how the light died out of her eyes and for a moment he thought she might burst into tears the way her lips trembled. Instead she pressed a hand to her mouth, then continued to chatter, almost feverishly, until they heard his father's measured tread crossing the flagged floor of the back kitchen. Steven watched speculatively as his mother rose to her feet and reached for another cup and saucer for his father.

'Eh, you're home at last, laddie. Na, na, dinna get up.' His father strode to his side and squeezed his shoulder. 'It's good to see you're back safely,' he said gruffly.

Steven knew he ought to tell them he was not here to stay, but the talk moved on. They both plied him with questions. He knew they were pleased to see him home, and yet he was certain there was an air of constraint.

'The farm is all right, isn't it?' The words burst out of him.

'Of course it is,' his mother answered swiftly. 'Why shouldn't it be?'

'I ... oh, I just wondered. I know I've been away, but I do read the papers and we do hear things. I know the government have been pressing everybody to produce as much food as possible. One or two farmers near to where we were stationed have been moved out of their farms. Some of us were sent to help get the harvest in when we were back in camp.'

He couldn't bring himself to tell them he knew the War Ag had threatened to take over Willowburn. It would distress his mother if she realized it was common knowledge down in the village and no doubt all around the parish.

'We've a grand litter o' piglets,' his father said. 'They were born three days ago, twelve of them and all alive and suckling. D'ye remember the gilt we had the spring you had to go into the army?'

'Yes, I do. We called her Sally.'

'Well, this sow was one of Sally's first litter. They're all good mothers.'

'Speaking of mothers, there was a cow calving in Keeper's Field. The calf was coming backwards. She looked as though she'd been calving for some time.' He didn't hear Fred come in. 'I gave it a pull. Surprisingly the calf was alive, but I wondered if the cow had hurt her back or if she was just exhausted. She didn't get up while I was there – she'll probably need a drink...'

'Interfering already are ye!' Fred growled angrily. He was still wearing his boots although they were thick with manure from the midden. 'Have you told him?' he demanded. There was no welcome home from Fred, Steven noticed, not even a hello.

'Oh, Fred, Steven has only just arrived, and look at your boots!'

'Don't nag,' Fred glowered. 'He's been here nearly an hour. I saw him coming up the road.'

Home an hour after five years away, Hannah thought, and Fred resents even that.

'What have you to tell me?' Steven asked, looking round the three faces in turn.

'Nothing,' his mother said shortly, setting her mouth in a tight line. 'It's nearly dinner time. We can talk later.'

His father was silent, rubbing his forehead, his

eyes fixed on the table top. Hannah had only given him an edited version of Fred's threats, but he still looked troubled. She knew how much he hated quarrels.

'If you won't tell him, I will.' Fred jerked his head towards the door.

Steven wondered how he could have forgotten his half-brother's sullen manner. He remembered how frustrated and angry he used to get when Fred failed to do his work and then blamed him. His mouth tightened, but he rose and followed Fred outside. He was beginning to understand the reason for the tense atmosphere now. He guessed Fred was bent on making trouble of some kind, almost before he had put a foot in the door, but there was nothing new in that. He had no inkling of how much trouble though.

Three

Steven stood outside the door of the sturdy stone-built farmhouse where he had been born and stared incredulously at his half-brother. He couldn't believe Fred could dictate who should, or should not, live at Willowburn.

Their father had followed them outside and Steven turned to look at him. His heart sank at the sight of his father's haggard face and the look of defeat in his eyes. He looked beyond them to the fields sloping upward towards the head of the glen. They were green and fresh after the city streets with their shells of burnt-out homes and factories. How often he had dreamed of the Scottish hills and glens during the hellish years spent fighting for his country and for the freedom of people like Fred. It was the dream of returning to the farm and the home he loved which had sustained him in his darkest hours.

In the tense silence he could hear the familiar gurgle of the burn which ran by the stack-yard boundary beyond the house. He had played there as a boy. He knew every inch of Willowburn Farm. He had spent the first eighteen years of his life here. As soon as he was fourteen he had worked in the fields and the farm steading. All that was before the war. It seemed like another life.

His eyes narrowed as Fred's words echoed in his brain as clearly as they had five years earlier.

'I'm not going to the army. I'm staying here. He'll have to go.'

'But Steven isn't eighteen yet.' He recalled his mother's anguished protest.

'I don't care. He'll be eighteen in two more weeks.' He knew Fred had wanted rid of him even then.

Steven had a mouth curved for laughter, but his upper lip curled in contempt as he brought his gaze back to Fred's sullen face. Had his brother hoped he would perish in a foreign land as so many others had done – as his best friend Sam had done? He would never forget those last hours he had lain side by side with Sam, knowing his friend was dying. No medal on earth could replace a friend like Sam.

Anger began to burn in him. He drew himself to his full height, his chin jutting out proudly. Fred's piggy eyes narrowed warily and he took a step backwards. Steven raised an eyebrow. His blue eyes flashed.

'Coward,' he hissed between his teeth. 'I suppose you always were, but I didn't know that when you were bigger than me. Did you hope I'd be killed like Sam? Did you hope I'd never return home?'

'So what if I did?' Fred sneered. 'There's no place for you here. We don't need you. Willowburn is my birthright...'

'The farm still belongs to Father, and he's my father too, or had you forgotten?' Steven looked at his father, willing him to raise his eyes from contemplation of his boots. His father's gaze remained lowered.

'I've made him a partner in the farm,' he muttered slowly. 'I would have made you a partner too, laddie...'

Steven's heart sank. 'Would have?' What did his father mean by that? A shaft seemed to pierce his heart as he stared at his father's bowed head. Willowburn was the place he had remembered when he wakened and before he went to sleep, the home he had fought for and dreamed about.

'Father?' he prompted with a note of desperation.

Slowly his father raised his head, lifted his cap a little to scratch his forehead. It was a habit Steven remembered well. 'Father?' he repeated.

'We-ell...' Eddy Caraford cleared his throat. 'I've told Fred we need ye, lad. I'm not so young as I was. There's more work than we can manage, especially now the land girls will all be going home. I expect Edna will be leaving now the war is over.'

'No!' Fred protested hotly. 'I told you! I don't need him here. There's no place for him. We've got a tractor now. Anyway, Edna is staying.'

'None o' the other girls stayed very long,' his father reminded him sharply, 'and they can't do the work Steven can do.'

Fred flushed. He considered himself the boss and he was not used to his father disagreeing with him these days. He sensed Eddy's disapproval and his resentment of Steven increased.

'If he's so good at working, he can get a job somewhere else, him and his medals and promotions,' he jeered.

He talks as though I'm not here, Steven thought, and guessed Fred had stated his opinions before.

'We ought to be keeping more cows and an extra sow or two...' Eddy said, meeting his younger son's direct blue gaze. 'You were good with animals, Stevie. And I remember you learned to plough when you were only thirteen...'

'We have the tractor for ploughing now,' Fred exploded. 'I've stayed here and worked while he was roaming about the world. Willowburn is mine. You said you'd tell the landlord to make me the tenant before *he* came back.'

'I can't tell the landlord anything, I can only ask. It's out o' my hands,' his father said firmly. 'When I mentioned having a joint tenancy the land agent said you needed to prove yourself. He preferred to wait until we knew whether Steven was coming back.'

'It's nothing to do with him! You could have persuaded him to put my name on the tenancy if you'd tried,' Fred argued belligerently.

'I made you a partner to encourage you to pull your weight, Fred. It hasna done much good so far,' Eddy said wearily.

Steven's gaze darted from one to the other. He saw the strain in his father's face and he felt defeated. Fred had always been a bully, but he never thought he would try bullying their own father, even less that he would succeed. Thinking back, he knew Fred had always expected to get his own way, even when he was young. His mother reckoned it was because Fred had lost his own mother when he was a baby and his father had tried to compensate for the loss. Fred had played on that from an early age, manipulating their father to get what he wanted. If there was no place for him at Willowburn, what would he do when he was finally demobbed? Farming was the only thing he'd ever wanted to do. He could have attended Dumfries Academy and had an education as his mother had wanted him to do, but he had longed to work with his father, learning to plough and to sow, to shear the sheep and help with the lambing.

Even at school Fred had been lazy and he had never been clever enough to pass for the academy, but he hadn't wanted his younger brother to have the opportunity either. Steven allowed himself a glimmer of a smile as he remembered it was the one and only time he had welcomed Fred's support. He grimaced at the memory now.

Fred glared at him. 'You needna smirk. Farming's not the easy life you had here before the war,' he said. 'It's bloody hard work and...'

'Nay, lad,' their father protested, 'farming was never easy and Stevie buckled to and got on with things. He was keener to farm—'

'He knows nothing about the way things are now,' Fred snapped, glaring at his half-brother. 'There's men in suits who come breathing down our necks, telling us what to do, ordering us to plough pasture that's never been ploughed before and—'

'My heart bleeds for you,' Steven drawled with rare sarcasm. 'I told you the first time I

44

came on leave that farmers all over the country were ploughing up pasture, and even ancient parkland, to grow more cereals because the country needs food, but you wouldna even keep an extra cow. It's only the inefficient farmers who have visits from the War Ag. I heard they'd threatened to turn you off. You would never have bought a tractor or learned to plough if the government hadn't made you grow cereals. It was only my mother and her poultry that saved you from being turned out of Willowburn.' Steven regretted his outburst immediately when he glanced up and saw the colour had drained from his father's face. He looked more like seventy-nine than fifty-nine. The war had not been easy for him. He guessed Fred still didn't do his fair share of the work.

'I suppose *she* told you that,' Fred snarled furiously, jerking his head towards the kitchen.

'No, Mother never mentioned it. She didn't need to tell me. It's the talk of the county. Even when I asked about it in my letters she avoided answering. You should know she's always been loyal, even though...'

'Loyal! She'd had one husband, but she still poked her nose in where it wasna wanted as soon as she got a chance o' trapping another fool into marriage.'

Steven saw his father wince, but he jerked upright.

'Nay, that's not the way of it...' But Fred ranted on.

'She should have stayed a widow and got on with being a bloody housekeeper. That's all she

45

was good for, but she wanted...'

'Fred! That's enough of such talk! You should be ashamed.' Eddy Caraford's face was chalky white now, and he sagged back against the house wall, one hand clutched to his chest. For once Steven was too incensed to pay attention to his father. In the army he had earned respect for his self control, his handling of tricky situations. He rarely panicked or lost his temper, but his half-brother's insults regarding his mother made his blood boil. Fred's sneering smirk was the last straw. His fist struck at the thick lips almost before he realized what he had done.

'Why you...!' Fred wiped a hand across his split lip. He saw blood. Instantly he lowered his head. Just in time Steven remembered that nasty habit of old. He jumped aside, remembering how painful Fred's headbutts had been in his tender young stomach. Now he wanted to laugh as his brother sprawled heavily on the dusty yard. Only the anger still coiling in his stomach prevented his mirth.

'Dinna fight. Ah, lads, there's nae need to fight. Surely there's been enough o' that,' Eddy said in genuine distress. He had never known Steven strike his elder brother before.

'You're right, Father.' Steven grimaced. 'I've seen enough to last me a lifetime.' He looked more closely at his father's drawn face and saw the way his hand clutched his chest. 'Are you all right, Father?' He frowned in concern.

'Aye, I'll be fine in a minute. Hush now, lad-die, don't worry your mother.'

'We-ell, if you're sure you'll be all right?'

46

'Aye. We could do with ye back home, laddie, but I canna do with fighting. I'm too old for...'

'Don't worry, Father. I haven't had chance to tell you yet. We've been drafted to Palestine. We'll be gone about a year to eighteen months, I think, then...'

'Good riddance!' Fred muttered, glowering at him as he dusted himself down.

Steven ignored him. 'It will give us all time to decide what's best, Father.' He squeezed Eddy's shoulder, grabbed his khaki haversack and slung it over his back. 'I couldn't promise we wouldn't brawl again –' he glanced at Fred in contempt – 'and I dinna want to cause you a heart attack, so I'll not stay where I'm not wanted.'

'Eh, lad, ye canna leave. This is your home and your mother is cooking ye a good roast dinner.'

'It's better if I go now, Dad. Tell Mother I'll see her before I leave and I'll explain about Palestine. I didna want to go there, but now I see the way things are it will give me time to think about the future.'

'But ye've only just arrived. Where are ye going?'

'Where I've always been welcome.' He strode off down the lane, away from the farm, away from the place he had dreamed of during the war.

He regretted his outburst and his loss of temper as he walked down the road away from Willowburn. Deep down he was hurt that his father seemed to accept Fred's decisions. After all, they were both his sons and he and his father

47

had worked well together. He had always thought they were close. He hadn't even said goodbye to his mother and he regretted that now, but his pride wouldn't allow him to return while Fred was around. He would go back and see her when he had calmed down. He wished she had told him that Fred was a partner in the farm. She ought to have warned him that Fred was angling after getting the tenancy in his own name too. Maybe he should have realized Fred wouldn't want him back at Willowburn after five years of being an only son. Right now he felt rejected, cast adrift like a ship without a rudder. What did the future hold for him now?

His commanding officer had tried to persuade him to make a career in the army, but his heart wasn't in it. He craved for the countryside; he wanted animals around him and land to plough and work and care for. He wanted to farm.

It was a mile and a half down to the main road and another couple of miles to Martinwold Farm, where the Oliphants stayed. They lived in the original farmhouse which adjoined the dairy, and the byre beyond it. As owners, the Turners occupied a newer, more imposing house, which was separated from the farmyard by a large garden. Steven knew Sam's parents would give him a warm welcome and a bed for the night. He had spent many happy hours wandering around Martinwold when he and Sam were boys, but he had seen Sam's parents only once since his friend's death. It had been a brief, sad visit. This time he knew they would have questions to ask, and they would want to hear all he could tell them about Sam's time in the army, including his death.

Throughout the years of fighting he had never allowed himself to think the Germans might win, not even when Sam and so many other fellow soldiers had been killed. Returning home to Willowburn had been his goal. Now there was a gaping hole in his life. He felt hollow inside as though his heart had been ripped out of his body. What had he to look forward to? He had been bitterly disappointed when he heard his regiment was being posted to Palestine instead of being demobbed. Now it didn't matter. Nothing mattered. His future was blank, his hopes and dreams smashed. He felt like sitting down under the hedgerow and bawling his eyes out, but he hadn't done that since he was six years old after a particularly nasty bit of bullying from Fred and one of his pals.

It was hot and he was thirsty and dejected. He had no reason to hurry anywhere. He laid his knapsack down on the grassy bank and scrambled through a gap in the hedge. He knew the fields like the back of his hand. At the bottom of a gentle slope the burn flowed crystal clear. At least he could quench his thirst. His stomach rumbled and he thought himself a fool for leaving before he had sampled his mother's home-cooked dinner. Even with the rationing she always managed to make a good dinner and he knew she would have been hoarding some small treat for his homecoming. Fred's glowering face was enough to turn the milk sour and it would probably have given him chronic indigestion, he thought, consoling himself. But he should have taken more time to talk to his mother. He knew his father loved him in his own way, but not enough to cross swords with Fred apparently. But his mother had always loved him unreservedly, even when he had scraped the knees out of his first pair of long trousers when they were brand new. He smiled wryly at the memory as he ran down the slope to the burn.

He knelt over the side and cupped his hands, drinking in the cold clear water. He sat there gazing around him, but all this seemed no longer part of him, or his dream for the future. His heart felt like a stone. Somewhere a blackbird was singing. He lay on his back with his hands behind his head, gazing up into the summer sky, his mind wandering hither and thither as he struggled to come to terms with the empty future.

Four

Steven had no idea how long he had lain there thinking. He thought he heard someone calling his name and sat up and listened.

At the top of the slope his mother stood waving to him. He got to his feet. There was no way he could go back with her after fighting with Fred. He had seen the distress in his father's lined face and he had a feeling he was not as well as he ought to be. He cursed himself for losing his temper.

'Wait there, Stevie,' his mother called, 'and I'll come down to you.' She disappeared through the hedge. When she reappeared she was carrying a basket. He climbed towards her, taking the basket in one hand and steadying her descent with his other.

As they reached the burn again, she said breathlessly, 'I still ride my old bicycle so I hoped I'd catch you up, laddie. I would have missed you if I hadn't seen your knapsack by the hedge.'

'I'm sorry, Ma, I didna mean to leave without saying cheerio.'

'I know that, Steven.' She sighed heavily, then looked him in the eye. 'I knew Fred would stir up trouble, but I didn't expect he'd start before

51

ye'd had time to get your feet under the table and have a meal.' She frowned anxiously as her eyes searched his face.

He summoned a grin.

'Is that food you've got in the basket? It smells good.'

'Aye, it is,' she said, pursing her lips. 'The dinner was nearly ready, but Fred couldn't wait until we'd eaten. I've left them to get their own. It's roast lamb, but I didn't wait for the tatties to finish cooking in case I couldn't catch up with ye. Such long legs ye have now.' As she talked she lifted a clean tea towel from the basket and unfolded it. Steam was still coming from the hot lamb and he could smell the home-baked crusty bread.

'Eh, Ma, it makes me ravenous just to smell it.'

'Eat up then. I've brought plenty. They'll have to scrape the bone for once. It serves them right – well, it serves Fred right. You'll have to forgive your father, laddie. He never could stand up to Fred's demands, even when he was a wee bairn, and now that he's become a man Fred bullies Eddy as he used to bully you and poor Sam. I've tried to love him, indeed I did love him when he was a bairn, but it's hard to respect a person who is so idle and selfish.'

'Never heed Fred, Ma. Enjoy your dinner while it's still hot. It tastes like nectar from heaven.'

'Nectar indeed!' his mother scoffed, but he knew she was pleased.

He grinned at her.

'You always had a fancy way with words, Stevie. Mr Forsythe, the schoolmaster, said so. He thought it was a sin when we didn't send you on to the academy.' She sighed. 'Fred was jealous even over that. I don't know where he's sprung from. He's not a bit like your father. His mother was my half-cousin and Eleanor was a sweet, gentle lassie so he didn't take it from her either. Mind you, her father was an arrogant bully of a man. There's no wonder his wife died so young. I expect Fred has inherited his ill nature frae him.' Almost without pausing for breath, she said, 'I brought you a bottle of tea.' She fished a woollen sock from the basket and extricated a bottle of tea. 'Drink it up, laddie. I'll make myself a fresh cup when I get back. There's apple pie for afters. I couldn't bring the custard.'

'Aw, Ma, you're spoiling me,' Steven said, and stretched out a strong young arm to give her a hug.

'You're a good laddie,' she said huskily. 'I'm glad ye're safely home after all that fighting. Sam was a grand laddie too. Your father and me both took it badly when we heard he'd been killed, but I thought I'd die when we got the telegram to say you were missing, presumed dead.'

'Aye, well, it seems none of us should presume anything,' he muttered.

Hannah heard the bitterness in his voice and knew he had good reason for it. He was the one who should have been allowed to stay at home to work the farm. Her mouth firmed, but before she could speak Steven told her his news.

'The fighting isna over for our battalion yet, Ma.'

'Where are they sending you? To India? Steven? Tell me...'

'No, we're to go to Palestine...'

'Oh,' Hannah said uncertainly. 'I'd hoped this would be the end and you'd come home.'

'Home?' Steven raised an ironic eyebrow. He grimaced and wished he hadn't spoken when he saw his mother's eyes bright with tears. Patches of pink coloured her cheeks and she swallowed hard. He couldn't think of anything to say that would comfort her now that Fred had knocked the bottom out of his world. One thing was certain, he'd never be able to call Willowburn his home while Fred lived there.

Hannah laid her hand on his arm. His mother was always soft and smiling, but now her lips were set in a firm line. He'd never seen her look like that before. He didn't realize he sometimes had that same determined expression.

'Listen, Steven, I've suspected for a long time that Fred didn't want you back at Willowburn. He's always been jealous, but he's grown greedy lately. He wants everything for himself. I've tried to talk to your father about it, but he hoped things would get back to normal once you returned home. I think that's why he didn't try to persuade the land agent to include Fred's name in the tenancy. Fred has been pestering for it almost since the day you left. He wears your father down with his lazy ways and his constant demands. Eddy was looking forward to you coming home, but he will see now that there would be nothing but quarrels, even if Fred doesn't carry out his threat to force him to sell up and pay him his share in cash.'

'Is that what he's planning if I return to Willowburn? That's blackmail!'

'It's jealousy and spite.'

'But he'd have no job either if he forced father to sell out. The money wouldna last him long.'

'That's what I said, but he muttered something about going to Canada with his share. Edna, the land girl, has relatives there and she talks a lot about visiting them.'

'I'll bet Fred wouldn't stay long if he went,' Steven scoffed. 'He'd soon find he had to work for a living anywhere else.'

'It would do him good. Your father is working far too hard, trying to make up for his idleness. I fear it's taking a toll on his health. We've both worked far harder than Fred to keep the farm going, and he knows it, but he doesn't care.'

'Most of the people round about know it too, Mother.' He patted her hand. 'Fred is the only one who never realizes how lucky he has been.'

'I know that. He says some nasty things, but I'm not afraid of Fred. Although your father appears to give in to him, I trust him to do what's right for both of you in the end. He's a good man, Steven, but he tried too hard to make up to Fred for losing his own mother and he's grown up expecting to always get what he wants.'

'Well, he certainly doesna want me back at Willowburn, that's for sure. It's all I've thought about for five years and now –' he turned to look her in the eye – 'when I see he's still the same,

55

and when I remember how frustrated I used to get, I can understand Father looking so tired and weary. I'm almost glad we're being sent to Palestine after all. It will give me time to think about my future. Maybe my CO is right, perhaps I should make a career in the army,' he added bitterly.

'Oh, no, Steven! No, you'd never be happy away from the land and your animals.'

'We'll have to see about that.' He had spoken on the spur of the moment, and with bitterness. He frowned when he saw her face. 'I didn't mean to upset you, Mother. I've never wanted to make a career in the army, but I see now that Fred and I would never get on together at Willowburn, not even if Father did make us equal partners. In fact, I expect that's what Fred is afraid of. I should have known how it would be, especially after he's had things his own way for five years.'

'We understand how you feel, laddie.' His mother sighed. 'I don't trust Fred. I think he'll keep making threats whenever your father willna let him have his own way. I wish he'd never made him a partner.'

'I don't think he'll make Father sell up to pay him his share as long as he's sure I'm not coming back to Willowburn,' Steven said slowly. 'He knows which side his bread is buttered.'

'I suppose you're right. He would like everything in his name, including the tenancy. He's not satisfied with just a share, he wants it all. He wouldn't get that if he left, would he?' Steven saw she looked happier with that idea. 'I doubt if the land agent would grant him the tenancy anyway. He must notice things have deteriorated.'

'I hope Father would never leave everything in Fred's name, for your sake, Mother.' He looked at her with concern. Willowburn was her home too and her life.

'Don't you worry about me, Stevie. I've survived worse blows than anything Fred could do.'

'You mean when you were widowed?' Steven asked curiously. His mother had often talked about her childhood, but he knew nothing of her adult life before she had married his father, except that she had been married young and lost her husband. 'Was it very bad?' he asked softly.

'It seemed like the end of the world at the time.' Hannah's eyes held a faraway look. 'Tom was far too young to die.'

'Tell me about it. How did he die?'

'He was at the mill that day. He worked there during the week. A man drove in with a wagon. Something startled the horse. It bolted. The wagon tipped over and pinned Tom underneath. It was so simply done and so final.' Her voice shook, but she raised her chin and carried on. 'It was an accident and I had to accept it was God's will, but we had only been married two years. I was twenty-one. I wanted to die too.'

'Oh, Mother...' Steven laid his hand on hers; they were clasped together on her knee. She gave him a wavering smile.

'It's all right, laddie. I got over it in time and at least we had two wonderful years together. That's more than some people will have had during this awful war.'

'I suppose so,' Steven agreed doubtfully. 'Where did you live then?'

'We had a smallholding, not far from Willowburn. It was only six acres, but Tom used all his savings to buy it and he worked four days a week at the mill. We had some pigs and I kept a lot of poultry and a house cow. We grew vegetables for sale. And we had two beehives and sold the honey. It was hard work, but we made a living and were happy. We had both known Eddy and his family for years and I was delighted when he married my cousin Eleanor. Her mother had died when she was ten so she had often stayed with us. We were like sisters. Her father was a horrid man so she liked to get away.' She sighed heavily.

Steven remained silent, hoping she would tell him more.

'When Tom was killed, Eleanor and Eddy couldn't have been kinder, or more helpful, but it was not the same without him, working all day on my own, then the long winter evenings with nobody there. I know it would have been a struggle, but I felt it would have been better if I'd had Tom's child to love. I was dreadfully restless and unhappy, and very lonely.'

'No wonder,' Steven said quietly. 'I had no idea.'

'Well, I survived, as people do. I sold the holding to the estate, and our few animals. I put the money in the bank and got a job. I'd never done anything except help my parents on their farm, and then on our own holding, so I wasn't trained

58

for anything, but I was always good at cooking. I went to work for an elderly man as a live-in housekeeper. He had a fairly big house, but he was quite frail and he needed company and looking after. His two sons both worked in England.' She sighed. 'Life has a strange way of working out. Two years later Fred was born and within the month Eleanor was dead from some sort of infection. Old Mr Matthews was very frail by then and he had been kind to me so I couldn't leave him in the lurch to go and help Eddy. He paid various women to care for Fred. None of them stayed long. Caring for a young baby is a twenty-four-hour job. Eddy had his own work to do and he had adored Eleanor so he was absolutely distraught. About four months later old Mr Matthews died and Eddy asked if I would go and keep house for him.

'He paid me, of course, and it seemed the right thing to do for both of us, but especially for Fred. He needed a routine instead of a string of changes and strangers. He was a lovable wee boy then and – and I suppose I was needing someone to love.'

'There's nothing lovable about him now,' Steven muttered.

'I know. As I said, I think he's taken after his grandfather. It's taken Eddy a long time to accept that, but recently I think he's come to see it for himself. I'd been there nearly five years before Eddy and I decided to marry and make the arrangement permanent. Neither of us expected another grand passion. We'd both had that and the sorrow of parting.' She chewed her lower lip.

'Did you ever regret getting married a second time, Mother?'

'Oh, no. I'd never have had you if I hadn't married Eddy. Anyway, we knew each other well and he was always a kind man, far too decent to deal with the likes of Eleanor's father. We got on well together and were good friends; we had a lot in common and we respected each other. I'd grown to love Fred too. I couldn't imagine ever wanting to leave him. I suppose we both spoiled him a bit,' she added ruefully. 'He started school and he hated it. Then you came along. That's when the jealousy and resentment started I think. I believe he thought we loved you more than him because we made him go to school while you could stay at home with us.'

'And the jealousy has been growing ever since if you ask me,' Steven said darkly. Then he smiled, a swift lightening of his whole face which always transformed him. 'I'm glad you told me how things were for you and my father.'

'Yes. Remember, Steven, there are many kinds of love. Over the years your father and I have found something deeper and possibly stronger than the passionate young love we'd both known. We have a lot to be thankful for.'

'Well, I certainly don't want to be the one to rock the boat then. I don't want you and Father to quarrel over me, nor do I want to cause him to have a heart attack by quarrelling with Fred.'

'Don't worry, laddie. In spite of his faults and the way he's indulged Fred, Eddy loves you and me too much to give him all his own way.

Sometimes it's easier for him to shut his eyes to Fred's faults, but I can't do that this time. You're my own flesh and blood and I shall do what I can to help you.'

'I don't want to become a bone of contention, Mother. Anyway, I've been reminded of the frustration I used to feel with Fred. It's funny how you forget the things you don't want to remember. I saw how it upset Father too. That's why I came away.'

'I don't want him upset either, but I know how much you still yearn for a farm, so listen to what I have to say, Steven, then you can decide what to do with your future. When the First World War finished, the government divided some of the largest farms into smaller holdings for men returning from the war who wanted to farm. They were all good farms. There's some near Annan, and Gretna and Canonbie, aye, and near Dumfries. I expect they're in lots of counties. They're in the hands of the Department of Agriculture for Scotland. They must take on new tenants when the old ones die or move on to a bigger farm.'

'You mean the same as the Councils have smallholdings to let in England?'

'I don't know what they do in England, but I reckon you must stand as good a chance of getting a holding to rent as anyone else when you've spent five years fighting for your country. I've thought about it a lot, even before Fred dropped his bombshell this morning. I'd like you to make enquiries and put your name down if they have a waiting list. I expect you'd need references, but maybe your sergeant will speak for ye, and the schoolmaster.'

'Ah, Mother, I'd need more than references to get a tenancy, however small the farm might be. I'd need to buy stock to make an income before I could pay the rent. I'd need at least one horse and cart for the work.'

'You stand as good a chance as anybody,' Hannah said, tilting her chin stubbornly.

'Tell me what an army sergeant or a school-master would know about farming and whether I'd be any good at it?' Steven gave a hollow laugh. His mother meant well, but she was confirming what he knew already. They had all accepted there was no place for him at Willow-burn if Fred had anything to do with it.

'Maybe Mr Turner, the Oliphants' boss, would give ye a farming reference? He knew you and Sam when you were lads. He knows you've always wanted to be a farmer.'

'He might, but even if I got an interview for a smallholding they'd want to know how I planned to get the stock to start up. It would take nearly everything I've saved to even buy a horse and cart.' He sighed heavily. 'I saved most of my pay, but sometimes we needed to spend money on beer to drown our troubles or to commiserate with a pal.'

'I understand that, Steven.' She patted his arm. 'And I've taken every penny of the money you sent home to the bank. I have a wee bit saved of my own too. I still have some of the money from the sale of Tom's wee holding, and Mr Matthews left me two hundred pounds in his will. Tom had a life insurance, for when we grew old...' She lifted her eyes to the trees and fell silent.

Steven was too sensitive to interrupt her memories. Eventually she brought her gaze back to him. She plucked a piece of grass and twirled it round and round.

'Where was I? Oh, yes, Tom's insurance. We never dreamed it could end so soon. The insurance company paid up though. I'd paid for the funeral from the wee bit we'd put by. I put everything in a bank account and it's been there ever since. Fred bullied your father into buying the tractor so that took most of Eddy's spare capital. He was probably right about us needing a tractor with the extra cereals and ploughing, but he's sly. He realized Eddy didn't have the knack for tractor driving, but he's still had nearly all the horse implements converted to fit on to it. So, you see, your father is dependent on him. Fred has him exactly where he wants him now. And he hardly does any work unless it involves sitting on the tractor.'

'Things are worse than I realized,' Steven said slowly. 'No wonder Fred feels he's in charge and doesn't want me back. Working the tractor would be no problem to me. I had to learn to drive a truck as soon as we got into the army.'

'He'll know that. So you see why I want you to try for a smallholding and use my bit o' money to buy stock and equipment. Your father knows about it and he says it's up to me what I do with it. Until today I know he longed for the day when you would return to Willowburn, but he'll see what I've been trying to tell him now.

There'd be no peace for any of us. If anything happened to me, Eddy would get my bit o' money, but I know what Fred is like and he'd winkle it out of him if he found out. So you see I'd rather you put it to good use, Stevie.'

'Oh, Ma, I can't take your money!' Steven protested.

'Yes, you can. If you add it to your savings, you'll have enough to get started in a small way. You'll still have a struggle, but I think you'd manage if you could get a tenancy. Anyway, I'd already written to the bank manager before Fred delivered his ultimatum. I want you to go to Annan and sign the papers to move it into your name. If you're going to Palestine make sure you go to the bank before you leave.'

'No, Mother, I canna do that. You might need it yourself...'

'I'll cross that bridge if I come to it. I don't think your father is in the best of health. He gets so tired and that means he depends on Fred more than ever. If Fred gets his wish, he'll have the tenancy of Willowburn in his own name, or at least he would if the agent would agree. I don't think they get on so well. Do you remember how Mr Griffiths used to drop in for a cup of tea and a chat with your father when he was passing?'

'Yes, I remember him well.'

'We hardly ever see him now, and when he calls Fred is always sullen or argumentative with him.'

'That's a pity. Father seems...' He frowned. 'He seems smaller somehow, not frail exactly, but not the strong, fit man I remember walking

64

all day behind the horses.'

'I know that, Steven, and that's all the more reason for me to do what I can for you and get my own affairs sorted. You needn't worry about me. Ever since Fred refused to join the army, and you had to go, I've seen how things are with him – selfish to the backbone. I've worked hard to keep our heads above water and anything I've earned I keep for myself. I buy a few national savings stamps at the post office every week when I take eggs to the village. The sixpenny stamps are building up a little nest egg. You mark my words, laddie, if you look after the pennies the pounds will look after themselves.'

'I understand how things are with Fred, but I still don't want to take your money, Ma.'

'I'd feel better if I knew it was in your name. I hope I never need help, but I know you'd never see me starve. I'd have no faith in Fred though, for all I've done more for him than I have for you. There's a callous streak in him. In fact –' she lowered her voice although there was no one but the birds and an odd rabbit to hear – 'he was downright brutal with one of the land girls we had and she was a lovely lassie. There doesn't seem to be any tenderness in him.'

'Mmm. I heard there'd been some gossip. Things were hushed up, weren't they?'

'Aye, her father is a vicar in England and he didn't want any trouble or unpleasantness for his lassie. But don't sidetrack me. Will you put your name down for a government smallholding, Steven?' Her tone was brisk now. 'I believe they're the only solution if you want to farm, unless you want to get a job as a dairyman? They get good money when they are in charge of a big herd, like Mr Oliphant.'

'Aye, the money is good, probably better than being a small farmer, but you're never your own boss. The cattle never belong to you however well you care for them, and it's seven days a week all year round for somebody else's benefit. When you take on a big dairy, like the Oliphants, you have to provide your own helpers too. I'd always expected we would all work together like that at Willowburn, for our own benefit.'

'I know, laddie, but promise me you'll get your name down as soon as you can? Even if you are going to Palestine there's no harm in letting them know you're interested.'

Five

The first person Steven saw as he made his way up the road to Martinwold Farm was Mr Turner, the owner. He was driving a Ferguson tractor with a young woman perched on the mudguard. He scrambled up the grassy bank to let them pass, but the tractor drew to a halt.

'Hello, young Steven,' Mr Turner called jovially. 'You're home in time to help with harvest, I see. I didn't expect you to still be in uniform though.'

'Afternoon, Mr Turner. I haven't been demobbed yet. We're being drafted to Palestine.'

'Ah, that's a shame, lad. I expect you were looking forward to being home and getting on with farming Willowburn,' Mr Turner said sympathetically.

'I thought I was, but it seems I'm not needed there.'

'Not needed? By God you are needed all right...' He broke off, frowning when he realized Steven was serious.

'Maybe not wanted is what I should have said,' Steven said abruptly, and began to walk on.

'Eh, wait a minute, Steven. I know your father has missed you and he could do with you back home. Britain will need all the food we can produce for years to come, and Willowburn could do a lot better if that brother of yours would get himself out of bed in the mornings and get on with things. You were always the worker, I remember. They need you, lad.'

'Yes, I could see that, but we could never work together. Fred made it clear he doesn't want me interfering.' He hesitated, remembering his mother's advice. This might be the best opportunity he would get to talk to Mr Turner. 'Mother thinks I should try to start up on my own when I do get demobbed. She suggested I apply for one of the government smallholdings.'

'Did she now?' Mr Turner seemed surprised. 'We-ell, maybe she knows best,' he added thoughtfully. 'I don't imagine Fred is the easiest of fellows to get along with and if there's strife in the home it doesn't make for peace and happiness.'

'I suppose not.' Steven grimaced. It seemed everyone thought he should leave Willowburn to Fred. 'If I do put my name forward for a government holding, I should need a reference from someone in farming...' Steven flushed and broke off.

Mr Turner looked at him keenly.

'If you're asking me for a reference, Steven, you can give my name, but let me know about it. We need young men like you if this country is to get back on its feet. There are changes ahead, and there'll be opportunities for young men keen to work hard.'

'Thanks, Mr Turner.' Steven smiled for the

first time. 'You don't think it's such a daft idea then?'

'No-o, but you'd need capital to get started.'

Steven nodded and would have moved on, but the girl leaned down and waved her hand in front of his eyes. Natalie Turner was not used to being ignored by young men.

'Don't you remember me, Steven?'

He blinked and looked at her properly.

'Natalie...?' The last time he had seen her she had been about twelve, the same age as Sam's little sister. As he looked at her generous curves and fashionable hair, done up in a roll around her head, he shook his head in disbelief. 'You've grown up. You and Megan were starting at the academy the last time I saw you.' He blushed faintly as he met her glance and what some of his army pals called that 'come-to-bed look'.

'Natalie's left school now,' her father said. 'She's going to secretarial college at Carlisle in September. I've been telling her women are training for careers and earning their own living these days.'

Steven smiled. The Turners had been wealthy landowners before the war and he guessed Mr Turner would be making the most of every opportunity when food was in such demand. He treated his farm as a business. As an only child Natalie would make some man a wealthy wife. He doubted if she would need to earn her own living for long.

As he walked on towards the farm steading and the old farmhouse where the Oliphants lived, he pondered on the changes war had brought. At one time Mr Turner would never have been seen in work clothes, or on a tractor. Megan and Natalie had never mixed in the same circles as children, but Natalie's parents had not wanted her to be too far away from home during the war, so they had paid for her to attend Dumfries Academy. Megan had passed examinations to go and both girls had lived in the hostel during the week.

He quickened his pace, wondering if Megan had changed as much as Natalie Turner. She had never sent him a photograph of herself. She had been smaller, more slightly built, than most of her school friends. He still pictured her in her short navy gymslip with her hair in two thick auburn pleats. He grinned as he remembered how strenuously she'd denied her hair was auburn whenever he'd teased her. Megan had had freckles and a snub nose and big green eyes with thick lashes the same colour as her hair. He wondered whether she was still as shy. Her letters had always seemed confident and mature, even when he and Sam first went away. She had a way with words. They had looked forward to her weekly letters. He would always be grateful that she had continued writing to him after Sam's death. She brought things to life so that he could picture them in his head; she made him smile when she described the idiosyncrasies of people they knew.

'Steven!' Before he could knock on the door, Mrs Oliphant had flung it open and was holding out her soft plump arms to give him a hug. 'I was just filling the kettle when I saw ye walking across the yard. Oh, but ye're a smart young fellow in your uniform.'

'Come on in and let's have a look at ye, Steven,' her husband called from the kitchen. 'You're just in time for some tea before we start the milking.'

Steven followed Mrs Oliphant along the stone-flagged passage into the big kitchen. It had an open range like his mother's with a rag rug in front of it and a big tabby cat curled up asleep. John Oliphant came round the table and grasped his hand in a fierce grip, reaching around to pat his back with his other brawny arm. Megan stood back smiling shyly and he seized her and swung her around as he and Sam had always used to do, but as soon as he felt her soft curves against him he realized she was just as much a young woman as Natalie Turner, even if she was small and slender and less sophisticated. He had made her blush with his exuberance. Her mother made things worse.

'Hey, lassie, there's no need to blush for Stevie,' she said with a chuckle. 'You've known him all your life.'

'I was surprised that's all. You didn't say you were coming home so soon in your last letter, Steven.' Megan's brows were raised in question.

'No, I hoped I'd be demobbed and home for good, but we're being sent to Palestine.'

'Aw that's a real shame,' Mrs Oliphant said. 'Draw in your chair, laddie. Pass another cup and saucer and a plate, Megan. Help yourself to a scone. There's not much butter with the ration-ing. We have to scrape it on and scrape it off again, but we've plenty of home-made jam.'

'Aye, help yourself, lad,' John Oliphant said. 'I'm right glad to see you. Your ma and pa will be disappointed ye're not home to stay though. They could do with ye at Willowburn now your pa's not so fit.'

Steven stared at the scone on his plate and didn't answer. Megan looked up and saw the pulse throbbing above his jaw, she noticed the stern set to his mouth too. She exchanged a glance with her mother.

'I expect Fred's annoyed because you're not coming back to do the work yet?' Chrissie Oliphant prompted.

'He's more annoyed that I didna get myself killed like Sam.' He couldn't keep the bitterness out of his voice.

'Oh, Stevie, dinna say that!'

'Well, it's true. He's made it plain there's no place for me up at Willowburn. He would like to get the tenancy in his name.'

'The laird will never agree to that! What does your father say?'

'Father doesn't seem able to cope with him. He always hated arguments.'

'He always gave Fred too much of his own way,' John Oliphant said, 'even when he was a laddie. Nobody can make up for him losing his mother. It was God's will and he couldn't have had a finer mother than yours.'

'I – er ... I blotted my copy book.' Steven looked-ed up almost defiantly. His gaze met Megan's. 'I punched Fred in the face, gave him a split lip. It upset Dad.'

72

'It would. You were always such a calm laddie. What happened?'

'Fred meant to butt me in the stomach, as he used to do at school. I stepped out of the way in time and he sprawled in the dust.' He saw laughter spring to Megan's bright eyes and knew she didn't hold his brawling against him. He glanced warily at her father. He had clapped a hand to his mouth, trying to stifle a roar of laughter.

'I'd have loved to have seen it,' John gasped. 'Fred's had that coming to him for a long time.'

'He has that, big bully that he was with you and Sam,' Mrs Oliphant said. 'Don't worry about it, your pa will get over it. He's lucky you've waited so long to stand up to Fred. Now you eat up. I'll fill up your tea cup.'

'When do you have to go back?' Megan asked.

'Tomorrow night. To be honest I wondered if I could cadge a bed for tonight. I don't want...'

'Of course ye can have a bed, laddie,' Mrs Oliphant assured him.

'Ye're more than welcome, lad. I'd enjoy a proper chat with ye.'

'Yes, I know,' Steven said, nodding.

John Oliphant would want to know how his only son had died. Well, he could tell him truthfully; Sam had never lacked courage and he had died bravely like the man he was. Those few last whimpers and his own tears were between him and Sam and God above, though he had wondered if there was a God as he and Sam had laid side by side waiting for darkness to fall.

'Can I lend a hand with the milking?' he asked. 'I'll need to keep in practice.'

73

'You certainly can, laddie,' Chrissie Oliphant said. 'I'll find you some of John's clothes to change into. They might be a bit short in the arms and legs. I can't believe what a fine figure of a man you are these days.' She went to find him a pair of wellingtons.

'We'll give you a rest from the milking to-night, Mum, if Steven will carry the milk instead of me?' Megan grinned up at him. 'That's a harder job than milking the cows, but it's my job until I go to college in the autumn. It saves us having a boy living in and Dad pays me the wages instead. It will help with my expenses for books and things.'

'I don't mind carrying the milk to the dairy.' He looked down to her upturned face and chuckled. 'At least I shall manage to pour the milk over the cooler. However do you reach it?'

'Dad fixed me up with a wooden trestle to stand on.'

'I should think it's still hard work lifting buckets of milk up to the pan?'

'I'm tougher than I look.' She tossed her head and her eyes sparkled.

'You're not much taller than when I went away, not like Natalie Turner. I didn't recognize her.'

'You've seen Natalie?'

'Yes, she was riding on the tractor with her father. She had her hair in a roll. You've cut your hair too, Megan.'

'I couldn't keep schoolgirl pleats for ever.'

'No, I suppose not. It suits you anyway, the way it curls round your face and on to your shoulders, but I shall miss not having those long pleats to tug.' He smiled, then sobered. 'You should have sent me a photograph.'

'I pin it up in a bun under a hat when I'm in the byre.' She pulled a face at him. 'Like Granny McKnight used to do? Do you remember?'

'Yes, I do. That was before Mr Turner installed the milking machine. I remember she milked cows as fast as everyone else, even your Dad, although she was an old woman. She was always threatening to chase Sam and me with the byre broom, or tan the hide off us.'

'Funny,' she said innocently, 'she never threatened me.'

'That wee dimple still betrays you when you're trying not to laugh, Megan. You never could keep a straight face when you played tricks on Sam and me.'

The light died from her eyes.

'I still miss him terribly, Steven. We haven't even a grave.' Her voice wobbled and he wanted to hug her. At one time he would have done so, but he remembered the feel of her and her blushes. She was growing up.

'I miss him too, Megan,' he said quietly. 'I reckon I always shall.'

'I know.' She swallowed, then gave him a wavering smile. 'Come on. I'll show you where the milk pails are.'

'Sometimes we were sent out to farms to help with hay or harvest when we were in camp. I never missed a chance to look around. I've dreamed of nothing else but getting back to farming. Now...' He shrugged his shoulders.

75

'Now my future is blank.'

'All the local farmers think you should have been the one to stay home and farm. None of them have much respect for Fred, or his methods, but that doesn't help, does it?'

'No. I'd like a good long walk around the old haunts after the milking is finished. Will you come with me?'

'After supper, I'd love to. That's if you're sure you don't want to go dancing. There's one on at the village hall?'

'I'd rather go for a walk,' he said, smiling, 'but if you...'

'No, I just thought you might be missing the social life.'

'I can't tell you how much I've longed for the hills and glens of home or how much I appreciate your letters, Megan. I hope you'll still have time to write to me when you go to college?'

'Of course I shall.' She blushed shyly. 'I love getting your letters too.'

Steven was kept busy emptying the milking units and carrying the milk to the dairy while Megan and her father milked the cows down each side of the byre. By the time they had washed down the stalls and taken the cows back to pasture they were hungry for supper.

'Natalie Turner called while you were all at the milking,' Mrs Oliphant told them as she carried a steaming dish of cheese pudding to the table.

'Natalie? She called here?' Megan echoed in surprise.

'I think she hoped to catch Steven. Her father is letting her borrow his car tonight. She wondered if you would like to go to the dancing in Dumfries.'

'Oh, Megan,' Steven said contritely, 'you should have told me you and Natalie usually go to the dancing.'

'I've never been to a dance in town.' Natalie Turner barely gave her the time of day. Her heart sank. It was Steven that Natalie wanted to drive to the dancing and she was used to getting her heart's desire.

'It's all right,' Mrs Oliphant said. 'I told Natalie you had other plans, but I said you would telephone her if you decided to go to the dance instead. She said something about using her influence to help you with your little project, Steven.'

'Did she...?' Steven frowned. 'I asked Mr Turner if he would give me a reference if I put my name down for the tenancy of a government smallholding,' he explained.

He had been looking forward to an evening walk with Megan up the glen and through the long wood where they used to gather the bluebells and play at pirates, but he didn't want to offend the Turners. He didn't know who else he could ask to give him a farming reference. He didn't know anyone else with Mr Turner's influence so it wouldn't do to offend his only daughter.

Six

Steven was quiet as they all tucked into their evening meal, but when they were all replete he began to tell John Oliphant about his mother's suggestion that he should try to get a government smallholding to rent. He had always been able to talk to Sam's father and he knew he would give him an honest opinion.

'She wants to give me her savings to help me get started with a couple of cows and some hens and a sow, but I can't help feeling it would be wrong to accept her offer, even if I was lucky enough to get a government holding.'

John Oliphant considered for a minute or two.

'I reckon your mother is right. You should stand a good chance of getting the tenancy of a government holding after serving your country for the past five years. As to the financing I'm sure she knows what she wants to do with her own money, Steven. She obviously feels she can trust you. I'd say it would be all right to accept her help so long as you never forget what she's done for you, and you're willing to help her in return if ever she needs you. Sometimes we have to take a chance in life.'

'That's what young Crosby said about his father's buses,' Steven said. 'He's full of plans

78

too. I hope I'd never neglect my own mother, whether I borrow her money or not,' he continued slowly. He looked around the table at them all and nodded his head. right then, I'll make enquiries about the government holdings and if you can put up with me until Monday morning, I'll go into the bank and do as she asked before I catch the train back to camp.' He sighed. 'It will take forever to build up a farm like Willowburn from nothing.'

'You have a lifetime ahead of you, laddie,' John Oliphant said. 'Deal with things one at a time and plan carefully. You'll be proud to be your own man and I reckon you'll do all right for yourself one day.'

'I agree with John,' Mrs Oliphant said, nodding. 'Besides, Steven, supposing you did come back to live at Willowburn. How would you and Fred get on when you both want to get married? Where would you live? Could you ever agree about the work, or about money? I don't think Fred would be easy to deal with. I think your mother is wise to separate you now, even though your father would have liked you at Willowburn and even if it does mean a struggle at the beginning. I agree with John. I'm sure you'll work hard and make a success, and you'll have the satisfaction of knowing it's all your own efforts.'

'I hadn't thought as far ahead as needing a house to get married,' Steven admitted ruefully. 'I can't imagine anybody wanting me until I make a decent living.' He sighed unconsciously. 'Goodness knows when that will be, if ever.' His brooding gaze slid to Megan, then away again.

'You'll probably do better than you think, lad,' John Oliphant consoled him, 'and at least you'll be free to make your own decisions.'

'If I'm lucky enough to get a tenancy,' Steven reminded him.

'I wonder how Natalie thought she could help you get one,' Chrissie mused, curiously.

Steven looked at her. 'I've no idea.' He shrugged. 'I asked her father for a reference. Do you think he'll change his mind if we don't accept his daughter's invitation to go dancing?'

'Mr Turner isna likely to go back on his word,' John Oliphant said. 'We don't always agree about the way he likes things done with the dairy herd, but he's a man you can respect. He ruins that lassie of his, but if he's the man I think he is then he'll never allow young Natalie to influence him about business affairs.'

Steven glanced across at Megan as she sat listening and watching in silence. Her lovely eyes were troubled. He longed to banish the shadows.

'I would rather go for a walk than spend the evening in a stuffy dance hall. What about you, Megan?'

'I'd like to go for a walk,' she said promptly.

Chrissie looked at her daughter. It was as though a light had been switched on inside her, the way her smile lit up her face and made her green eyes sparkle. Her mother's heart felt a pang of misgiving. Megan had known Steven all her life, but she was so young. She had her career to consider and, on his own admission, it could be years before Steven could afford a wife. First love could hurt so much.

'I'll have a wee nap while you two are out,' Mr Oliphant said, 'then we can have a chat when you come back, Steven. Eh, but it's good to have you here, laddie.'

Natalie Turner couldn't believe her eyes as she turned from preening in front of her mirror and glanced out of her bedroom window. Steven and Megan were strolling up the sloping field where the cows were grazing. Why wasn't Steven getting ready for the dance? She stared incredulously. They stopped every now and then to talk. How easily they laughed together. Even from a distance Natalie could sense the warmth and companionship between them, but she couldn't believe any young man could prefer a walk with the daughter of her father's herdsman rather than go dancing with her. Fury swelled in her chest, her eyes narrowed and her lips pursed into a thin line. Steven Caraford hadn't been given a choice, that had to be the explanation. Chrissie Oliphant had not passed on her invitation. She'd deliberately kept it to herself. Silently she vowed to have her revenge. The Oliphants needed reminding they were only employees and employees could lose their jobs and be made to move on.

It was a beautiful summer evening and Steven felt calmed by the sights and sounds around him. Megan's easy companionship was like balm to his troubled spirit. They had known each other too long and too well for any pretence between

81

them. Even their silences were comfortable. He gave a sigh of contentment.

'I can't wait to be finished with the army and start living my own life back here in Scotland, even if there's no place for me at home.'

'But you have done well in the army, Steven.'

'I only did what scores of others have done,' he said simply. 'I didn't do it for promotion. I wasn't even sure I wanted to be a corporal.' He gave a wry grin. 'One good thing though, the pay went up from three shillings a day to four and three pence and it hasna been so bad. The others didn't seem to bear any resentment.'

'I'm sure your fellow soldiers respect you.'

'I hope they do because the CO hinted I could be in line for promotion to sergeant now we're being sent to Palestine. I was too disappointed at not being demobbed to pay much attention. All I'd thought about was getting back to Willow-burn.'

'I know. Your letters told me that, Stevie,' Megan sympathized, 'but perhaps your mother is wise. You would have hated constant quarrels. I think you will be happier farming on your own, even if you do have to start off small.'

'Ye-es, the more I think about it, I think you're probably right.' He sighed. 'It was a shock to find I wasna welcome though. One good thing is if I do get made a sergeant I'd get double what I earned as a private, and I have even more incentive to earn extra money now. It will be a long struggle, but I think I should enjoy the challenge and the freedom to make my own decisions.'

Steven helped Megan over the fence into the

wood where they had spent so many happy hours as children. It was inevitable that their thoughts should turn to Sam. They sat for a while on the little hill in the middle of the wood. It had been a fortress and a pirate ship, a desert island and a castle under siege. In fact, in their childish imagination, it could have been anything.

'Poor Megan –' Steven grinned, lifting her hand and stroking her fingers – 'we always left you to tag along, didn't we? Come on, we'd better make a move. Race you to the edge of the wood.'

'Oh,' Megan gasped as they reached the far side. 'I'd forgotten we'd have to cross the burn and they've taken away the planks we used to use.'

'We'll just have to jump across then,' Steven said. 'We had to face worse obstacles than this in the army.'

'It's all right for you with your long legs,' Megan said indignantly, giving him a poke in the ribs.

'Be good or I shall leave you here,' he teased her, just like he and Sam had done when they were children.

Megan sighed. 'We had some happy times, didn't we?'

'Aye, and nobody can take away our memories, Meggie. Right, I'll roll that big stone into the middle of the burn. Then you can jump from it to the other side. I'll go first and catch you.'

'All right, but if you let me fall in I shall get my own back,' she warned, her eyes glinting. She watched Steven leap across with ease. She stepped across to the stone and balanced precariously. She still had more than halfway to jump.

'I don't think I can jump that far.'

'Of course you can,' Steven reassured her. 'Grab my hand as you jump.'

Megan jumped, Steven grabbed her and together they fell backwards on to the bank of the burn, breathless and laughing. Their eyes met. Time seemed to stand still. Steven was intensely aware of Megan's small soft body lying half on top of him. He knew by the flare of emotion in her eyes that she was fully aware of his feelings, and possibly even shared them. But this was not the time or the place to find out, certainly not with Megan, his trusting young friend. He scrambled to his feet and helped her up. There was a slight tension between them now, but he kept hold of her hand and they continued their walk. Gradually the old easy familiarity was restored, at least on the surface, and when Natalie Turner saw them returning they were walking hand in hand, happy and smiling, with the ease of old friends.

Steven enjoyed the weekend. He accompanied Megan and her father to morning service at the parish church. He thought his mother might be there too, but she wasn't. The Turners were in their usual pew at the front and he knew he had offended her when Natalie scowled at them on her way out.

On Monday morning he was up early to help Megan and her father with the milking before he left. The Oliphants were allowed to keep a pig and a few hens and they had free milk and potatoes, all as part of their wages. Chrissie made them a huge breakfast of porridge and cream, followed by her famous tattie scones, bacon, eggs, mushrooms fresh from the field and newly baked soda scone.

Natalie rarely ventured near the farmyard, but she was determined to waylay Steven on his way from the dairy. She had got up earlier than usual too.

'Father says you're leaving today. I'll drive you to the station, Steven,' she said.

He looked at her, one eyebrow raised and his head on one side as he tried to decide whether it was a command or an invitation. Then he gave a crooked smile.

'That's kind of you, Natalie, but I must decline your offer. You see I have some business to do before I catch my train and I made my appointment to fit in with the bus. Another time perhaps?' Without waiting for an answer he went on his way back to the byre with the empty buckets leaving Natalie frustrated and angry.

Later, he offered no objections when Chrissie Oliphant suggested Megan might accompany him on the bus. 'Miss Byers has ordered some knitting wool for me and you could collect it while Steven is seeing to his own affairs. It would be nice for him to have someone to wave him off at the station.' She turned to Steven. 'It will be a long while before we see you again, laddie. Just remember there'll always be a welcome for ye at our fireside.' Chrissie was sincere in her offer, but she was secretly relieved that Steven would be tied up with the army for another eighteen months. While he was away she hoped Megan would settle down at teacher training college rather than throw away the opportunity of a good career.

Steven thanked them for their hospitality.

'You've earned it, lad. You've helped at every milking,' John Oliphant said. 'You've given Chrissie a wee holiday.'

'You have indeed, Steven.' She hugged him warmly and he sensed the tears were not far away as she pretended to brush a speck off his uniform. He guessed she was thinking of Sam.

Megan enjoyed the journey on the bus down to Annan, squashed between the window and Steven. It made her heart flutter to be pressed so close against him, but when it came to saying goodbye at the station she couldn't hold back a few tears. Steven cupped her face in his hands and kissed them away.

'Goodbye, Megan,' he said huskily. He looked down into her face as though memorizing every feature. 'Write to me?'

Megan trembled, praying fervently that he would come back safely.

'Of course I will,' she whispered, then to her eternal joy Steven bent his head again and kissed her mouth with lingering tenderness. The train was starting to chug away before he jumped on board and she stood, waving, until it was out of sight.

About a week later John Oliphant hurried up to Martinwold house in agitation.

'Can I speak to Mr Turner please? It's urgent,'

he gasped the moment Natalie answered his ring on the doorbell.

'I'll give my father your message,' she said haughtily. 'He's engaged right now.'

John hesitated, but he couldn't argue with her.

'It's urgent,' he repeated anxiously. 'One of our best Ayrshire cows was lying dead in the field when I gathered in the others this morning. I think she had milk fever, but your father should know right away. He'll need to call the vet to do a blood test in case it's anthrax. I can't move her until we know, but we don't want to leave her lying there any longer than necessary for passers-by to see.'

He would have waited at the door for Mr Turner's instructions, but Natalie nodded, her eyes gleamed and she turned away and closed the door in John Oliphant's face. She knew how much store her father set on appearances. He would hate anyone to see that his herdsman had left dead animals lying around so she deliberately ignored the urgency of the message. She skipped upstairs to her bedroom, instead of returning to the dining room where Murdoch Turner was reading the morning paper and sipping leisurely at his third cup of coffee.

Mr Turner enjoyed riding his big chestnut hunter and he frequently galloped over his own fields, often stopping to inspect a fence or examine a crop, or simply to enjoy his property. It was after midday when he galloped home along the edge of the cow pasture next to the road. He was dismayed when he saw a dead animal, now bloated and grotesque only twenty yards from the roadside. He was furious. How could John Oliphant have missed her? He must have known she was missing from her stall when he brought the rest of the herd in for the morning milking. Why had he not searched for her? Why had he not reported it? Was the man growing careless? He rode angrily into the yard, slid from his horse and hammered on the farmhouse door with his whip.

Chrissie Oliphant answered immediately. She saw at once that something had annoyed their boss and her heart quailed. She knew the dead cow was one of the best in the herd, but she had shown no sign of milk fever when John had looked round the herd just before bed time.

'Where's your husband?' Mr Turner demanded.

'He-he's been hanging around in the yard all morning waiting for ye. He-he didn't want to move the cow in case it was anthrax. He thought you would get the vet to see her first, though he's fairly certain it was milk fever. She's only been calved a couple of days.'

'How the h—?' He bit back the expletive as he focused on Chrissie Oliphant's anxious face. He frowned. 'How could I get the vet until he told me the...?' He avoided another oath with an effort. 'When he never told me the cow was dead?' he snapped.

'B-but he went up to the house straight after milking to tell you...' Chrissie said in bewilderment. 'He was upset. He doesn't like to lose a cow any more than you do, Mr Turner.' Chrissie pulled herself erect, bristling in defence of her husband now. John was a good, conscientious herdsman. 'Shall I go and find him for you?'

'No, I'll look for him in the yard.' Mr Turner hurried away.

He was still seething when he returned home for his dinner. Natalie would never forget to give him a message like that. She would have known how important it was to deal with the dead animal immediately. John Oliphant must have forgotten and now he had the effrontery to blame his daughter.

Natalie was not at home for lunch so he couldn't get the matter off his chest. When he did see her later that evening she didn't answer his question directly.

'You've had the Oliphants a long time, Father,' she said. 'They probably regard the cows as their own property by now and think they can do what they like. Perhaps it's time they moved on? Gosh, I'm tired, I think I'll have an early night.' Without waiting for a reply she went off to her room with her new library book.

Murdoch Turner was still annoyed with his herdsman when he went to bed. He was getting undressed when he realized Natalie had not actually answered his question about John Oliphant leaving a message. He admitted it was not the death of the cow that had vexed him. Such things happened in the best of herds and at least it had not been anthrax. It was the fact that it had lain out in the field on public view most of the day and John Oliphant had failed to see it, or had forgotten to tell him. He scowled and stopped in the middle of slipping his braces from his shoulders.

'What's wrong, dear?' his wife asked. 'You look like a thundercloud. Have you got indigestion?'

'Of course not.' He looked at her. 'Do you know if anyone came to the house asking for me at breakfast time this morning?'

'Only John Oliphant. Natalie attended to him. There was no one else as far as I know. Why?'

'I see...' He frowned thoughtfully. 'Do you think Natalie has it in for the Oliphants for some reason?' he asked slowly. 'She's hinted more than once that I should replace them.'

'Oh, surely you wouldn't do that! They're a decent family and both John and Chrissie are hard workers. They care for the cattle as though they were their own.'

'Yes, you're right of course.' He felt calmer now. He tried to treat his workers well, but he didn't like people letting him down. He felt it was a reflection on his judgement. 'I wonder what they've done to upset Natalie,' he mused.

His wife smiled. 'I doubt if the Oliphants have done anything except have a handsome young soldier as their guest. Didn't you notice how Natalie mooned about looking out for Steven Caraford when he was staying with them? Your daughter is no longer a wee girl, Murdoch. She's a young woman and she's not used to being ignored, however unintentionally. I suspect Steven was a challenge to her vanity. You'd better get used to her eyeing up young men. Now, finish getting undressed dear and get to bed.'

The following morning, Mr Turner's anger had cooled, but he let Natalie know he knew about her subterfuge and he didn't like it. His sense of justice reasserted itself too, much to her chagrin. He lost no time in apologizing to his herdsman, but he could not admit to John Oliphant that his daughter had been at fault.

The months flew past and Megan settled into her new life at college, much to her mother's relief. Chrissie knew the regular exchange of letters with Steven still continued, but she didn't mind that so long as Megan got through college and completed her teacher training. She was as proud of him as she would have been of her own son when Megan told them he had received promotion and was now Sergeant Steven Caraford.

Megan shared the news with Maryanne, a fellow student who came from the other side of Dornielea village. They always travelled to and from college together. The other students teased her about her mystery boyfriend in the army. They didn't know Steven always kept his letters light and friendly, with no hint of the deeper feelings Megan longed for. The memory of his kiss at the station was like a secret treasure.

Seven

The eighteen months passed quicker than either Steven or Megan had thought possible. Megan was almost halfway through her second year at college and looking forward to going home for Christmas when Steven wrote to tell her his battalion would be home soon. She wondered how he felt and what he meant to do. She knew he had written to the Department of Agriculture ages ago, asking for his name to be included in a list of prospective tenants for one of their small-holdings. The reply had been brief and dis-appointing, advising him to write again when he had a firm date for his return. His most recent letter was more optimistic.

I have written to Mr Turner to remind him of his promise to give me a reference, and I'm fairly sure my commanding officer will give me a good character reference, although he has asked several times if I wouldn't reconsider and make the army my career instead. He doesn't understand how I long to get back to Scotland, and how much I want animals of my own to care for and land to keep them on.

Dearest Megan, there are other things I

long for too, but I'm in no position to mention them until I know what the future holds and until I can offer security. I fear that may not be for a long time yet.

Megan read the letter repeatedly. What did Steven mean by other things he longed for? Was it possible he returned her feelings and yearned for her as she did for him? Was she reading too much into his letter? What if he loved someone else and had to wait until he had more money? What if...? Megan tortured herself with questions, her hopes soaring one moment and drowning in doubts the next.

The local land officer rated Steven's chances of renting a holding as low to nil as far as he was concerned. Even though he knew Steven would be home soon, he didn't bother to include his name in the shortlist for the senior officer's consideration when a holding became vacant.

'I thought I'd seen an application from a young soldier on top of the pile?' the senior land officer remarked during a discussion of the applicants. 'What was his name? And why isn't he on the shortlist?'

'His name is Caraford. I didn't think he would be up to making a living from farming after six and a half years in the army,' his colleague replied.

'But he was farming before he joined up according to a letter I read.'

'I believe so. I don't know the fellow, but I do know his brother and his parents. Their farm was almost taken over a couple of years ago. The brother is an idle, sullen fellow. He refused to plough up permanent pasture to grow his quota of cereals until we ordered him to do it.'

'But everybody was asked to plough extra land for maximum food production.'

'I know that. He knew that. He didn't care. The father seemed a decent enough fellow, but I got the impression the son was in charge. The wife rears poultry and keeps pigs. It was mainly due to her efforts they got away with a warning. I don't suppose the brother in the army will be any better, especially after being away so long. Shall we discuss the next applicant?'

'No, not yet,' the senior officer said, frowning at the papers he was studying. A few minutes later he looked up. 'My younger brother was killed during the war,' he said slowly.

'Aye, we lost a lot of good men. Do you...?'

'He didn't want to join the services, but they took him anyway. He wasn't in a reserved occupation you see.'

'Mmm, it was hard luck for some of them.'

'It was, whatever way you look at it, Mr Wilson. Those who have survived have sacrificed years of their young lives for their country. According to one of the references, this young fellow –' he glanced at a sheet of paper – 'Sergeant Caraford, would have preferred to stay home and farm. That's why he's applying for a holding now. Mr Turner gives him a good reference. He says he's willing to lend him a hand to get established, so he must have faith in his ability.'

94

'I suppose so,' Wilson agreed reluctantly. He didn't like his authority being questioned.

'His commanding officer gives him an excellent reference too.'

'He's an army man. He'll know nothing about farming.'

'Maybe not, but he should be a good judge of men in general. I expect he'll know who he can trust to do a good job. He says here that Caraford takes initiative and he always volunteered to help with hay and harvest on the local farms when they were in camp. That doesn't sound like an idle fellow.'

Wilson remained silent, scowling. He had already chosen the three men he thought should be on the shortlist. 'I believe there could be another holding coming to let,' he said. 'One of the tenants is seriously ill and they have no family to follow on. Maybe we could add Caraford's name to the shortlist for that holding?'

'Very well. How big is that one?'

'Thirty-five acres,' Wilson said shortly. It was less than half the acreage of the one under consideration.

'I see. Should I assume you have your own favourite selected for the larger holding?'

'The three I have selected are all good men in my opinion,' Wilson said stiffly.

'Very well, arrange the interviews for them.'

'What about Caraford then?'

'Put him on the shortlist for the next holding as soon as one becomes available. This way we need not delay the letting of the larger holding and if he proves as unsuitable as you seem to think there'll be no harm done.'

'Very good,' Wilson said, assuming he would be doing the selection for the next holding himself. He certainly wouldn't be doing any favours for a relation of Fred Caraford.

Megan gave in to Maryanne's plea to accompany her to the Dornielea Christmas dance, although she would have had more enthusiasm if Steven had been home in time. She was surprised to see Natalie there. She never attended any of the village functions or mixed with the locals if she could help it. She was even more astonished when Natalie made a point of coming across to talk, even taking a seat beside her. They rarely exchanged greetings. Tonight Natalie had brought a group of friends from the Carlisle hospital where she worked as a secretary to one of the surgeons.

'I had another letter from Steven a couple of days ago,' Natalie said as though making casual conversation, but managing to infer Steven was a regular correspondent.

Megan summoned a smile with an effort. Steven had never mentioned that he was keeping in touch with Natalie.

'We got a Christmas card too. He's really looking forward to getting home.'

'Oh, he is. He always replies straight away to my letters.' Natalie smiled sweetly.

'Aren't you going to introduce me to your friend, Natalie?' a deep voice said, over their heads. They looked up startled. One of the young men from the group had followed Natalie across the hall. She frowned.

'Her father works for us.'

Megan heard the disparagement in her tone and knew that Natalie Turner would have liked to have brushed her aside like dust underfoot, but the young man raised a questioning eyebrow.

'So? She has a name presumably?'

'Of course she does. Megan Oliphant. Doctor Gray,' she muttered, making the introduction with obvious reluctance. Megan gave him an extra-friendly smile, unaware that her green eyes were sparkling at Natalie's forced response.

'Lindsay Gray. Lint to my friends and colleagues. Pleased to meet you, Megan.' The young doctor grinned at her. 'May I have this dance, please?'

Natalie gasped. She had assumed he had followed her across the room to be sure of dancing with her.

'Thank you.' Megan rose, relieved to be rescued. She never felt easy in Natalie's company and she didn't entirely trust her either, though she had no idea why.

'How lightly you dance,' Doctor Gray remarked. 'It's like holding the fairy queen in my arms.'

'You're pretty good at the dancing yourself, Doctor Gray,' she quipped. She felt quite at ease with this smiling young man with the twinkling brown eyes.

'Oh, call me Lint. I saw you from my bedroom window this morning. You were walking across the farmyard carrying two large buckets with things like giant spiders dangling from them.'

'You're staying at Martinwold?'

'Only until tomorrow. I'm on duty over Christmas.'

'Oh, I see. It's as bad as being a dairyman. My parents have to milk the cows whatever day it is.'

'Do you work with them on the farm?'

'I always help when I'm at home from college.'

'What are you doing at college? Damn,' he said as the dance ended. 'Can I have the next one? Please? I'd like to get to know all about you.' The admiration in his eyes brought the pink to Megan's cheeks. She was unaware of Natalie watching them closely and with displeasure. She had heard from local gossip that Dr Gray came from a wealthy family. 'So? What are you studying, Megan?'

'I want to teach in a primary school,' she said. 'I enjoy being with children.'

'Children and animals?'

'Yes, I like animals too. I'm hoping I shall get a job in a country school, but I've another year at college to do after this one, and then I need to teach for a year to get my parchment, but at least I shall be earning then.'

'It's never ending, all the studying, is it?' he said sympathetically. 'I've a few years of training and studying ahead of me, but it's what I wanted to do so there's no use grumbling.' He sighed as the next dance came to an end. 'I'd better go back to the gang or Nats will be locking me out of the house tonight judging by the glowering looks she is throwing my way.' He

98

gave her an impish grin and Megan couldn't help smiling back at him.

She was surprised when he came to ask her for the last dance of the evening, almost running the last few steps in order to beat Maryanne's brother, Rufus.

'Can I give you a lift home?' he asked.

'Oh, no, thank you. I'm with a friend.'

'I rather think your friend has other plans for going home tonight.' He grinned and nodded his head in the direction of Maryanne and her dance partner.

'So she has.' Megan smiled, pleased her friend had enjoyed her evening.

'So you'll come with us? Natalie is driving her own car so she'll be taking Nick and she can take one of the girls too. The other two will come with us so you'll be perfectly safe.' He gave his disarming smile.

'I'm sure I shall. Thank you, I shall be glad of a lift.' She would have walked the two miles back on her own rather than go with Natalie Turner, but there was no reason why she shouldn't accept Lindsay Gray's offer, although she knew instinctively Natalie would not be pleased. Her mother always said it was because she was an only child so she was not used to sharing anything, but her father insisted it was because Mr Turner had spoiled her. Whatever the reason Natalie was not an easy person to like.

Natalie lost no time in writing to tell Steven that Megan had spent the evening dancing and flirting with Dr Lindsay Gray, one of her own

99

house guests.

'She enticed him away from our party and she even begged him for a lift home in his car. It was most embarrassing,' she wrote.

Steven knew Megan too well to believe she would beg a lift from anyone. She was a very attractive girl and he was certain he was not the only man who would think so. He guessed Natalie had exaggerated, but his heart was heavy as he thought of Megan dancing in another man's arms, and him seeing her home. He had been jolted into awareness when he had seen her on leave and held her in his arms. She was a lovely girl with her vivid colouring and sparkling eyes. Even as a child, her warm smile had always drawn people to her. He was even more disappointed when Megan did not reply to his last letter as quickly as she usually did. Obviously, she had other things to occupy her time and he had no right to claim all her attention.

Megan couldn't help feeling dejected when she realized Steven and Natalie were corresponding regularly with each other, although there was no reason why he shouldn't write to as many girls as he wanted. She felt he was not as much in need of her letters as she had believed. In fact, she wrote so regularly he probably found them a nuisance and he was too polite not to reply. Yet his letters had always been so chatty, almost as though they were talking together. She had no way of knowing Natalie had only recently acquired Steven's address when she had seen his letter to her father lying on the desk. She had copied it down and written to him immediately.

Steven knew he couldn't expect Megan to wait for him, even if he had had any prospects of taking a wife, and as time passed it seemed he had no prospects of anything. He was sure he ought to have heard from the Department of Agriculture about his application for a holding by now. All his joyful anticipation seemed to drain away as he contemplated a future without Megan and without any prospect of becoming a farmer. He didn't even have a home where he was welcome any more. He travelled back to Willowburn with his spirits as bleak as the short January day. Where else could he go until he found a job?

At least he had managed to build up his savings with the boost of his promotion to sergeant and his sojourn in Palestine. He clenched his jaw. He would pay for his board and lodging so Fred wouldn't be able to say he was free-loading. His mother would need persuading to accept money from him though. It would be difficult to keep away from the animals, but he recalled Fred's angry resentment the last time he had been home and all he had done was assist an animal in pain and save the life of her calf. He was not afraid of Fred, nor even unduly concern-ed by his attitude, but the atmosphere between them made life unpleasant for everybody and he couldn't expect his father to deal with Fred's jealousy at this late stage in his life.

As soon as Steven set foot in the door of the familiar old farmhouse, his mother was there to greet him and his heart thawed a little at her welcoming hug.

'Come and sit down at the table, Steven. I saw ye walking up the road so the tea is brewed and ye'll be ready for a hot drink inside you.'

'I am that.' He smiled at her. 'What's Fred saying about me coming here?'

'Fred? What should he be saying? This is your home, Steven. Where else would you stay? Besides I don't think he's so bothered now he knows you're not intending to work at Willowburn. There's an official-looking letter for you by the way. It came yesterday. Here it is.'

Steven took the large brown envelope with a mixture of excitement and trepidation. Could this be what he'd been praying for?

He slit it open and scanned the typed page. He looked up, his blue eyes alight with hope.

'Another holding has fallen vacant and I'm on the shortlist this time, Mother! I've to go for an interview the day after tomorrow.'

'Ah, that's good news.' Hannah gave a huge sigh of relief.

'It doesn't mean to say I shall get it,' Steven cautioned. 'I'm only on a shortlist.'

'You must take the van. You'll need to be on time and you would have to change buses at Annan.'

'I don't want to cause any upset and Fred would have something to say if I do that.'

'I bought the van myself to deliver my eggs when I got too many to take on the bus. It's been handy. You must take it.'

Steven took her advice and arrived at the

government offices in good time.

'If you'll take a seat, Mr Caraford,' a pleasant young woman said. 'Your appointment is with the senior land officer and he was delayed on the journey down this morning. He will not keep you waiting long.'

Steven couldn't remember when he had last felt so nervous. His mother had pressed his suit specially, but he doubted if that would help much. He tugged at his collar and tie as though it was choking him.

'Mr Burrows will see you now. Please come this way.'

The woman showed him through to another room.

The interview was long and the searching questions were wide-ranging. Many of the topics seemed to have nothing to do with farming, but the man's manner was pleasant, almost conversational, and Steven began to relax. He was articulate and he had kept himself up to date with both world affairs and the state of farming, as well as reading books for pleasure. When it came to a discussion of how he planned to stock and finance a holding he was grateful for his mother's financial help and pleased he had managed to swell his bank balance even more during the past eighteen months, even though he had grumbled at being sent abroad instead of being demobbed. Sometimes things did work out for the best. Mr Burrows nodded his approval as he listed his priorities.

'Well, I think we can offer you a tenancy, Mr Caraford, but the holding is less than half the acreage of the last one you applied for. It is just thirty-five acres. The house and garden are not in the best of order but the rent will take account of that until the next review is due. The previous tenant was ill. Cancer I believe. The original farm was called Schoirhead before it was divided into five holdings. Three of them had new cottage type houses and a small range of new buildings. The farmhouse was split into two. One half of the house goes with this holding which is Number One or Schoirhead. It is separated from the neighbouring house and garden by a high stone wall. The farm steading has been maintained in good order. You may decide to wait for a larger holding to become vacant, but I cannot guarantee you would get it. My advice would be to take this one and see how you get on. The rent is one pound seventeen shillings and six pence per acre per year, payable in two halves in May and November. All this will be confirmed in writing.'

'Thank you. What is the date of entry?'

'The rent is paid until May but the widow of the previous tenant found she couldn't stay there without her husband so the house is empty. You may look at the holding at your convenience. Legally the tenant is still responsible for everything until term day, including any frozen pipes and the water bowls in the byre, so the widow may be happy for you to take over earlier.'

'That would suit me too. I am free immediately.' Steven felt his excitement rising.

'You will need to pay Mrs McKie, the outgoing tenant, the value of unused fertilizer and various other items, mainly the farmyard manure. I'm afraid it has been allowed to accumulate. Mr McKie was a highly satisfactory tenant prior to his illness. You will be given a copy of the conditions on your way out.'

'The first thing I shall need is a horse and cart, a wheelbarrow and a good strong fork by the sound of things,' Steven said, trying hard to keep from smiling as his spirits soared. He was young and fit and he would relish the satisfaction of spreading the manure on his fields. His land.

'The first thing you must do is inspect the holding and study the lease carefully,' the senior land officer warned, but with a smile tugging at the corners of his mouth at Steven's youthful enthusiasm. 'If you decide to take on the tenancy, there will be papers to sign. I would advise you to consult your solicitor before committing yourself, especially if you have any doubts regarding the valuation. Your reference from Mr Turner was excellent and I notice he is willing to offer you his support. You may wish to consult him too before you sign anything.'

'Thank you, sir. I shall follow your advice, but I think this is the opportunity I have been waiting for and it couldn't have come at a better time, so it will have to be pretty bad for me to refuse the tenancy.'

'The land is very good I believe, but the meadow near the river has been known to flood. The farm steading will benefit from a coat of whitewash as you will see.'

'I understand, sir.' Steven nodded.

'Normally we would expect a tenant to take

possession on term day, the twenty-eighth of May, so that is when your lease will begin officially, but if you reach an agreement with the widow you will need to pay Mrs McKie a proportion of the rent which was paid by her late husband.'

'Would it be possible for me to see it today, sir?'

'I should think so.' Mr Burrows smiled at his eagerness. He was certain this young man deserved an opportunity to farm. 'The keys to the house are with the next door tenants, a Mr and Mrs...' He scrutinized a sheet of paper. 'Ah, yes, Mr and Mrs McGuire. Their address is Number Two, The Loaning. I understand Schoirhead means land above the harbour, though there doesn't appear to have been a harbour in that area. Perhaps it was a landing stage at one time, or maybe the Solway smugglers used to land their contraband there.'

Steven thanked him and tried hard not to grin from ear to ear as he left the building. Thirty-five acres was less than half the size of Willowburn, but it was a start and it would be his very own place. He longed to tell somebody. He wished Megan was at home, but he knew she must have already returned to college after the Christmas holidays. He would take a good look at the place, then, once he was sure, write and tell her all about it, although her letters had been less frequent recently and he felt there was a cooler tone to them. First, he must find a telephone kiosk and let his mother know his news and his plans to inspect the holding right away.

He could barely contain his excitement as he gave the Willowburn number to the operator.

As he had expected, his mother was relieved and delighted. 'Take your time and have a good look at everything, Steven.'

He jumped into the van. Half an hour later, after he had driven through Annan, he realized it would only be a short detour to call on the Oliphants. Sam's parents would be as pleased as his mother. Mr Oliphant was often free for an hour or two in the middle of the day to compensate for the early start and late finish to his day. It would be good to have his opinion.

A little while later he was turning into the Martinwold road end. He jumped out of the van and ran up the path. Mrs Oliphant had seen him arrive and she met him at the door. He followed her into the kitchen.

'Megan!' he exclaimed with delight. 'I didn't expect to find you at home from college.'

'She's had the influenza,' Mrs Oliphant said. 'She's fretting because she's missing lectures, but Dr Burns says she's had a bad attack and she must stay in and keep warm.'

'I'm all right,' Megan insisted, 'just a bit wobbly. I'm definitely going back on Monday. You look as though you've got good news, Steven.'

'I have.' Steven moved to her side and took one of her hands in both of his. 'I've got a tenancy for a holding. I was longing to tell you, so I'm glad you're here, except I'm sorry you're ill. I hoped your father might be free to come with me. I'm on my way to look at it now.'

'Oh, Steven, that's wonderful,' Megan said,

her green eyes shining with happiness for him.

'That's tremendous news, laddie.' Chrissie Oliphant clapped him on the shoulder. 'Exactly what you hoped for. I'm pleased for you.'

'We-ell it's only thirty-five acres, but it's a start and I reckon it's as much as I can afford to stock to begin with.'

'I'm sure you'll do fine. I must hurry up and finish the rag rug I'm making. It will be just the thing for your new fireside.'

'You're making it for me?' Steven asked incredulously.

'I can't think of anybody who deserves it more. Besides if I know men it's the outside that claims all the money and attention, but it's nice to have a place to warm your feet on a cold night.'

'It is that. Mother says I can take my bed from Willowburn so if I've a table and a chair –' his blue eyes twinkled – *and* a rag rug, I shall be all right. By the sound of things I shall have to muck out the sheds so my first priority must be a horse and cart.'

'There's John coming round the corner,' Chrissie said, glancing out of the window. 'I'll give him a shout. Oh ... he seems to be discussing something with Mr Turner.'

'Is he there too? I ought to tell him I've been successful,' Steven said. 'According to the land officer, the reference he gave me helped a lot.' He looked back at Megan. 'I do wish you could have come with me, but you do look pale.'

'Aye, this is the first day she's been downstairs. Better not take any risks, lassie,' her mother advised, seeing the longing in her daughter's eyes. 'The soup is nearly ready, Steven. Ask John to come in and you can both have a bowl before you leave.'

Steven went to join the two men. They could tell by his expression he had had good news.

'Have you got a tenancy, laddie?' John Oliphant asked eagerly.

'I have.' Steven grinned. 'It's only thirty-five acres, but it's big enough to start off. I want to thank you, Mr Turner, for the reference you gave me. I know it helped to get me the interview.'

'I'm glad you've been successful, Steven.' Mr Turner shook his hand and beamed. 'You deserve it. I know you'll not let me down.'

'Not if I can help it,' Steven promised. 'I called in to see if Mr Oliphant was free for an hour. I'm going there now to have a look. The last tenant has died. The rent is paid until May, but the widow didn't like staying on her own so I can probably take possession as soon as everything is agreed and signed up.'

'That's splendid. I'll not keep the two of you then,' Mr Turner said.

'Mrs Oliphant says we've to go in for some soup before we set off,' Steven said.

They were almost finished their soup when the telephone rang. Chrissie Oliphant went into the hall to answer it.

'That was Mr Turner,' she said. 'He would like to join the pair of you. He says he'll drive you all there in his car. He'll pick you up in ten minutes. So come on, Steven, eat up some soda scone and cheese and I'll make you a cup of tea and fetch you a slice of apple pie.'

She didn't mention that it was Natalie Turner's idea that her father should accompany them, or that she intended going too, although she was also supposed to be off work after a bad cold.

Eight

John Oliphant was surprised when he opened the back door of his boss's car and saw Natalie sitting there.

'I've left the front seats for you two old men. Steven, you can sit in the back with me,' she ordered imperiously.

Steven raised his brows, then he frowned. He didn't care for the knowing look in John Oliphant's eyes or the half smile twitching the corner of his mouth. Natalie Turner was the last person he had expected to show interest in a neglected smallholding. She didn't even take an interest in her father's prosperous acres so why did she want to come with them? He had not even seen the place himself. He was irritated, but he couldn't afford to offend Natalie when it was her father who had been instrumental in helping him get a start on the farming ladder.

The moment they arrived at Schoirhead Steven was eager to view the buildings and discover what facilities he would have. He had also intended walking over the land with John Oliphant, but he doubted whether that would be possible with Natalie tagging along. The house was the last thing on his mind. He knew his mother would come to look and they could see it

111

then, but it was the only thing which interested Natalie.

'I'd need to get the key from next door,' he said, frowning.

'Well, go on and get it then. It's freezing out here.'

Reluctantly he went through the garden and the small orchard to the neighbouring holding. Mrs McGuire eyed him warily, but she gave him the heavy iron key.

'We only have one door each. This used to be the back o' the hoose. You've got the kitchen and the front room o' the original,' she informed him abruptly.

He smiled and thanked her and promised to return the key before they left.

Natalie was standing shivering in the tiny porch. Surely she must realize an empty house in January would be cold, he thought impatiently. He handed her the key.

'You have a look round while I inspect the loft above the pigsty. It might be suitable for rearing some chickens. I shall need something to bring in an income as soon as possible.' He turned away, ignoring her pouting lips and the invitation in her eyes. He managed to get John Oliphant on his own up in the small loft.

'I can't see half of the place with Natalie here,' he said in a low voice. 'Anyway I need to get out of this suit and get my boots on to walk over the fields. I'm sorry if I dragged you here. I'll have to come back and have another look tomorrow.'

'I understand, lad,' John Oliphant said. 'But I'm pleased you asked me anyway. Your father and mother will want to look.'

When they climbed down the wooden steps, Natalie was waiting. She almost dragged Steven to the house.

'You come and see it too, Daddy. It's a mess, but I've seen some lovely wallpaper in one of the shops in Carlisle.'

Steven's eyes widened. The house would be lucky if he had time to give one of the rooms a coat of distemper, but he had to admit the place did look forlorn and neglected.

'Empty houses always look miserable,' John Oliphant said. 'It will be fine once you move in.'

There were a few cobwebs and a layer of dust over everything, but Steven was surprised to find the kitchen had a small Aga stove with two ovens instead of an open range. It was very scruffy and he wondered whether it worked. It had two big hot plates. Maybe it wouldn't be as cosy as an open fire and it certainly needed a good clean, but he could imagine what a benefit it would be to keep the house warm and this might help revive a sickly piglet, or a starved lamb, if he decided to keep a few breeding sheep. The previous tenant had left a pine dresser, which took up most of one wall, but it looked solid enough and it would provide useful storage. It had probably been too large to take with her. There was a big pine table too, which would suit him fine if it had a good scrub with scouring powder. A door opened into a white-washed larder.

'Of course all this will have to be gutted out,' Natalie said. 'It will give more space if we knock down the larder wall too.'

'I can't do that!' he exclaimed. 'There's a list of conditions in the lease. They even have a note of the number of coat pegs and they must be replaced if a tenant removes any of them.'

'You must remember, Nats, Steven is only renting the place,' Mr Turner said. 'He can't knock it to bits, even if he wanted to.'

Steven wandered across the small hallway and pushed open the door of a sitting room. It faced south to the garden and he thought it would be pleasant in summer. Natalie followed.

'This room might be all right with some thick velvet curtains and some a pretty wallpaper. The polished floor surround is not so bad, but that grate will have to go. You'll need a three-piece suite in here, Steven. I've seen lovely uncut moquette suites for thirty-nine guineas.'

'Thirty-nine guineas?' Steven almost choked.

'Yes, and you'll need a carpet of course. The bathroom is downstairs. That's not very convenient, but there's a box room upstairs so you could make another one in there. The water has been turned off so we can't use the toilet. There's no washbasin either. It's so tiny.'

'At least it's indoors,' John Oliphant said with a chuckle. 'When we were married we had to go down the garden and the bath was a zinc tub in front of the fire.'

Natalie gave him a scathing glance. She had never lived anywhere else but Martinwold, with its upstairs bathroom and a downstairs toilet. She was unaware that two of her father's tenants still had no bathroom and considered themselves

114

lucky to have an indoor water closet.

'The stairs are a bit steep,' she said. 'The last tenants left the stair carpet, but it's a horrible colour. You'll need to change that.'

Steven turned away, caught John Oliphant's bemused glance and rolled his eyes heavenward.

'I can't afford to spend any money on the house,' he said firmly.

'Oh, come upstairs and don't be an old misery,' Natalie said.

They all trooped upstairs to the small square landing. There were two big bedrooms, each with an Adam-style fireplace. There was a huge wardrobe in one bedroom. Although Natalie referred to the little room as a box room, it had a small iron grate and it was big enough for a single bed and a chest of drawers. Again, she started listing the things he would require, including new carpets and a bedroom suite in figured walnut that she had seen for forty-nine guineas. Steven gaped at her.

'I'm bringing my bed from home,' he said brusquely, 'and there's linoleum on the floor – that will have to do.'

'Don't be such a meanie. Daddy will loan you the money if you haven't enough, won't you, Daddy?'

'No!' Steven said emphatically. 'I don't want to borrow any money if I can help it. If I ever do, it would have to be for something essential for the farm. My first priority will be a horse. I saw an old cart in the shed. I believe I could patch it up to make do for a year or two. The last tenants have left a wheelbarrow as well, and a shovel and some small tools.'

'I expect the widow had no one to help her clear out or muck the sheds if she had no family,' John Oliphant said. 'I noticed an old chicken brooder. I'm sure Chrissie could fix it up with some felt curtains. You'd only need a new oil heater for it.'

'I saw that.' Steven nodded. 'I can pay for the material if you think Mrs Oliphant would fix it for me.'

'Bring it the next time you visit,' John Oliphant suggested. 'It would be easier for her if she has it near at hand.'

'But, Steven,' Natalie protested, tugging at his arm and reclaiming his attention, 'you have to consider the kitchen at least.'

'It looks fine to me, except it needs a good clean and a coat of distemper.'

'Oh, don't tease. You know you will need an electric cooker and you may as well get one of the new electric washing machines. You should get one of those with electric ringers, then you don't have to turn the mangle.'

Steven stared at her. He hadn't thought about washing. His heart sank. Come to that he didn't know much about cooking either. His earlier elation was draining away as he listened to Natalie's critical comments and expensive ideas. It would take him years before he could afford all the things a wife apparently expected.

'Don't look like that.' Natalie shook his arm impatiently. 'You can get a brand new cooker with four rings for forty pounds and I know Mother paid about that for her new washing machine.'

'There's a copper boiler and a tub in the wash house and I'm hoping that old stove will do any cooking I'll be doing,' he said dully. 'Now I want another quick look outside, then we must get back in time for Mr Oliphant to start the milking.' Steven avoided Natalie's pouting face, but he caught her father's eyes on him as they trooped outside.

'The place needs a lot of hard work,' he said thoughtfully, 'but it's better than I expected.'

'Oh, Daddy! Better than you expected? It's nothing but a dump!'

'The buildings are in good structural repair. All they need is cleaning out and a good coat of limewash and a lick of paint on the doors and windows,' Mr Turner said firmly. 'It will take time, but I know you never shied away from hard work, Steven. We'll talk again when you've had a walk over the land. I may be able to let you have one or two implements for the horse now that we've moved on to tractors. It would be a big benefit if you had a milking machine. You'll have everything to do yourself.'

'I need to buy some cows to milk first,' Steven said. 'I have to creep before I can walk.'

'Well, at least you've got your head screwed on the right way,' Mr Turner approved.

'Oh, Father!' Natalie exclaimed irritably.

'You'd have the poor lad bankrupt before he got started if he listened to you, Nats. You'll have to learn to budget before you think of getting married,' he added sternly, but Natalie only pulled a face at him.

117

Steven guessed she'd never gone without anything she fancied, in spite of the rationing and clothing coupons and all the shortages other people had had to suffer, and were still enduring.

Back at Martinwold, the road forked as they approached the farm with one drive to the Turners' house and the other to the farm.

'You can drop us here,' John Oliphant said. 'It will save you turning in the yard.'

'Very well,' Mr Turner said. 'Let me know if there's anything I can do to help, Steven, and good luck.'

John Oliphant and Steven walked together towards his van.

'You'll come in for some tea, laddie, before you leave?'

'No, thanks,' Steven said flatly. 'I'd better be getting home. Mother will be waiting to hear the details.'

'You sound a bit down. Were you disappointed? Or is there something else bothering you?'

'No, not really,' he said, then sighed. 'It's just that Natalie pointed out all the faults. I don't care about the house as long as I've a place to sleep, but she made me realize it could be years before I can afford to make it a comfortable home. Are all women so demanding?'

'They like a bit of comfort, but we've never bought any new furniture yet and I reckon we're happy enough. Never heed what Natalie says. She's a spoiled brat. She must spend half her time window shopping in Carlisle when she's supposed to be at work. She fancies you, Steven. That's why she's letting you know what the house will need.'

'Natalie Turner fancies *me*?' Steven laughed in disbelief. The idea was crazy, but he saw John Oliphant was serious. 'There's no fear of that,' he added soberly.

'Don't be so sure. You're a good-looking fellow and you've done well in the army. She's not used to being overlooked. You'll have to pay her more attention. When she thinks she's got you where she wants you, she'll probably lose interest. The Natalies of this world crave attention and she has enough of her father in her to relish a challenge.' John Oliphant grinned.

'It will be years before I can afford a wife. Anyway I don't want to offend Mr Turner and he wouldn't thank me for flirting with his only daughter, even if I wanted to. I'll get away home now. Thanks for coming.'

'Eh, laddie, I was pleased you asked me.' John Oliphant's eyes shadowed. 'Sam would have been really pleased for ye,' he said gruffly. 'If ever we can help, you've only to ask.'

'Thanks,' Steven said simply. He slid into the van and drove away, his mind going over the day's events.

Megan was bitterly disappointed when Steven didn't come in for afternoon tea with her father. She had washed her face, put on a clean skirt and jumper, and brushed her hair until it shone. It was the first day she had felt like doing anything with her appearance since she'd had the influenza. She listened eagerly to her father describing the little farm that would soon be Steven's

119

home. She longed to see it, but when her father mentioned Natalie Turner had been there her heart sank.

'Natalie went with you?' She couldn't hide her dismay.

'Aye, she did.' He frowned. 'It would take a richer man than Steven to keep up with her ideas.'

'What has it to do with her?' Megan asked, but she didn't need an answer. She knew already that Natalie was attracted to Steven. The Turners would probably want someone richer for their only daughter, but Steven was intelligent and ambitious, and he was a fine-looking man, even if she was prejudiced. If Natalie had set her heart on having him for her husband, Mr Turner would do a great deal to help him on his way, if only for Natalie's sake. Some day Martinwold would belong to Natalie and her husband. It was a prize worth winning.

Megan felt tired and depressed. She knew it was not all due to her recent illness. She had waited eagerly for Steven's return, longing to hear his ideas for the farm, but he had discussed them with Natalie and her father instead. No wonder he hadn't bothered coming in for tea. She sighed, remembering how foolishly she had allowed herself to dream. Except for his kiss at the station, he still seemed to regard her as Sam's wee sister. He hadn't been home five minutes and already Natalie Turner was claiming his attention.

The following morning Steven waited to drive

his mother to Schoirhead, but his initial enthusiasm had been dampened by Natalie's criticisms yesterday. It was not that he cared about her opinion except that she was a woman so presumably she knew what most women would expect. Even so, he wished she had never seen Schoirhead. He was prepared for hard work and a struggle to get himself established, but she had left him in no doubt of how little he had to offer a woman. Would Megan have considered the house a dump? he wondered.

'Put these in the van, will you, Steven?' His mother interrupted his thoughts.

He looked at the large cardboard box in surprise.

'What's all this?' he asked, taking it from her, as well as the bucket swinging from her arm. There was an assortment of brushes, cloths, scouring powder, a packet of soda and various other cleaning materials. 'I haven't signed on the dotted line yet,' he protested. 'I'm waiting for your verdict.'

'I know,' Hannah said, chuckling, 'and much notice you'd take of my opinion. This is your chance, laddie, and I know you'll seize it. I'll do a wee bit of cleaning while you're looking round the fields. The minute you get permission officially, you'll be moving in if I know you. So you'll need a clean kitchen and a bedroom to sleep in. There's another couple o' boxes in the kitchen if ye'll carry them out for me? We'll kindle a fire to boil a kettle for a cup of tea.'

They were almost ready to leave when Eddy

121

Caraford came round the corner from the stack-yard.

'If you can hang on a minute, Steven, I'd like to come with you.'

'You would?' Steven couldn't hide his delight. His father was interested in his future after all. 'We'll hang on as long as it takes, Dad. I'm glad you want to come.' His enthusiasm returned.

'I'll have a quick shave and change my collar then,' his father said and disappeared into the house.

'I can ride in the back of the van, Mother, if you will drive?' It occurred to him how well she had adapted to changes during the war. He remembered when she had driven him and Fred to the village in the pony and cart, but she was the one who had saved up and bought the second-hand van and learned to drive. His father seemed wary of anything mechanical, but he would always be one of the best stockmen in the area. Neighbours often came for his advice over a sick calf or a difficult calving.

'I'm glad your father is coming. He's worried about you, Steven.'

'Mmm. I'm glad too. You drive as far as Gretna, then I'll take over. Schoirhead and the other holdings are on a narrow back road.'

'Schoirhead must be getting near the water then? Are the fields wet?'

'One of them floods occasionally. The land officer said it was all fertile loam so it should grow good grass. Mr Turner has offered me one of his tractors and a trailer, but I don't want to start borrowing things unless I have to. Anyway, a well-schooled horse would walk on while I throw the manure off the back of the cart. A tractor can't do that. I'd need to get on and off every few yards.'

'I hadn't thought of that,' his mother mused. 'Fred uses the tractor for everything these days, but he never did like the horses and he always has Edna running after him so he doesn't do any jumping on and off. I've packed some sandwiches. I think there'll be enough for your father too.'

When they arrived at Schoirhead Steven looked at his mother.

'If you go next door to ask for the key you'll meet my neighbours, Mr and Mrs McGuire,' he said. 'She looked very stern and disapproving when I returned the key yesterday.'

Hannah hurried away. It would be such a relief if this venture worked out well for Steven. In her heart she had known for a long time that he and Fred would never be able to work together at Willowburn. Steven unloaded the van while his father walked along the row of sheds, peering over the half doors in the triangular yard. It was an unusual shape for a farmyard but he guessed it was the only way to divide the original yard. The dairy washroom, with the steam chest and tubs, was almost an extension to the house. Next to it was the dairy where the milk was cooled and filled into churns for taking away to the creamery, and beyond it was a byre with stalls for eight cows with a feed passage in front and the usual channel and walkway behind. At the end of the byre there was a taller building with stabling for two cart horses and a pony, with a hayloft above. Then came the midden, piled high with manure, and an upside-down wheelbarrow as though someone had used the last of his energy to empty it and left it there.

'At least the midden has a wall all round or the manure would be spread all over the yard by now,' he said wryly as he joined his father.

'Aye,' Eddy Caraford agreed, 'but ye'll have plenty of work to get it all spread, and didn't you say there's two fields to be ploughed, Steven?'

'Yes. One is three acres and the other is nearer five I think. It's compulsory to sow them with cereals for one more year, after that I can sow them with grass again so long as I plough up an equivalent acreage. It will suit me until I get enough stock to graze them all and it's a chance to reseed with some of the newer varieties of grass. I reckon I've enough money to buy a sow and four milk cows or in-calf heifers so long as I don't need to pay more than forty-five to fifty guineas each. There's an old cart in one of the sheds. I think I can mend it well enough to do for this year.'

'Mmm...' His father nodded thoughtfully.

A gate next to the midden opened into a small stack-yard with half of a rick of hay and a small straw stack. Beyond that a track led to the fields. Along the other side of the triangular yard there were three sheds for carts and implements, but two had been used as housing for animals and the manure was three-feet deep or more in them. Next came three pigsties with a low loft above. A gate into a small orchard separated the sties

124

from the high stone wall which divided the garden and the adjoining holding. Steven wondered what it would be like having a neighbour so near.

'Here we are,' Hannah said as she came hurrying through the garden with the key to the house. 'Your new neighbour seems pleasant enough, Steven, but she's a lot older than I expected and her husband looks crippled with arthritis.'

'He is,' Steven agreed. 'Come and see the house.'

'The kitchen is a good size, and it's light and airy,' Hannah said as she looked around. 'That's a grand solid table and dresser somebody has left. A good scrub will make all the difference.'

Steven felt a wave of relief at his mother's sound common sense. Natalie's criticism still niggled more than he cared to admit. He wished they could have brought Megan with them. She was young, but she was down to earth like his mother.

Hannah shooed them away to inspect the fields while she unpacked the boxes she had brought.

Steven enjoyed his father's company as much as he had when he was thirteen and learning to plough. They went round each field in turn, inspecting the fences and looking over at the neighbouring fields too.

'The conditions for maintaining fences and ditches are written into the tenancy agreement. We can use timber if we need it, but we can't sell any of it, and same with stones. The mineral rights and everything else belongs to the landlord.'

'Willowburn lease is similar,' his father said. 'Fred wanted to chop down the trees in the wee copse, but I told him he'd get us put out.'

'Why would he want to do that?' Steven asked, puzzled.

'He intended to saw them up and sell them for firewood to make himself some spending money, with coal being rationed, you see. The previous tenant has kept the fences better than he's kept the sheds,' he said, changing the subject.

'I think he was too ill for any heavy work by the end. Anyway, the manure is part of the tenant's valuation so it will not cost me as much to take over if I do the spreading myself.'

'You always did look on the bright side of things, Stevie,' his father said. 'I reckon you'll do all right. I've been thinking ... How would you like to have Daisy? She's getting old, but she's a steady worker and she always worked well for you when you were at home.'

'What would Fred say to that?' Steven asked cautiously, but his heart was singing. His father wanted to help him and he knew Daisy had always been his favourite Clydesdale.

'Fred has no time for the horses. He says they eat their heads off. It'll take about three acres to keep Daisy between grazing and hay, but I reckon she'd be worth it until you can afford a tractor.'

'Thanks, Dad, if you're sure?'

'Aye, I'm sure. You can have the single-furrow plough as well, if you like. It's no use to us now. Fred bought a new plough for the tractor. You'll need to borrow another horse to work beside Daisy for the ploughing.'

'Daisy solves my first problem and it will save a chunk o' my savings. Now I might be able to afford a gilt as well as a sow.' Steven grinned. 'I'll get my bike out when we get home. I'd like to go down to the Oliphants.' He wanted to tell Megan about his plans before she returned to college. He felt more optimistic now and Megan had always shared his dreams – and many of his fears – though he was finding it a bit different talking to Megan in person since he kissed her. She was a desirable young woman, although he tried not to dwell on such thoughts. He sighed. It would be years before he could consider asking any girl to marry him and he couldn't expect Megan to wait.

He pulled his attention back to the land with an effort.

'This is the field that floods sometimes,' he told his father as they walked beside the river-bank. 'You wouldn't think the water would rise high enough.'

'Water is a powerful beast,' his father warned. 'I've heard the tides can come up mighty fast and you're not far from the Solway Firth. It grows good pasture though. Your cattle should do well here.' He looked at the dark skeletons of the trees against the grey of the January sky. 'There must be a fair bit of wind the way the trees are leaning, but if you keep the hedges thick the cattle will have shelter.' He sighed heavily. Fred had refused to learn to lay hedges or to keep the ditches and drains clear and he felt it was all getting beyond him. He wished Steven had been joining them at Willowburn, but he knew the atmosphere between his two sons would lead to nothing but quarrels. He had had enough of that when Eleanor's father had kept trying to interfere and tell him what to do, but he had been a young man then and he had coped with the stress. In his heart he knew he should have been firmer with Fred when he was younger instead of always trying to compensate for the loss of his mother.

On the way back they saw one of the other smallholders spreading farmyard manure prior to ploughing his field. He came to the fence to talk to them.

'You the new tenants for Bob McKie's place?' he asked curiously.

'I'm seeing the solicitor and signing up today,' Steven said warily.

'Aye, Mistress McGuire said ye were a wee bit of a lad, but we're needing some young blood around here. I'm Bill Kerr frae Number Four, The Loaning.' He spat on his hands and wiped them down his brown cords before extending one in greeting.

'I'm Steven Caraford and this is my father Eddy. He farms at Willowburn, about six miles north of here.'

'Pleased tae meet ye. We like to help each other when we can, but we mind our ain business. Let me know if there's anything I can do for ye. My son Jimmy is a mechanic and he works in Annan, but he helps me when he can. By the way I've two fine collie pups left if you need a dog? You can take your pick at a guinea each. They're well bred and their mother is a good worker.'

'Thanks, I'll think about it,' Steven said slowly. A dog would be company when he was living on his own and useful if he did take on any sheep to eat the grass until he could buy enough stock of his own, but he needed to watch his money carefully until he had all the essentials.

'I'll buy him a pup,' Eddy Caraford said, 'if ye'll take a pound.' He pulled his old leather wallet from his inside pocket and took out one of the two-pound notes.

'But, Dad...' Steven protested.

'It'll be company for ye, and you always liked to have our Bess beside ye when ye were at home.'

'Right, that's a deal.' Bill Kerr grinned and reached for the proffered note. 'I'll keep it until you move in, Steven. Mistress McGuire will tell you which is my place. Would you like a dog or a bitch?'

'A dog, I think. I'd like a bitch, but she might take a bit of watching with so many neighbours. I don't want to spend my time rearing pups, at least not for a while.'

'I've enjoyed our walk, Steven,' Eddy Caraford said a wee while later. 'I missed our chats when you went away. I'm sure you'll make a go of things here. You were always a thinker as well as a hard worker.'

'Thanks, Dad. I'm glad you came today.'

They had taken longer than they expected and they were hungry by the time they arrived back

129

at the house. Hannah had kindled a fire in the front room and the kettle was propped on the grate and singing merrily.

'You'll have to sit on the floor or on one of the window sills,' she said, bustling in with a basket of sandwiches, a bottle of milk and three white enamel mugs with blue rims.

'What have you been up to when you didn't want us near the kitchen, Mother?' Steven asked with a grin.

'You can peep in at the door, but I don't want you making footprints when I've just scrubbed the floor. That dresser has come up a treat and it's a grand sturdy table. I found two old chairs in the wash house. Even the cooker looks nearly presentable since I took some steel wool to it. It's not one o' them you have to burn coke, is it, Steven?'

'It's an Aga so I think it does need coke. Mrs McGuire said there's a bit left in the wee shed next to the wash house, but I have to apply for a ration to order more. They had one at a farm where I helped with the harvest when I was in the army. They never go out so long as you remember to fill them up every night and morning.'

'I'll need to show you how to make broth, and a casserole with plenty of vegetables. They would simmer nicely in the oven. I've measured the windows. I'll see if I've spare curtains that would do until you get a wife, then she'll likely make her own.' She smiled at Steven and was surprised when the colour rose in his cheeks.

'If I can ever afford to keep a wife,' he mutter-

130

ed, then, almost in the same breath, he added, 'I thought we might take the old brooder back with us while we have the van here. Mr Oliphant said his wife would make some new felt curtains for it.'

'All right,' Hannah said, eyeing him closely. Had mention of a wife brought the Oliphants to mind or was it coincidence? She knew he had continued to write to Megan since Sam's death, but she was away at college now.

'Sam's ma is making me a rag rug for the kitchen.'

'That's kind of her, Steven. Chrissie Oliphant always treated you like a second son. She must miss Sam terribly. Has Megan been helping her?'

'I think so, when she's at home from college anyway.'

'I ordered fifty day-old chicks for you when I ordered ours. They were a wee bit cheaper to order them altogether – fourteen pounds, two and sixpence a hundred. You'll need the brooder if you want to rear them here. I expect you'll want some eggs to sell to bring in some ready cash?'

'Oh, yes, I shall certainly keep some poultry. I'll keep anything if it will earn me a penny or two. I might even consider a hive of bees in the orchard, so long as the McGuires don't object.'

'I got two grey blankets for you, from Binns's sale, and a pair o' cotton pillow cases.'

'How much were they?'

'The blankets were eight shillings and eleven pence. They're not as nice as the white ones, but they were a bargain. It will be cold living here on your own. You'll need plenty of bedding.'

'Thanks, Mother. I'll pay you when I've been to the bank. I shall need to set up an account with a chequebook.'

'Och, Steven, we don't want money for the blankets, or the chicks,' said his mother. 'You'll have enough to buy. I've been gathering a few things together while you've been in Palestine; towels and a few pots and pans. We'll move them all down as soon as you get word you can move in.'

'I can't take them all for nothing...'

'Eh, laddie, your mother enjoys helping you get things together. We both want to see you settled and happy. I'll have a talk to Fred. I reckon we can spare a couple of cows to get you going.'

Steven looked at his father in surprise.

'I ... er ... I don't want to cause any more trouble with Fred.'

'You deserve all the help I can give ye, laddie. Fred should understand that. He's been easier to get along with now Mr Griffiths has agreed to make him a joint tenant. He would have liked it all in his name, but the agent told him he'd need to make some improvements and prove himself a worthy tenant first.'

Nine

The daylight was fading and it was milking time by the time they returned to Willowburn.

'I would help you with the milking, Mother, but I don't think Fred wants me near the farm,' Steven said.

'I know, laddie. Sometimes he tells me not to poke my nose in when I criticize, but he and Edna are so untidy and careless I can't help it occasionally. You can collect the eggs and feed the hens for me if you like. Then you should get away to the Oliphants with the brooder.'

'All right,' Steven agreed readily.

He whistled cheerily as he fed the hens and put the water towers inside to protect them from the frost. He hoped he would manage things as well as his mother. She always had some eggs, even in winter, when it was natural for hens to stop laying. He remembered how difficult it was to teach the pullets to go into their huts at night. Instinct didn't seem to tell them they needed protection from the foxes. When he was little they had all helped shoo them inside, even Fred. He wondered how he would manage them on his own. There were always some wanting to roost in trees or on rafters in the barn. Usually they ended up having their feathers clipped so they

133

couldn't fly so high. Bess, the collie dog, had been almost as good at rounding up the hens and the ducks as she was at herding the sheep. He smiled when he remembered how ready his father had been to buy the pup for him. He hoped he would be able to train it. He was well aware of all the work which lay ahead, especially for a man on his own, but he couldn't afford to employ a boy until he had a steady income.

He was smiling when he drove into the yard and knocked on the door of the Oliphants' house. As he had hoped, it was Megan who answered.

'Steven! I-I didn't expect to see you.' She seemed flustered.

'Aren't you going to ask me in?'

'W-well, y-yes, but Dad and Mum are at the milking.'

'Yes, I thought they would be. It was you I came to see, to tell you about Schoirhead. I've been back there today with my mother and father. I've signed the agreement and posted it off so there's no going back.' He grinned as he followed her along the passage and once into the kitchen he seized her round the waist and hugged her exuberantly – just as he had done when they were young. 'I feel as though I'm setting out on an adventure, Meggie.'

She smiled and shook her head at him. He reminded her of the carefree schoolboy he used to be. Does he still think of me as the twelve-year-old I was when he went away? she wondered, but she was glad he had come.

'Have you been to see Natalie?' she asked

before she could stop herself.

'Natalie? Should I need to see her?' He pulled a face. 'She went with us yesterday. She thinks the house is a dump. Apparently Mrs McGuire overheard her, or so she told Mother. She was not impressed.' He chuckled. 'There's a high wall between the houses. It might stop the Mc-Guires looking, but it doesn't stop Ma McGuire listening.'

'I expect she's bound to be curious about her new neighbours.' Megan smiled as she looked up at him.

'You're still very pale, Megan. Are you feeling any better?'

'Yes, I'm improving. I must get back to college for Monday. I can't afford to miss any more lectures. As it is I shall need to catch up.' She knew she was chattering. She felt a mess in her old skirt and woollen jumper. She hadn't even bothered to braid her hair today. She push-ed it back from her shoulders irritably.

'Don't do that, Megan,' Steven said softly. 'I like your hair loose and soft around your face.' He reached out and stroked the red-gold tresses gently. 'You have lovely hair, but I hardly ever see it like this.'

'It feels a mess. It's needing washed.'

'It's not a mess at all.' Steven smoothed her hair down each side of her face, then he leaned down and kissed first one cheek and then the other. Megan blushed prettily and he laughed and let her go, but she wished he had kissed her lips. She wondered how many girls he had kissed when he had been in the army. They had

135

shared so many confidences in their letters, but Steven had never mentioned any special girl-friends. She ached for him.

They sat side by side in front of the fire and she plied him with questions about the small-holding and he told her his plans and about his father giving him Daisy and buying him a collie pup and the offer of two Willowburn cows.

'Oh, how lovely, Steven. I'm sure your father loves you, but it must be difficult for him living and working with Fred. He was never very pleasant to Sam and you, was he?'

'No, I expect it's his nature.'

'I hope I get to see the wee dog next time I'm home. You will tell me all about him when you write, won't you? Will you still have time to write?' she asked wistfully.

'Of course I shall, and I hope you'll have time to reply.'

They were still talking when John and Chrissie came in from the milking, looking cold and hungry.

'I've asked Steven to stay for supper, Mum. Is that all right?'

'Of course it is,' Chrissie said warmly. 'It's a bitter night out there.'

'I've brought the old brooder,' Steven said, flushing. 'Maybe that's not all right? Mr Oliphant said you might be able to make some new curtains for it?'

'That's fine, Steven. I repaired ours last year and I've plenty of the green felt left. John will help you lift it into the shed before you leave.'

Megan was lifting a meat and potato pie from

the oven and Steven went to help her with a dish of carrot and turnip and a bowl of Brussels sprouts with white sauce. Meat was still rationed, even on farms, but most places grew their own vegetables.

'That's a thing I shall have to do,' he mused. 'Dig the garden and get some vegetables planted. I might need some advice.'

'It's a pity you're away at college, Megan. She's a grand lass in the garden,' John Oliphant said.

'I shall write and ask for instructions then, Megan,' he said, enjoying the warm and friendly atmosphere.

Steven had settled into his new home by mid February. His mother fretted because things seemed stark and bare and the weather was bitterly cold. In December the government had nationalized the railways and the ports; the coal mines had followed in January. Adding to the misery of the food rationing, the dock workers had now gone on strike and troops had been brought in to distribute the meat supplies and prevent cargoes rotting in the ships. None of these things troubled Steven. He was thankful he was no longer in the army, especially when he read of the continuing troubles in the Middle East. He had all the essentials and he was too busy working to worry about the house. He was glad of the warmth of the cooker when he came indoors and it was easier than he had expected to keep it going day and night, but the bill for the load of coke had seemed enormous.

His mother had been down twice with the van loaded with furniture and utensils. Steven had been astonished to see Fred accompanying her the first time she came, apparently to assist with unloading the pieces of furniture. There was a huge wardrobe in the bedroom already, left there by the people who originally owned the farm, according to Mrs McGuire. Fred opened the doors wide, but his demob suit and the few other clothes looked lost in its cavernous interior and his half-brother was not interested in the rich red mahogany which gleamed from Hannah's polishing. Fred poked curiously into every room, but he made no comment. Steven thought he was making sure he had not taken anything of value from Willowburn and he felt a wave of thankfulness that he wouldn't have to cope with Fred's moods every day.

'I hope it makes him realize how lucky he is,' his mother said. 'He has a clean and comfortable home and not a thing to do. You'll be sure to come up on Sundays for your dinner and bring your washing?'

Steven wondered whether he would have the energy to cycle six miles there and six back again after loading and spreading manure all week, but he knew he would have to try. He had no telephone at Schoirhead but few people used one unless it was essential. His mother and Mrs McGuire seemed to be getting on well and they had exchanged numbers in case of an emergency. Steven smiled to himself, wondering how they thought he had survived in the army.

On his second evening at Schoirhead he went

down to see the Kerrs to collect his collie pup. They made him welcome and introduced him to their son Jimmy, who was a year younger than himself.

'How would you like to buy a second-hand motorbike?' he asked with a grin and Steven remembered he was a mechanic.

'I'd like it fine, but I've to count my pennies until I get some cows and some money coming in.'

'It would be handy for you getting home and to the markets.'

'Aye, it would, but the bus or my bike will have to do me for a while,' Steven said ruefully.

'Sorry, mate.'

'Shall I tell you if I come across another bargain?' Jimmy asked.

'Give me six months or so to see how things are going.'

Steven was glad of the little dog's company.

'I have named him Shandy,' he wrote in one of his letters to Megan. She seemed interested in everything he had to say about the farm and he wished she had been able to see it instead of Natalie. Her criticisms still irritated him, especially when he looked around the empty rooms. At least the rug from the Oliphants had added a spot of cheerful comfort to the kitchen and his mother had displayed some plates and bowls on the Welsh dresser.

'What does Shandy look like?' Megan wrote back. 'I'm longing to see him.'

'He's a black and tan collie with a white bib and a white tip to his tail,' he wrote back. 'He

139

has the brightest eyes and he watches everything I do. Sometimes I think he can tell the time the way he pricks up his ears when he thinks I should move on to the next job, especially when it is time to eat.

'Mrs McGuire is always grateful for my help with some of the heavy jobs and Shandy looks up at her with such a beguiling look, she always finds him a treat of some kind. I think I am lucky with my neighbours. Now I'm getting to know them, I'm sure you'll like them too. Mr McGuire's arthritis seems worse with this cold weather and he can't do much himself. So far his wife has kept me supplied with eggs and milk and she made me a rice pudding the other day. Thanks for explaining about the scrambled eggs, Megan. When you have time I shall be glad to have more easy recipes. I didn't know you had learned to cook. I wish you were here to do it for me.'

Megan wished she was there too. Did Steven really mean that or did he simply mean he wanted someone to cook for him? Her heart ached at the thought of him being alone in a cold empty house, but she knew he couldn't afford a housekeeper. Money must be tight until he had an income coming in. She wished she had been nearer to lend a hand, but it would be a year come June before she finished at college. There was no telling where she would get a job teaching to get her parchment either. She wondered whether Natalie had been down to see Steven since he moved in. It would be so easy for her, especially now she had a car of her own.

* * *

Steven had emptied the midden and one of the sheds and the McGuires had offered to lend him their elderly gelding to work beside Daisy for the ploughing.

'I'm taking a day off to go to Annan market before I start the ploughing,' he said to Mr McGuire. 'I intend to buy two dairy cows. It will take most of the day by the time I walk them home. I wondered if you would keep an eye on Shandy for me. He's too young to be any help yet.'

'But you'll have to milk twice a day, clean the byre and wash up in the dairy as well as doing the ploughing. And what would ye feed them on?' Mr McGuire sounded alarmed.

'There's half a haystack and the loft above the stable is full of hay. I paid for it in the valuation when I took over the tenancy,' Steven said, assuring him the cows would not go hungry. 'I need to start producing something to sell.'

'Aye, aye, I suppose so. I could sell you a load or two of turnips. We'll not need them all now we've only half the cows.'

'That would be ideal,' Steven said, and immediately negotiated the price.

'What it is tae be young and fit?' Mr McGuire sighed enviously, eyeing his two walking sticks with a scowl. 'I don't know how we'd manage if the wife couldna milk the cows that's left. We've only four now. Last winter we had seven or eight milking, before I became sae crippled.'

'Maybe the pain will ease when the better weather comes,' Steven said comfortingly.

'That's what I thought last summer, but it didna help much. Anyway, laddie, I'll write down the name of a fellow who has a wee lorry. Mention my name and he'll give you a fair price to bring your beasts home. It's six to eight miles to walk them back frae the market. It will save you time.'

'Thanks. I'll look out for your man.'

Steven enjoyed the atmosphere and excitement of the market. He inspected all the dairy animals carefully, avoiding the three farmers his father had warned him about as well as the dealers. He made his selection. His first choice was an Ayrshire heifer, newly calved with a full neat udder. He was disappointed when she made five guineas more than he could afford. The next one was an Ayrshire cross Shorthorn, ready to calve her second calf and Steven bought her for 45 guineas. Several others that he had marked out made too much money and it was getting towards the end of the sale before he managed to buy a second animal, a newly calved Ayrshire cow for 49 guineas. As he turned away from the ring, a man tapped him on the shoulder.

'Are you Steven Caraford?'

'I am. Should I know you?'

'Your neighbour, Annie McGuire, telephoned me last night. She mentioned you might be looking for transport.' He grinned. 'She said I was to give you a fair price. I've a couple of heifers to deliver down your way. If you'll help me load them, I'll give you a lift home in the lorry.' Steven readily accepted the man's price and the lift home, and sent a silent prayer for the

McGuires. He would be glad to get home and settle his animals in their newly bedded stalls. The cow's udder was swollen with milk and she would welcome the relief of being properly milked. Optimistically he had set up the milk cooler and a churn in the dairy before he left. Tomorrow he would send away his first milk for sale when the lorry collected McGuire's. Jubilantly he looked forward to Sunday and telling his father he was in the business of farming at last, even if it was a very small step up the ladder.

Eddy Caraford was delighted with his news. He knew most of the local dairy farmers and he seemed to approve when Steven told him the names of the two whose cows he had bought. 'I'm glad things are beginning to work out, lad. We've some heifers coming to the calving. I'll send you four Willowburn cows as soon as I can arrange it. It takes as long to wash up the dairy and clean the byre for two as it does for six and you'll get a better milk cheque. Thank goodness for the Milk Marketing Board. We know we can rely on getting the money at the end of the month these days.'

'That would be brilliant...' Steven began, then he noticed Fred's sullen mouth and narrowed eyes. He knew that look. Clearly Fred didn't object to him taking away his bed and bedding but he resented him getting any help to make a living. He changed the subject. The last thing he wanted was another quarrel or anything which would upset his parents.

* * *

As soon as Steven set off home, Fred exploded.

'I thought we'd agreed Daisy and the plough would be enough for him. If you send him cows, he'll never be finished wanting more.'

'Steven has never asked for anything,' Eddy said firmly. 'It was my idea. He deserves his share and I want to help him get a decent start.'

'He's had enough,' Fred snarled, and stomped out of the house, his mouth set. He'd expected that he had seen the last of his half-brother when he was posted to France, but he'd always succeeded at everything he attempted, even surviving. Deep down he knew Steven had as much right to their father's stock as he had. Eddy had been less easily manipulated since Steven came back. He didn't want to antagonize the old man completely, but neither would he agree to him sending any of the Willowburn cows to swell Steven's bank balance. He considered what could be done.

Fred was not intelligent, but he was sly. He devised a plan which would benefit himself even more than his cursed half-brother.

'Father, if you insist Steven must have four cows,' he said later that evening, 'I'll go to Annan market and buy him four. I can get them delivered straight to his farm.'

'But we don't need...'

'You keep saying we should have more milk so we'll keep our own heifers,' Fred interrupted sharply, although they all knew he would not be the one to milk them if he could avoid it.

'All right,' his father agreed. Maybe Fred really was getting keener to expand their own herd now that his name was on the tenancy and they had had a good run of dairy heifers this year. 'Make sure you choose four decent animals. Steven always preferred Ayrshires.'

'I'll see to it.' But there was a spiteful gleam in Fred's eyes.

Many of the Cheshire dairy farmers concentrated on producing as much milk as possible so they did not rear calves from their own herd as replacements. This meant there was a constant demand for dairy heifers from further afield. There were several reputable cattle dealers who regularly attended markets in the North of England and Scotland in search of good dairy animals to fill orders for farmers further south. They made their living by buying and selling. Unfortunately, there were always one or two who were less reputable. Fred had heard of one in particular who bought up cheap animals anywhere he could get them, often bringing them over from Ireland, to sell on to other dealers in England. He strolled around the market pens until he spied the man in a pen of twenty cattle of indeterminate breeds and ages – black, roan, red, white.

'What're ye asking for them?' he demanded officiously.

The dealer eyed him silently, chewing on a straw. 'Thirty-eight guineas for the four older ones, thirty for the rest.'

Fred smirked to himself. He knew Steven had been prepared to pay fifty guineas for decent animals.

'I'll take the four older ones, but you'll have to make 'em twenty-five guineas.'

'Twenty-eight guineas and I pick two of 'em,' the man said slyly.

'It's a deal,' Fred said with glee. He didn't care if the man picked the poorest of the bunch. They were all ill thriven compared to the rest of the animals at the market and he knew neither his father not Steven would have given them a second glance. 'When will they calve?'

'That one calved this morning.' He shrugged. 'That's probably why she's discharging. The two blue-roans should calve in the next couple o' months.' The dealer gave a hollow laugh. The farm where they had come from had lost most of the calves due to contagious abortion. He rarely sold direct to farmers, especially locally, but he didn't like the attitude of this arrogant fellow. Fred knew his father would not approve, but his dear parent would never see them if they were delivered directly to Steven. He searched around for a haulier to deliver them.

'My lorry is a bit small, but I reckon it will hold your four scraggy mongrels,' the young driver said bluntly when Fred approached him. He scowled at him but his price was too reasonable to refuse.

'This is the delivery address. Send your haulage account to me at this address.'

'What? Are you sure this scrawny bunch are for Schoirhead? I delivered two cows there last week. One o' them was better than this lot put together.'

'That's none o' your business,' Fred snapped.

'He's lucky to get them. He's not paying.'

'This lot could prove dear at a gift,' the haulier muttered. 'You're sure he'll take them?'

'Beggars can't be choosers,' Fred snarled, and strode away.

The haulier frowned uneasily, but he had his instructions.

Fred had a deal of his own to do if he was to make his parents believe he'd paid a decent price for Steven's animals. Besides, he was determined to make a bit of cash on the side for himself and his stepmother was fussy about her bookkeeping since the government had insisted on everybody keeping accounts and paying tax since the war started.

Even at the pedigree ring, the dealers all kept a sharp eye open for a bargain and this one watched in astonishment when he saw Fred bidding against the man at his side. They both wanted the fine young Ayrshire cow. The auctioneer knocked the animal down to Fred at 58 guineas. Minutes later, the dealer couldn't believe his eyes. He watched Fred selling the cow privately at the ringside to the farmer who had been second bidder. What was the young fool playing at? He must have sold the cow for less than he'd just paid for her. He edged closer round the ring. He saw a bundle of notes changing hands. Fred put them carefully in his inside pocket.

'Queer way to do business,' the dealer muttered, shaking his head.

Across the ring Mr Turner and his herdsman, John Oliphant, also watched curiously as they waited for three of their own animals to come into the ring to be sold.

Fred had made sure he paid the dealer and the auction company by cheque. The total sum from the two cheque stubs would amount to a 170 guineas and that was the only proof of his purchases he intended to produce for his stepmother and her precious records. She would assume he'd paid an average of 40-odd guineas for Steven's animals. He smiled slyly to himself. The sale note from the auction company would be conveniently lost and there was nothing to say he had sold the cow to another buyer for cash. He patted the wad of notes in his breast pocket and gave a snort of satisfaction.

At Schoirhead the driver opened the back doors of the cattle lorry. Steven stared at the scraggy, ill-thriven animals. He couldn't hide his dismay.

'Is this some sort of joke? Are you sure these are for me?'

'Aye, I'm sure,' the driver said, watching him anxiously.

'I can't believe my father would send me cattle like these.'

'The buyer wasna old enough to be your father, but he gave me your address. This is the name he gave me to send my bill.' He pulled out a second piece of paper.

'Fred!' Steven groaned. 'He's my half-brother. I'll bet he bought the cheapest animals he could find. A single cow from Willowburn would be better than all this lot.' He pushed his cap back from his head and rubbed his temple. He was tempted to send them to Willowburn and tell

148

Fred what he should do with them. Then he thought about his father. Would he be hurt by his rejection? He sighed. 'I suppose they'll grow once they can get out to some good pasture,' he said resignedly. 'We'd better get them unloaded. These two look more like Galloways than dairy beasts and they're a long way off calving. The udder on one of the other cows is so swollen she can barely walk. I'll milk her straight away. The sooner they all get some hay and water and a bedded stall to lie in the better, poor devils.'

'Do you mind if I leave my lorry here while I pop round to see the McGuires?' the driver asked once he had helped Steven tie the animals in the byre. 'Old McGuire is a cousin o' my father's. I hear he's been crippled with his arthritis this winter.'

'He has. He'll be pleased to have your chat.'

Steven reckoned it would snow before morning and he was glad to get into the warm kitchen as soon as he had taken care of all his animals for the night. After he had eaten his supper he settled himself beside the Aga with his writing pad and fountain pen to write to Megan. He didn't try to hide his bitter disappointment. It was a relief to be able to confide in her.

I would have been happier with one cow from Willowburn rather than these four ill thriven rats. I can only pray they don't bring any disease with them for they don't look that healthy to me and one is discharging badly.

149

Megan's heart sank when she read Steven's letter. She longed for him to make a success of his little farm. She knew as well as anyone how easy it was to spread tuberculosis, mastitis and other diseases into a herd if cattle were introduced from a dubious source. Her father, and both sets of grandparents, had been dairymen all their lives and she had been brought up understanding about animals, especially cows. It was the main reason her mother had been so keen for her to go to college so that she would have an easier way of earning a decent living. Fred was sly as well as jealous. Megan had no doubts that he had deliberately done the cheapest, meanest deal possible, but surely even Fred would not buy unhealthy animals? Maybe they just needed some good food. Her father often said some farmers half starved their animals in winter if they had had a poor hay crop.

Ten

Flurries of snow accompanied the bitter wind, but they all knew it was bound to come when it had been so bad in England in February with blocked roads and railways and even Buckingham Palace lit by candles.

Steven spent a great deal of time breaking ice on the water bowls, even though they were in the relative warmth of the byre, but it was essential that the cows should have water if they were to produce any milk. He had to take a sledge hammer to the thick ice on the water trough in the yard before he could lead Daisy out to drink and he did the same for the McGuires, earning their gratitude yet again. Each morning it was the same all over again but none of this made Steven feel as sickened as the sight of the two scraggy blue-black mongrel heifers. He wouldn't be able to pretend to be grateful when he saw his parents and he couldn't bear to see Fred's sly smirk.

He went round to see Mrs McGuire.

'Would you mind telephoning Willowburn please? Tell Mother I shall not be up for Sunday dinner tomorrow. There's plenty to do here keeping the animals watered and fed and I reckon we could have more snow.'

'We could, I suppose,' Annie McGuire said, eyeing him shrewdly. 'I'll let her know.'

After passing on Steven's message, she mentioned the new cattle.

'Tom Green, the haulier, is a relative o' ours. He's a bit concerned about the animals he was asked to deliver to your laddie from one o' the dealers. He said Steven looked horrified when he saw them.'

'Surely they weren't as bad as that, Annie?' The two women were on first name terms now.

'I only know what Tom said and he's a fair judge o' men and animals. Steven hasn't even mentioned them to us. He hasn't invited McGuire round to see them like he did with the two he bought himself.'

'We haven't seen them,' Hannah said slowly. 'Maybe we should come down to Schoirhead. I could cook the Sunday dinner there. It will make a change if Steven doesn't want to cycle all this way. Will you tell him we're coming down if the snow holds off, please, Annie?'

'That's a grand idea, Hannah,' Eddy said, pleased with her suggestion. 'I can see his cows and how he's getting on.'

Fred was furious on Sunday morning when he heard their plans. His father would be sure to inspect Steven's animals. He would know immediately they were nothing like the quality he would have bought himself. He would never have given them a glance.

Hannah noticed the blaze of anger in his eyes and the tight lips.

'You can come with us if you like, Fred. Edna is spending today visiting friends so you'll be on your own.'

'I can make my own dinner,' he snarled ungraciously. 'I don't see why you have to waste petrol trailing down there. It could snow before night.'

'Your father wants to see the cattle he's paid for,' she said.

'*We* paid for them. I'm a partner too,' he reminded her sullenly.

'You're a partner because your father has been so generous to you. Surely you must see Steven deserves something from his father too?' she prompted gently.

'I've earned my share. He's never earned anything for this place.' Hannah's blue eyes met his steadily, but she simply shook her head in despair. Does fighting for his country count for nothing with people like Fred? she wondered.

Steven had received a letter from Megan on Saturday morning. She always cheered him up and helped him look on the bright side and she was right. He was still ashamed to own such scraggy animals, but the two milking cows had settled in and were milking steadily, even if the yields were a bit low, and his own two cows were doing splendidly. He was proud to be sending away a morning and an evening churn on the milk lorry now, even though neither of them were full yet. He was looking forward eagerly to getting his first milk cheque at the end of the month.

He hoped Shandy would not chew any more chair legs when his parents came to visit, but he was sure they would love him. Mrs McGuire seemed to get on well with his mother and she had invited them all round for afternoon tea before they returned to Willowburn.

'Well, Steven I'm pleased to see you're happier than I expected,' Hannah greeted him with relief, thinking Annie McGuire must have exaggerated.

'Mmm.' He grinned at her. 'I had a letter from Megan yesterday and she always cheers me up.'

'How much longer has she to do at college?'

'Another year come the summer, then a year's practical teaching. I can't imagine Megan being strict enough to be a teacher.'

'I hear she's grown into an attractive young woman. I saw Mrs Andrews yesterday when I was delivering my eggs. Her daughter Maryanne is at college with Megan. She says she's very popular with the students who come to the dances from the agricultural college. Her own laddie, Rufus, has a fancy for her himself.'

'Does he?' Steven muttered.

His mother bit back a smile. The Oliphants were a decent, hard-working family and she would welcome Megan as a daughter-in-law if Steven got around to seeing her in that light before it was too late, but it would be a while before either of them could think of marriage by the sound of things.

'Shall we go and see what you've been doing, Steven?' his father asked. 'Let your mother get on with cooking the dinner. I'd like to see the cattle Fred bought. He says he's forgotten the name of the farmer who was selling them.'

Steven chewed his lower lip. He was sure his

father would be as disappointed as he had been. Eddy was unprepared for the shock which awaited him.

'Good gracious! Surely these are not the animals Fred bought? The haulier must have made a mistake.'

'I'm afraid there's no mistake,' Steven said unhappily.

'How could he waste good money, any money, on such rubbish?' Eddy's face paled with anger as he moved along the byre to take a closer look. 'Oh my God...' he breathed.

Steven knew his father never blasphemed.

'What's wrong?' he asked tensely. hurrying to his side. 'Oh no!' He could have wept. There, lying in the channel, was the hairless fetus of a calf. 'She's aborted! They were all right at milking time. This is one of the things I feared when I saw them.'

'You've reason to be afraid with a bunch like this.' His father almost spat the words. 'This is a dealer's rubbish or my name's not Eddy Caraford.'

'I admit I was disappointed when I saw them,' Steven said, 'but I thought they might grow when they got out to grass. I-I hadna bargained for this though.' He stared at the lifeless fetus with despair in his eyes.

'Have you a spare shed, Steven? I'll help you get these two heifers into it. Keep them away from the rest and pray they haven't spread any disease already.'

'But what good is that now?'

'You can see this one aborted well before her

time. The heifer has no udder yet and she'll have no milk. Take my advice and get them out of here. Keep them away from the rest and fatten them up if you can. They're half Galloways anyway by the look of them. They would probably kick all the way through milking. You're better without them.' He rubbed his forehead and shook his head. 'I can't believe Fred would spend all that money on animals like these.'

Steven frowned, gnawing the inside of his cheek, his jaw clenched.

'I wish I'd never seen them. It will take months to get them fit for sale, even as store beasts.'

'We'll put them into one of the sheds you've mucked out and give them some bedding,' his father said decisively. 'I'll go to Annan market myself and see whether I can persuade the seller to take them back.'

'Even if you find him, he'll never do that!' Steven gave a hollow laugh.

'I can always ask. Fred reckoned he couldn't remember the man's name and now I know he didn't want to remember. This lot are the tail end of a cheap dealer's gatherings,' he muttered in disgust.

They untied the two young heifers and chased them into one of the newly cleaned sheds. Steven had never seen his father so tight lipped and his face was worryingly grey and pinched.

'If you've any Jeyes' Fluid, we'll disinfect the byre where these two have been,' Eddy said grimly. 'Can you lend me a pair of wellingtons? Make sure you don't walk through any discharge and spread it to the rest.'

'You really think it's serious then, Dad, not just due to the heifer being shunted about in lorries?'

'I hope I'm wrong, lad, but you can't afford to risk it,' his father said, shaking his head slowly. 'Nobody could, let alone somebody just beginning in farming. If it is contagious abortion it can ruin a man if it spreads through the herd. You end up with calves born early, usually dead, and then the dam doesna milk. It's a vicious circle.'

Before he went to bed that evening Steven wrote to Megan, telling her about his parents' visit.

I don't know whether I'm more worried about the possibility of these beasts bringing disease to the place before I even get started farming, or about Dad. I've never seen him look so disillusioned and disgusted. When he saw the fetus lying in the channel I thought he was going to have a heart attack. He looked so drawn and pale, as though his very soul had been torn out of him. We were invited round to the McGuires, but he refused to go. All he wanted was to get home as soon as they had eaten their dinner. It spoiled our day. I saw Mother giving him anxious looks. I expect he would tell her everything on the way home. It's never easy to keep anything from Mother. She has a way of worming things out of us – well not out of Fred apparently. He's too sly, even for Mother.

He told her about Shandy's antics and his neighbours. He read the letter through, but before he sealed it he added a postscript.

I know it's a while until Easter, but I wondered if you would come to a dance with me when you come home for the holidays. I could cycle up to your house, but I'm afraid we'd have to walk to the village hall and back. I've no hope of affording any sort of vehicle for a long while at this rate so I shall understand if you choose to go with your young doctor friend, instead.

When she read the letter Megan's spirits fluctuated between feeling desperately sorry for Steven's struggles to get established in his wee farm and soaring with happiness that he was beginning to see her as a woman at last. It was the first time he had asked her out on a proper date. She danced around her tiny room hugging her pillow, wishing she was already in his arms. She came to a sudden halt.

What did he mean about her young doctor friend? She frowned. Only one person could have told him about her having a lift home with Doctor Gray and that was Natalie Turner. They must keep in close contact. Had she been trying to stir up trouble? If that was her intention it had backfired. It had probably made Steven realize she was no longer a schoolgirl, but it also meant Natalie wanted Steven herself or why would she want to cause a rift between them?

It would be years before Steven could seriously consider marriage, even without Fred's dirty tricks holding him back, but if he married Natalie her father would give him all the help he needed and probably get Steven a large farm to rent, she thought dejectedly. Marrying Natalie would be the easiest and the quickest way to becoming an established farmer. Resolutely, Megan refused to think about Natalie Turner. Steven had invited her to go dancing and that's what mattered. Lost in her youthful dreams, Megan was oblivious to the snow storms which were affecting the whole country. It didn't enter her head they might have dire consequences for Steven too. People were miserable enough without the atrocious weather; the rationing was already serious and the strikes and fuel shortages had added even more restrictions.

Fred had never seen his father look so grim and silent as he did when he returned from Steven's. He knew the reason, but he felt no remorse. It didn't occur to him that it was not only the condition of the cattle which dismayed Eddy Caraford. He was an honest and trustworthy man himself and he was sickened by the knowledge that his elder son would play such a mean and shabby trick. He could no longer turn a blind eye to such faults. In his heart he had known for a long time that Fred resembled his late father-in-law rather than himself, and he bore no resemblance at all to the gentle woman who had been his mother.

Eddy knew Hannah blamed herself because she was responsible for Fred's upbringing, but he knew she had always been fair and kind to both his sons. He could not have managed without Hannah. He could no longer hide from the truth. He had done his best to set a good example. He had done everything he could to compensate for the loss of Fred's mother, and to show him he was loved, but Fred had become increasingly selfish and demanding as the years passed. Enough was enough. He had to accept the true character of his elder son and do something about it before it was too late.

'On Friday I'm going to the market myself,' he said to Fred. 'You bought those ill-thriven beasts from a dealer. I shall find him, even if I have to ask everybody I meet. I shall ask him to take them back.'

'You must be mad!' Fred said, staring at his father as though he had grown horns. He gave a harsh laugh. 'Even if you find him, he'll never take them back. You're crazy.'

'I'm not expecting he will, but I intend to try. You paid a ridiculous amount for them anyway. I thought you were a better judge of cattle than that. If he won't take them back, I've told Steven to send the two blue greys as store cattle and I shall buy him two decent animals in their place.'

'You can't do that!' Fred blustered. 'Remember I'm a partner. I have a say in what happens.'

'I haven't forgotten I was fool enough to make you a partner. I thought I could trust you. Now I know I can't. There'll be little profit for any of us this year unless the dealer will repay me for Steven's animals.'

'Suit yourself.' Fred smirked. He had all the

160

profit he needed for a while with the cash he had hidden away. That had been a nice little deal he'd done at the ringside. Even his clever little stepmother hadn't suspected he had tricked them all.

Steven smiled and his spirits lifted when he received Megan's reply to his letter.

I shall look forward to going to a dance with you, Steven, but if you intend doing the American jitterbug you will have to teach me first. Though I'm not sure if our local bands will be able to play the music. I hope you will not find us all too tame after army life.

I have another bit of news. Dad has bought a second-hand car and he has promised to teach me to drive during the summer holidays. He knows you can drive so he may offer us the car – not that I mind walking, as you should know, but I hope the weather is not as bitterly cold as it is here tonight. We are all wrapped in our eiderdowns as we try to study for our exams.

Steven always felt better for Megan's cheerful letters. She wrote as she talked and he could almost imagine she was at his side. He would never admit it to his mother, or anyone else, but he did find the silent house rather lonely during the winter evenings. He had grown used to the company of his fellow soldiers during his years in the army. He had yearned to be free then, but it seemed there was a price to pay for freedom too. He found himself longing for Megan's companionship – and more. The blood stirred in him as he remembered the feel of her pliable young body against his own. She was so small and neat, and yet she was remarkably strong and tireless.

Looking back, he thought he had always felt a tenderness for Megan, but recently he recognized there was more to it. When he thought of the hard work and small rewards which lay ahead, he wondered whether he had made the right decision. During these first few weeks all he seemed to do was spend his precious savings. They were already into March and he had hoped the spring grass would soon be showing signs of growing but the heavy snow and the bitter March winds had blighted his hopes for an early spring. He was glad to buy all the turnips the McGuires could spare to feed his few cows.

'How long has Mr McGuire been lame with the arthritis?' he asked his wife one morning as he shovelled turnips into his cart.

'Och it's bothered him for years, but it got really bad about harvest time last year. That's why we sold half the cows and the reason we have turnips to sell. He would hate to leave here, but I don't know how he'll manage to carry on. He keeps saying he'll be better once the warm weather comes again, but I can't see him being fit to trudge behind the horses to plough our field for the corn and it's still a government regulation even though the war is over. Things are scarcer than ever.' She sighed heavily.

'I reckon we shall all feel better when we get

some spring sunshine,' Steven comforted her.

'Aye, I hope so. I've been baking scones. Come in and try one before you go back round to your own place, laddie.' She scurried back into the house, leaving Steven wondering whether he could manage to plough his own fields and help the McGuires as well. He guessed Mrs McGuire was hoping he would, but the year was getting on. He didn't know then that the ploughing would prove a simple problem compared with the other worries which awaited.

Eleven

Hannah was tense and worried as she drove Eddy to market the following Friday. It was already snowing heavily and she hated driving on icy roads, but he was insistent he must go today and in person. All week he had looked drawn and tired. Her heart ached for him. She knew how disillusioned he must feel now that he had seen Fred's treachery for himself. She had known it must happen one day, but neither of them had yet discovered the lengths Fred would go to cheat his own father.

'Are you sure we shouldn't turn back, Eddy?' she asked for the third time. 'The weather could be worse before we get home again.'

'They've had most of the snow in the south this year. We had the driest February I can remember in this area,' Eddy said. 'We're into March now, so even if the snow does get heavier it'll probably have gone by the time we return home. I can't delay another week or that dealer will have forgotten he ever sold those beasts to Fred. I expect he handles thousands. That's his business.'

Eddy found the dealer without much difficulty. He knew most of the farmers in the market, as well as the auctioneer and the market helpers and several of them had been surprised to see Fred doing business with the man. He had less success trying to persuade him to take back the cattle. In the end he offered to buy back the two cross bred heifers for fifteen pounds each.

'Fifteen pounds!' Eddy echoed incredulously. 'Fred paid over forty. That's daylight robbery.'

'Forty?' The dealer stared at him as though he had lost his senses. 'He paid twenty-eight a piece and the two milk cows were fairly decent animals for that price. I buy for another dealer. I don't usually sell to local farmers, but he was such a cocky fellow I thought he needed taking down a bit. Is he your son?' Eddy didn't answer. He frowned and rubbed his temple.

'Twenty-eight pounds,' he said hoarsely. 'For all four? Then what did he buy with the rest o' the money?' he muttered, more to himself than the dealer.

'As to that, he was doing some sort o' deal at the ringside. I couldn't reckon up what kind o' game he was playing, but if ye dinna mind me saying so, I wadna trust him wi' my money. I saw him buy a damned good cow through the auction, but he sold her again straight away. Privately. To the runner-up. He must have got less than he'd paid for her. It didn't make sense to me.'

'You didn't notice who the runner-up was, I suppose?' Eddy asked carefully. His face was white now and he gripped the metal bar of the pens tightly, feeling another dizzy spell. They were coming too often recently. The doctor had said it was tension and he ought to relax more.

Relax! How could he do that?

'It was a farmer. I think his name is McDougall, but I could be wrong. I see hundreds of cattle sold every week and I often buy through the ring.'

'McDougall?' Eddy repeated vaguely and blinked, trying to clear his head.

'So what d'ye want to do about the two bluegreys?'

'They're at my other son's. Collect them soon as you can. I'll give you his address. Pay him the thirty pounds. He can put the money towards a decent dairy cow.'

The dealer nodded.

'I'll pay him in cash when I lift them.' He jotted Steven's address in his notebook, then moved on to attend to other business, leaving Eddy Caraford still holding on to the rails as he struggled to make sense of Fred's actions.

A little while later he saw a neighbour of the McDougalls and without any prompting the man remarked on Fred's peculiar behaviour at the market a fortnight ago.

'Billy McDougall was delighted when your lad changed his mind about taking yon cow home to Willowburn. He'd bid it up as far as he could afford to go because she was a pedigree beast and he fancied the breeding. What was wrong with her? Your lad must have lost a guinea or two for Billy to buy her off him.'

'I don't know what was wrong with the cow. He didn't say.'

'Queer way to go on, if ye ask me. He wouldna accept a cheque so he was lucky Billy had just drawn the money from the sale o' his pigs. That's why he had enough on him to pay in cash. He said it was his lucky day.'

He moved on to talk to some other farmers. Eddy stood still, his mind refusing to accept what he had just heard. His head swam but there was no getting away from it - Fred was not only mean and spiteful with his own brother, he was a thief and a liar. Slowly he made his way back to the place he had arranged to meet Hannah. She was already in the van, drumming her fingers nervously, although she hadn't expected Eddy to return for another half hour or more.

'Eddy, you look frozen.' Worse than that he looked blue around his mouth. 'Let's get home. I don't suppose you found the man you wanted, but it's not worth all this worrying.'

'It will be a bigger worry if those dratted animals have carried any disease to Steven's place. I did see the dealer though and he's agreed to take back the two scraggy wee heifers but he'd only offer fifteen pounds each.' He hadn't meant to tell Hannah about Fred's dishonesty, but he couldn't keep it to himself. It was going round and round in his head until he thought it was going to burst. 'So he must have pocketed the cash...' Eddy's voice trailed away. He looked defeated.

Hannah was speechless. She couldn't believe even Fred would stoop so low. She reached out a comforting hand to Eddy, but at that moment a small lorry came skidding down the incline towards them. The driver couldn't control it on the slippery surface. It caught the rear end of the van and slewed it around before it continued on its way slithering down the hill. One rear wheel of the van was stuck in a shallow ditch on the opposite side of the road. Hannah and Eddy climbed out to survey the damage. The snow was falling faster now.

'Such weather for March!' Hannah muttered, setting her shoulder against the van in an effort to force it back on to the road, but she was too small and her strength too puny to have any effect.

'You get back in,' Eddy said, 'and be ready to drive it off as I lift, and keep it going until you have it under control. I'll catch you up.'

Hannah obeyed and on the third heave from Eddy the van shot forward, skidding until it was almost facing the way it had come, but Hannah managed to get it straightened up and continued driving as slowly she could. She was almost afraid to stop in case the van wouldn't draw away. She reached the top of the incline and pulled the van to a halt to wait for Eddy, keeping the engine running. Her fingers and toes were so frozen she had little feeling in them in spite of her woollen gloves and thick stockings. It seemed to take a long while for Eddy to manage the few hundred yards, but finally he climbed into the van.

'Let's get home,' he gasped and slumped into his seat. His face looked a strange purple colour now, but Hannah assumed it was due to the cold wind and the effort of lifting the van. She was truly thankful when they reached the road up to Willowburn. She noticed the milk churns still on

168

the stand at the road end and knew the milk lorry had not managed to get through yet, so some of the roads must be even worse than theirs.

It was a relief to drive into the open-fronted shed next to the house.

'Come on, Eddy, I expect you're as ready for a cup of hot tea as I am.'

He opened his eyes and looked at her vacantly. In the dim light of the garage it was difficult to see, but she thought his face looked grey and haggard.

'I can't let it go, Hannah. I've been thinking what to say to him. I have to confront Fred this time, and without Edna listening in. Those two are getting too friendly and too smug. I wouldn't be surprised if she knows what he's done and thinks he's smart, but she'll find out that a man who has no respect for his parents will have none for a wife, if that's what she's aiming for. She'll be as doomed to disillusion with Fred as I've been.'

'Oh, Eddy,' Hannah said softly, 'I've never heard you so cynical before. Don't think about Fred now. You look shattered to bits. Money isn't everything. Come inside and get something hot inside you, then you can decide what to do.'

Fred and Edna were already sitting at the kitchen table, their dirty dinner dishes strewn around them. They were drinking tea and they had eaten almost the whole of the cake which Hannah had baked early that morning. Fred eyed his father with sullen defiance. The sight of them sitting there so warm and comfortable seemed to light a torch in Eddy Caraford. He

169

looked at Edna.

'Get out to the byre and do the work you're paid to do. Now!'

The land girl stared at him in amazement. He was always so polite and gentlemanly. She opened her mouth to protest, closed it again, glanced at Fred and shrugged as she made for the door.

Hannah busied herself shoving the soup pan on to the hob and making fresh tea, but her heart was pounding. She had never seen Eddy so angry or upset. Fred didn't care for his father's expression either. He stood up.

'Stay where you are!' Eddy ordered 'I never thought I'd have a son who is a cheat and a liar. I expect you thought you were clever to send Steven the cheapest rubbish you could buy. It was a dirty, selfish trick.'

'It's as much as he deserves.'

'Shut up and listen to me for once. You're jealous and spiteful and you've never had any reason to be. Today I discovered that my own son is a thief and I can't forgive that.'

'What d'ye mean by that?' Fred demanded belligerently.

Hannah noticed the wary look in his eyes.

'I mean the cash you pocketed and said nothing about, pretending you'd spent it on cattle for Steven.'

'I did...'

'You bought a good cow and sold it again for cash. Where's the money now? I'll tell you where! You pocketed it. That's stealing, stealing from your own family.'

'I've earned it,' Fred sneered. 'Stop your

ranting, old man. You know you can't farm Willowburn without me. You can't even drive the tractor and...'

'I can manage without you,' Eddy snapped. 'You find yourself a job and see how you like working for a boss and earning your living. You're the one who should have gone to the army. I see that now. It would have done you good!' The veins were standing out on his temples as he became more and more agitated.

'Hush, Eddy, sit down and I'll pour you some tea,' Hannah said soothingly. She looked at Fred and jerked her head towards the door.

'You'd better get on with the work until your father calms down,' she said quietly.

Fred scowled at her. 'I'll go when I'm ready...'

'Get out! Get out of my sight,' Eddy shouted.

Then, before either of them could move, he seemed to crumple and crash to the floor. In a flash Hannah was kneeling beside him, her heart pounding. She stroked back the wisps of white hair. When had Eddy gone so white? She saw his mouth working, but no sound came and his face looked strangely lopsided.

'Phone for the doctor, Fred,' she ordered.

'He'll not come out in this weather...'

'Phone him! You must meet him with the tractor. Tell him ... Tell him I-I think your f-father has h-had a stroke.'

The next few days were a nightmare for Hannah as she watched over her husband with tender care. She had telephoned the McGuires with a message for Steven, telling him Eddy had

171

suffered a stroke but he was holding his own.

Steven longed to visit his parents. Instead he had to struggle with the snowstorms which blocked the roads and isolated him and his fellow smallholders from the rest of the world. He blamed himself for his father's stroke, but how could he have prevented him from seeing the animals Fred had sent. After all, it was their father's money Fred had wasted.

He longed to tell him the cattle didn't matter, nothing mattered in comparison to his health and peace of mind. Many of the phone lines were down and he didn't like pestering the McGuires to use their telephone. He wished he had put his name down for one of his own now instead of penny pinching.

'No news is good news, laddie,' Mrs McGuire comforted him.

'I know, but Mother could have talked to me whenever she needed if I'd applied for a phone connection.'

'Och, laddie, ye'd never have been in the house to answer it,' Mr McGuire said. 'You've spent every spare minute shovelling snow.'

This was true. The remaining prisoners of war from one of the local camps were working to clear the main road, but the side roads were piled high with drifting snow. All the Schoirhead Loaning smallholdings shared the same side road running from the main road almost to the shore. The milk lorry had been unable to get through to collect their milk. Steven's holding was the nearest to the main road, but it was still a couple of miles away. On the second day of being snowbound they all assembled at Schoirhead and worked together to dig their way through. Then they worked their way back making a track wide enough for a careful driver to get through with his horse and cart. After the next milking each of the farmers brought their milk across the fields to Steven's yard, where they helped him load the churns on to his cart. He and Daisy did a valiant job of getting the milk to the main road, but the frozen surface was treacherous and exhausting for both horse and man.

Mrs McGuire had telephoned the creamery and arranged for the lorry to collect the milk at the junction with the main road. She'd also asked for empty churns to be dropped off ready for the next milking. She contacted the grocer, promising they would give him their ration cards when he next delivered to the farms if he would send some emergency supplies to help them through the week. He met Steven with stocks of bread, flour, oatmeal, lard and various other commodities. The meat ration had been cut to a shilling's worth per week in January, but the butcher had sent what he could as well as two tins of corned beef to share between them all.

The Loaning wives did their best to repay Steven for getting their milk away. Mrs McGuire made him a large pan of barley broth, the Kerr family sent two fruit pies and the two other wives, whom he barely knew yet, had sent bread and scones, a dozen eggs and a savoury dish which he couldn't identify, but he was hungry enough by evening to eat almost anything.

'Everybody rallies round to help when there's trouble and we all like to repay a kindness,' Mrs McGuire said. 'Ye're young, but ye're truly one of us, laddie. At least your ma doesna need to worry about you going hungry. She telephoned this afternoon, but I told her ye were taking our milk to the main road. Your brother had taken his across the fields with his tractor.'

'Did she have any other news?' he asked eagerly.

'The doctor hasna been back on account o' the snow drifts, but he told her every day your father survives without having another stroke is a step nearer surviving. He still canna speak clearly though, and he gets agitated when your brother goes into his bedroom.'

Steven nodded. He knew now how Fred had cheated his father. He knew it was not the loss of the money which would have distressed his father, but the disappointment he must feel at being deceived by his own son.

'I told your ma you would come round here tonight and telephone her after you finished milking.'

'Oh, thanks, Mrs McGuire,' Steven said with real gratitude. He felt like hugging her.

'I thought ye'd be pleased. I took the liberty of asking the telephone people whether you could get a telephone installed. That's what you want, isn't it?'

'Yes, it is. What did they say?'

'You'd have to agree to a party line if you want one soon.'

'What does that mean?' Steven asked with a

frown.

'You'd share a line. We're nearest and we're the only ones using this one. I'm not sure how it works except that you can't use it when the other party is telephoning. We only use ours for emergencies and a few messages. You'd probably do the same so we dinna mind sharing a line if ye want to go ahead. They're going to write and explain, and tell us what it will cost.'

Later that evening, Steven went round to the McGuires and telephoned his mother, but he was conscious that the McGuires could hear his half of the conversation. He sensed how upset his mother was and it didn't sound as though she was getting much support from Fred or the land girl, Edna. He longed to go to Willowburn to see them, but, with snow still lying and his animals to tend, he knew it would be foolish to risk setting out on his bicycle.

'Come and have a cup of tea and a biscuit, laddie, and stop fretting,' Mrs McGuire urged as soon as he put the receiver back on its cradle. 'Your mother is a capable woman. She's bound to be anxious, but it sounds as though your pa is holding his own. She'll not want you worrying.'

Steven had always enjoyed writing to Megan and getting her letters, but he hadn't realized how much he needed her until now. He had been hoping for a letter from her, but the postman hadn't got through to any of the smallholdings for the past two days. He sat down with his pad and his Conway Stewart fountain pen. It had been a gift from Megan and her parents on his twenty-first birthday and he used it regularly. It was one of his most treasured possessions and he filled it carefully using the ink bottle.

Megan was shocked to learn Mr Caraford had suffered a stroke when the letters belatedly arrived from Steven and her parents. Fred's trickery was despicable and she gasped when she read Steven's account of him pocketing the cash. Although he had no respect for his half-brother, and he was often ashamed of him, Megan knew Steven was intensely loyal when it came to family, so she felt honoured that he trusted her enough to confide in her. She could tell he was terribly upset about his father.

At times like this Megan wished she had taken a job locally instead of having to stay away at college. She hadn't minded so much for the first eighteen months when Steven was still in the army, but knowing he was upset and on his own made her yearn to be nearer and to offer comfort and help. Then the doubts crept in as they did so often these days. She knew Steven valued her friendship or he wouldn't write so often or confide in her, but would he ever see her as more than the younger sister of his best friend? She knew he and Sam had confided in each other about many things and sometimes she wondered if Steven saw her as a substitute confidante. He never spoke of the future or of his feelings for her.

Pauline Cameron, one of her college friends, had an elder brother, Derek, who worked in a bank. He had been transferred to a branch about six miles away and he lived in lodgings so he often came to see Pauline. He had been taking them both out in his car, trying to teach Pauline to drive, but she was terrified the car would run away with her. When he asked Megan if she would like to try, she seized the opportunity. If she could get her licence, she was sure her father would let her borrow his car to drive down to Steven's when she was at home during the holidays.

Derek lost patience with his sister's nervousness, but to Megan's surprise he seemed happy to continue taking her for lessons. Pauline was content to sit in the back, but as the end of the Easter term drew close and examinations loomed she said she needed to stay in and study. It was true she found the work difficult, so Megan accepted her decision. She had no qualms when Derek suggested she should continue the lessons on her own. It never occurred to her that he found her attractive. Her only aim was to learn to drive so that she could visit Steven. She was hoping the weather would have improved enough for her to help him with his vegetable garden during her vacation and she looked forward to the two of them working together.

One evening Derek leaned forward and ran his hand down her leg to her ankle while she was driving. She gasped, but she was unable to shrug him off while she was driving.

'Don't do that, Derek! We might have an accident.'

'I couldn't resist. I've noticed what shapely ankles you have,' he said with a grin, watching her, waiting for her response.

She muttered and stared at the road ahead, her cheeks pink with embarrassment.

He laughed. 'I could almost believe you're shy, but Pauline tells me you had a boyfriend who was in the army?'

'Yes, I have, but he's not in the army now.'

She hoped that would quell any ideas he might be harbouring for a mild flirtation with her. When he started teaching them to drive Pauline had confided that he was pleased to fill his spare time with them because he had parted from his long-term girlfriend when he got promoted and had to move away. His familiarity made her feel uncomfortable so she was thankful when he reverted to his usual casual friendliness. Derek had a nice car and he was good-looking so she assumed he probably had lots of girlfriends. She decided she was being conceited if she thought he had any interest in her, other than as his sister's friend. She assumed the driving lessons were his way of repaying her for helping Pauline, who found the work and the exams such a struggle. The short drives continued when they could be fitted in and Derek behaved impeccably.

At last the exams were over. They were all in high spirits, preparing to go home for the Easter holidays. Megan had packed her case so she would be ready to leave early the following morning. She was surprised when one of the girls brought a message to say Derek was waiting outside in his car to take her for a last driving lesson before the holidays. The weather was still cold and snow lay in shady hollows beneath the hedges, but the roads were clear. She grabbed her coat and ran down to the front entrance.

'I wasn't expecting to see you, Derek.'

'You said you wanted to surprise your father with your driving and you've been busy with your exams lately, so I decided you should have a refresher before you go home.' He climbed into the passenger seat, indicating she should get behind the wheel. A group of her fellow students were strolling down the road and they waved merrily.

'I'll wait for you in the entrance hall in the morning,' Maryanne called. 'Don't be late. We don't want to miss the train home.'

'I'm all packed. I'll be there!' Megan called back.

'Turn left at the road end and we'll take a scenic route this evening,' Derek instructed.

'We shall not have long to view the scenery. It still gets dark early. It doesn't feel like spring yet.'

He continued to direct her along country roads she had never been before, but she felt more confident and in control now. She hoped her father would be impressed. They had travelled quite a distance when Derek told her to turn right into an even narrower road. As she drove along she began to feel uneasy. The road was so narrow there were passing places at the side. Megan shuddered.

'It's so dark and gloomy with the trees meeting overhead. It's like being in an eerie green tunnel and there's still snow on the tussocks of grass where the sun never penetrates.'

'Draw into the next clearing and I'll drive the rest of the way,' Derek offered. 'You're doing well. I reckon you should apply for your driving test.'

'Thank you.' Megan drew the car to a halt and climbed out of the driver's side. The dark woods on either side gave her a creepy feeling, but she stretched thankfully, realizing how tense her neck and shoulder muscles were. Before she could guess his intentions, Derek had moved round the car and placed an arm on either side of her, trapping her with her back to the car.

'How about a wee thank you then, before you go off for the holidays. I shall miss you, Megan.' His arms tightened and he pressed her close, much too close. 'I don't know how I shall survive without seeing you,' he muttered and clamped his mouth firmly on hers stifling her protests. His kiss deepened. Except for Steven's tender goodbye kiss at the station Megan had never had more than a peck on the cheek. She struggled, trying to shove Derek away, but he was strong and broad shouldered. She remembered Pauline telling her he had been in the rugby team at university. His grip tightened. He seemed excited, oblivious to her struggles. She began to panic. She couldn't breathe. The smiling young man she thought she knew had disappeared. She was frightened and his strength astonished her.

'Stop it!' she gasped when he lifted his head for a moment.

'I've been longing for this since the first night
180

I met you with Pauline.' His breath was hot against her cheek and his mouth moved feverishly over her face.

'Stop it, Derek! C-control yourself.' She was near to tears, but he continued to rain kisses on her face and then down to her throat. One of his hands was fumbling with the buttons of her coat and Megan was both angry and terrified now. She had no idea where she was and she realized Derek had brought her to this isolated spot deliberately. His intentions were obvious, even to her. It was lust Derek felt and nothing more. She struggled helplessly.

Twelve

As soon as the roads were clear enough, Jimmy Kerr offered to take Steven up to Willowburn if he could ride pillion on the back of his motorbike. Steven accepted gratefully. It was Jimmy's father who had bred Shandy and both father and son often stopped at Schoirhead to pass the time of day on their way past. They always enquired how the wee dog was doing and Mr Kerr offered some advice on training him.

Hannah Caraford was astonished and delighted when Steven walked into the kitchen at Willowburn that evening.

'Wherever did you spring from, laddie? How did you get here at this time o' night? Surely you havena come on your pushbike?'

'No.' Steven grinned at her. 'I got a lift on the back of an angel of mercy.' Behind him, Jimmy gave an explosive laugh and Steven introduced him.

'I've been called a good many names, but nobody has ever called me an angel,' he said. 'Wait until I tell Ma that.'

'Well, you must be something like that to come out on a cold night. I'm truly grateful to you, laddie. I'll make you both a hot drink and something to eat. Draw up a chair. You go up and see your father, Steven. He'll be really pleased you've come. He's managing to say an odd word now, enough to let me know when he needs a drink or the toilet. He has a long way to go, but his mind is clear and that's a great relief.'

'Where's Fred?' Steven asked warily.

'He and Edna are toasting themselves in front of the living room fire. I think they're listening to *Have a go!* on the wireless.'

'Fine. I'll go up to Father then.'

As soon as he entered the bedroom, Steven knew by the way his father's eyes widened, then lit up, that it had been worth the freezing ride on the back of Jimmy's motorbike. He went to the bedside and took his father's limp hand in both of his. He had difficulty speaking himself over the lump in his throat. His father looked so much smaller and so defenceless propped against a mound of pillows. He was trying hard to speak.

'Heifers? Is that what you meant, Father?' He nodded.

'A-aw-ay,' he croaked.

'Don't worry about them. The dealer collected them the day before we were blocked in with the snow. He paid me thirty pounds for the pair. He said that was what you agreed?' His father nodded. He seemed to relax. He tried to smile, or at least that's what Steven thought, but it was a lopsided grimace.

'B-uy ... c-c...'

'You want me to buy a cow with the money?' His father nodded and closed his eyes, exhausted.

Steven sat for a while on the edge of the bed,

183

but he guessed the effort to talk had tired his father. He heard his mother calling softly from downstairs and he stood up. His father opened his eyes and gave a grimacing smile, then he reached over with his left hand and clasped Steven's hand firmly.

'G-laad ... c-c...'

'I'm glad I came too, Father. The roads are getting better every day so I'll be back to see you before long. You rest now, and don't worry about any of us,' Steven said gently.

His father had never been a demonstrative man, but on impulse Steven bent and kissed him lightly on his brow. Eddy Caraford opened his eyes and Steven saw they were bright with tears. He squeezed his father's hands.

'Rest now,' he said gruffly. He closed the bedroom door quietly behind him. He gulped over the lump in his throat, then took out his handkerchief and gave a good blow before he returned to the kitchen to join his mother and Jimmy Kerr. He sensed his mother's keen regard.

'He's better than I dared to hope,' he said. 'I could guess what he was trying to say. Did the doctor think his speech will return?'

'He was here today and he said he was pleasantly surprised and he thinks Eddy may be able to communicate if he goes on as he is doing, though he'll probably never be able to hold a proper conversation,' she added sadly. 'Now drink up your tea, Steven, and eat some scone and jam. I've made up a parcel of food for you to take back if you can manage it on the

184

motorbike.'

'Oh, I'll find a way to manage it,' Steven said. 'Thanks, Ma.'

'Then I think you'd better be getting back. I do wish you had a telephone so you could tell me you were home safely.'

'I'll telephone you, Mrs Caraford,' Jimmy volunteered. He grinned at Steven. 'We'll not be able to stop off at the pub for a drink if we've to report in.'

'Don't worry, Ma. Jimmy is only teasing. We shall both be glad to be back home to a warm house tonight. And I've put my name in for a shared telephone line. I said it was urgent due to illness so I should have a telephone before long.'

'Oh, Steven, that will be such a relief.'

'Yes, it will. I never thought of anything like this happening. We shall not have to talk too long though, because the other party can't use their phone if the line is being used.'

'Just to be able to get in touch will be a relief. Annie McGuire has been very kind, but I hate to pester other folks.'

Fear leant Megan strength as she struggled against Derek's grip.

'Let me go!' she gasped. 'You have no right to treat me like this.'

'No?' He lifted his head and seemed surprised. 'I've been taking you out for weeks now.'

'B-but only to teach me to d-drive...'

'For goodness' sake, Megan! You must have guessed how I feel about you. A fellow doesn't waste his time and petrol driving a girl round the

185

countryside unless he expects something in return. Come on...'

'Y-you're despicable,' she said with a gasping sob. She turned her head sharply as he tried to kiss her mouth again. 'I-I thought you enjoyed teaching Pauline and me to drive.'

'Pauline knew I fancied you. That's why she stopped coming. I told her I'd rather be alone with you. You must have guessed?'

'She knows I-I h-have a b-boyfriend. Don't! Don't do that!' She pushed furiously at his groping hands.

'So you've just been using me?' She sensed Derek's temper was rising. Anger was a dangerous emotion. 'Then it's time I used you in return.' He fastened his fingers in her hair and wrenched it painfully, intending to turn her face to his while he held her hard against the car. Megan's only thought was to get away from him. In desperation she grabbed at his nose and twisted it sharply. He gasped in pain and his grip slackened momentarily. She darted under his arm and ran into the wood. She had no idea where she was or where she was going. She had to get away. Run! Run! The words pounded in her head. Get away from him.

It was even colder and darker amongst the trees and the undergrowth caught at her clothes, but in her panic she ran on blindly. She heard Derek calling her name, but it didn't occur to her that he might be suffering remorse. Her breath caught in a sob, but she kept on running until she was too breathless to go any further. She stopped behind a tree and listened. Gradually she stopped panting and her ears became accustomed to the night-time noises and scuffles, but there were no footsteps crashing through the wood in search of her. She had no idea how long she waited, but eventually she heard a car engine roar into life some distance away. She held her breath. Yes, it was moving. She could hear it driving slowly along the road at the edge of the wood.

The wave of relief was followed by an awful fear. How was she to get back? What if she couldn't find her way out of the wood? Her teeth were chattering with cold and fright. Supposing she died of exposure in the cold night air?

'Come on, Meggie, let me look at your knee and I'll give you a piggyback home.' She could almost hear Steven's voice all those years ago when she had followed him and Sam against their wishes. They had gone looking for birds' nests in the old quarry and she had missed her footing and fallen heavily.

'I c-can't walk,' she had sobbed.

'You can do anything, anything in the whole world, Meggie Oliphant,' Steven had said bracingly, 'if you're brave enough to try.'

She had looked up at him with a wobbly smile and tear-streaked face, but she had put her hand in his and allowed him to pull her to her feet.

She took a deep breath. She needed all her courage now. She didn't want to spend the night in the wood and end up a frozen corpse. She wanted to go home tomorrow. She wanted to see Steven again. She peered through the trees in every direction. She thought the sky seemed lighter when she looked in one direction, but it could have been her imagination. She had to try. Stumbling over tussocks and through brambles she kept her eye on that grey glimmer which was only slightly less dark than the rest. She couldn't believe she had run so far into the wood. Eventually the trees began to thin as she reached the edge. There was not a star to be seen through the thick curtain of cloud. She clamoured over a ditch on to the road. She had no idea which way to go.

The narrow road seemed unending on foot and several times she stopped to pull up her coat collar against the damp chill of the wind, or to rest her feet for a few minutes. Her shoes were never intended for a hike in the country and they were wet and muddy. She could feel her heels growing tender and knew she would have blisters long before she got back to the hostel.

Eventually she came to a junction with a slightly wider road, but the signposts had been removed during the war and had not yet been replaced on such minor roads. She couldn't remember driving this way. Mentally she tossed an imaginary coin, then set off resolutely, hoping she might come to a cottage or farm where she could ask directions. She cringed at the thought of questions though. Only a fool would be out walking and get lost on a night like this. She came to another junction and a more major road. She was still hesitating when she saw two lights winking and wobbling towards her through the darkness. As they drew nearer she realized they were bicycles ridden by two middle-aged workmen. She breathed a sigh of relief and stepped forward to ask for directions.

Megan's relief was short lived. The men estimated she was at least five miles from the main road and another mile or two to the college. She wanted to sink down on to the grass verge and cry like a baby, but common sense reasserted itself. She gritted her teeth. She would get nowhere sitting down. If only she had grabbed her hat and gloves and scarf when she ran out so joyfully to join Derek. Even if she came to a village and a bus route she had no money to pay her fare. Resolutely she lifted her chin. There was nothing for it but to plod on in the direction the men had recommended.

Her feet were blistered and sore from the rubbing of her damp leather shoes and her stockings were ruined from the brambles in the wood. Darkness had brought a chilling drizzle which penetrated to her bones in spite of her efforts to keep up a brisk pace. She had no idea how far she had walked. Except for the distant twinkle of a farm or cottage, she seemed to be nowhere near civilization. Her heart sank as she realized the hostel would be locked for the night long before she reached it, if she ever did. She was so weary and cold it was an effort to keep putting one foot in front of the other. These were country roads and petrol was rationed so she couldn't even hitch a lift. She was filled with despair.

At last Megan trudged through the gates into the hostel drive. The building was in darkness as she had known it would be. They were all supposed to be in bed by ten o'clock and that was hours ago. She felt like curling on to the steps and weeping. The rain was falling faster now and it had penetrated through her tweed coat and her jumper so she could feel the damp chill on her shoulders and her hair was dripping down her neck and around her face.

She knew there was a boiler house, but she had never investigated the sheds at the back of the hostel. She had to find shelter somewhere for the rest of the night. Her teeth were chattering with cold as she moved stealthily round the back of the building. As she reached the hostel laundry and the tiny kitchen which was for the use of students she saw a faint crack of light round the thick wooden door. She remembered one or two of the bolder students sometimes arranged to be let in that way if they were out later than they were supposed to be. She had never expected to have need of it herself. She tried the door but it was locked. She knocked gently, without much hope. She almost fell inside when the door opened immediately.

'Megan? Oh, Megan, is it really you at last? Thank God you're safe! Thank you, God,' Pauline Cameron muttered and put her hands together as though in prayer. She was in her dressing gown and slippers and she seemed as near to tears of relief as Megan herself. 'It's nearly two o'clock. I-I thought. O-oh ... I don't know what I thought.' She stammered feverishly as she unbuttoned Megan's coat and peeled it off. She reached to the pulley above their heads and pulled down a towel which didn't belong to either of them. 'Sit on that stool. Let me rub your hair. I'm frozen waiting in here so you must be like ice.' She pulled down another towel. 'Here, dry your face and hands. I'll kill that brother of mine.'

'H-how d-did y-you know...?' Megan could barely speak for her chattering teeth.

'He telephoned the payphone and asked one of the girls to get me. He was worried sick. He knew he shouldn't have left you – miles from anywhere and in the dark. He said he waited quite a while, but he couldn't find you. He went back again to see if you were on the road, but he thought you must have got a lift.'

'D-did he t-tell you what h-happened?' She took the towel from Pauline and rubbed vigor-ously at her hair, but she felt she would never be warm again.

'He said you'd had a quarrel and he was sorry he lost his temper.'

'I see. I-I think I turned the wrong way when – when I came out of the wood ... S-so m-many narrow roads and crossroads.'

'We must get you into bed and warmed up,' Pauline urged anxiously. 'I can only pray you don't get pneumonia. You were off with flu after Christmas. I've kept the kettle boiling. I'll fill my hot-water bottle for you. I filled yours hours ago and wrapped your pyjamas round it, but it'll be cold now. You ought to have a hot drink, but we've no milk for tea. Come on, we'll tiptoe upstairs and I'll get your bottle and fill it up again.'

'What about you, Pauline? You'll need a

bottle.' The bedrooms were notoriously cold and the windows were patterned with a layer of frost for most of the winter.

'I don't need it as much as you. You can't stop shivering. I'll never forgive Derek if you're ill after this.'

'It's not your f-fault. D-don't w-worry a-and th-thanks for letting me in and w-waiting up. Come on, l-lets g-get to b-bed.'

Megan was thankful to get out of her wet clothes, but her stockings had stuck to the raw blisters on both her heels and she winced as she pulled them off. The soles of her feet were sore and she had blisters on her toes. She pulled on her pyjamas and a cardigan and then her dressing gown. She took some thick socks from her case and put them on too, knowing she must get warm as soon as possible.

Poor Pauline, I must thank her properly tomorrow, she thought. It was a long while before she began to feel warm and it was almost time to get up by the time she fell asleep. She missed breakfast and would have missed her train if Pauline hadn't knocked on her door and brought her a glass of milk and a rasher of bacon sandwiched in a slice of bread.

'I managed to cadge these from the wee Irish maid,' she said, 'but you'll need to hurry if you want to catch your train. Maryanne is already down in the lobby with her case. She's panicking because you weren't at breakfast.'

'I didn't thank you properly last night, Pauline.'

'Och, there's no need. If it hadn't been for that

stupid brother of mine, we wouldn't have been in such bother. You look awful.'

'I feel it, but I would have been worse if you hadn't waited up and let me in. I do appreciate it, really I do.'

'You'd better get down to the bathrooms, though I reckon everybody else has finished with them by now. I'm not leaving until later so I'll keep Maryanne calm until you come down.' She disappeared.

Too late it occured to Megan that she should have warned her not to tell Maryanne what had happened. She was a blithe girl, but Maryanne loved to chatter and the last thing Megan wanted was for the folks back home to hear she had been out half the night.

The first thing Maryanne did when they were settled on the train was ask, 'Come on then, tell me where you and Derek went for your big adventure? What kept you out half the night? Was it exciting?'

Thirteen

Steven's father was still confined to his bedroom, but with Fred's reluctant assistance Hannah managed to get him into a chair in front of the fire. Doctor Burns had told him to move as much as he could to keep his muscles exercised and he was trying hard, but there were times when he was so frustrated by the paralysis in one arm and his leg that Hannah feared he would burst into tears. The weather was still bitterly cold, but Steven visited twice more on the back of Jimmy's motorbike. On the last visit Jimmy had arrived with a more powerful bike which Steven duly admired.

'I'll sell you my old motorbike at a bargain price,' Jimmy said. 'It'll be a lot better than your old pushbike. You'll want to keep visiting regularly I suppose, while your father is ill?'

'Mmm ... I wonder if he'll ever get the power back in his right arm. Mother says his right leg is weaker too, but he can stand on it so long as he has some support.'

'Ma says a stroke can ruin the life o' the fittest man,' Jimmy said sympathetically.

'How much do you want for your bike?' Steven asked.

'I'd let you have it for twenty-five pounds.'

'I'll think about it and let you know.'

'I'll tell you what, I'll bring it round to your place and leave it for you to try. See how you get on with it. I've another suggestion to make to you, Steven – well, more of a favour really.'

'I owe you plenty of those,' Steven said. 'I've been really grateful to you for taking me to Willowburn in this cold weather. What's the favour?'

'Well, you know how my father and the McGuires are behind with their ploughing due to the bad weather? And I believe you still have one of your fields to plough?'

'Yes, that's right, the smaller one.'

'My firm has a second-hand Fordson tractor in. I think my boss would let us hire it for a weekend to get the ploughing done on all three places. I can drive a tractor, but I don't know how to plough. Dad and me wondered whether you would have a go. He said you'd made as good a job as he's seen in the field you've ploughed with the horses.'

'That's nice of him,' Steven said, 'but I've never ploughed with a tractor. Anyway, we'd need a plough to fit on to a tractor. The horse plough is no use.'

'Oh, I never thought about that.' Jimmy frowned thoughtfully. 'I'll have to ask my boss if he can fix us up with one to fit the old Fordson. If he can, will you have a go?'

'I suppose I could,' Steven said slowly. 'Yes, of course I will. It may take a bit of getting used to, but if Fred can do it then so can I.'

'Good for you!' Jimmy clapped him on the

back. 'Dad and Mr McGuire say they will pay for the hiring, if you'll manage the ploughing. Oh, and it would have to be on a Saturday afternoon and Sunday while our firm is closed.'

'A Sunday?' Steven frowned. His mother never approved of Sunday working if it could be avoided. He chewed his lip. 'Yes, all right. Let me know if you can fix it.' After all, the fighting had not stopped on Sundays during the war and this was an exceptional year. They all needed to get their land worked ready for sowing now the snow had cleared.

'You're a pal,' Jimmy said. 'And if you like my bike when you've tried it out, I'll make it twenty-two pounds, ten shillings.'

'All right. I'll have a go and see how I get on with it.' Steven returned Jimmy's irrepressible grin. A motorbike would certainly be faster than his old pushbike and he wanted to visit Willow-burn as often as he could.

Megan found a letter from Steven waiting for her when she arrived home for the Easter vaca-tion. Her mother chewed her lower lip, seeing how eagerly she opened the letter and how her eyes lit up. Megan was pleased Steven had not forgotten he had invited her to the dance. She had thought he might, considering all the worry he must have concerning his father, but her blistered feet were so painful she contemplated making an excuse. If she refused this invitation, he might think she didn't want to go with him; he might never ask her again. She longed to be with Steven, to dance in his arms and have him walk her home. Her father watched the troubled expressions chasing each other over her face as she read the letter.

'Are things all right with Steven? How is his father?'

'Steven's fine. His father is making progress, but it's very slow.'

'That's good then. Didn't you promise to help him with his vegetable garden during your Easter holiday, Megan?' John Oliphant asked. 'If you arrange a day to suit all of us, I'll give you a ride down to Schoirhead in the car. I might even let you have a go at driving there. Your mother bought some L-plates. She says she's going to learn to drive if you can do it.' He gave his wife a teasing grin.

'I am. I mean it. I can't have my wee lassie beating me to something like that,' Chrissie said, squaring her shoulders as though for battle.

Megan smiled at her mother. 'There's no reason why you shouldn't drive, Mum. Steven's mother does.' She had wanted to impress her parents with her driving, but now she didn't care. She shuddered at the memory of her last lesson.

'I'd like to see how Steven's little farm looks now he's had time to sort things out a bit,' her father said. 'We could take the brooder back if we tie it to the boot.'

Normally Megan would have been delighted by her father's offer, but she felt utterly miserable. Apart from being tired from lack of sleep, she ached everywhere after last night's marathon walk and her feet were seriously painful.

'You don't seem very enthusiastic, lassie,' Chrissie said, frowning. 'In fact, you look exhausted. Were the exams very difficult? Have you been working too hard?'

'No.' Megan shook her head. She knew she would have to tell her mother about the blisters because she felt like an old woman hobbling about, but she had to keep the details to herself. 'I went for a walk last night to blow away the cobwebs.' She gave a wan smile. 'It came on wet and it took ages to find the way back. I, er ... I got a couple of nasty blisters.'

'Soak them in a hot mustard bath and then put some plasters on if they're very sore. I expect a good night's sleep will sort you out,' Chrissie said briskly.

Megan was aware of her mother's scrutiny. Chrissie knew instinctively that Megan was not telling her the whole story, but her daughter would soon be twenty. She had been married by that age and she had resented her mother asking questions. Even so, she was shocked when she saw the state of Megan's feet and she couldn't help wondering what had actually happened.

They were surprised when Steven arrived on a motorbike to collect Megan for the dance.

'You didn't tell me about that in your letters,' Megan said.

'I wanted to surprise you. I've only just bought it from Jimmy Kerr. It will be handy for getting to Willowburn to visit Dad. I thought it would be better than walking to the dance, if you can trust me enough to ride pillion, Megan?'

'I don't mind at all, but Dad has offered to lend

you his new toy.'

'You would be warmer in the car, Steven,' Chrissie said anxiously. 'Megan is dressed for summer in that dress.'

'Oh, Mum, we are going to a dance and I shall be wearing my winter coat.'

'Mmm, you look very pretty anyway, Megan, but your mother is right, it would be warmer in the car.' He smiled and his eyes crinkled mischievously. 'And I suspect the truth is she doesn't trust me with her wee girl on the back of a motorbike.'

'Well, they are such dangerous things,' Chrissie said defensively.

'There's the key for the car, Steven,' John Oliphant said. 'You try it out and tell me what you think of it.'

'Thanks, I will,' Steven said. 'It would be a shame to get Megan's dress in a mess.'

Megan had only worn the dress once. It was pale green and fitted her slender waist beautifully before it swirled out into a wide skirt, ideal for dancing. The colour matched her eyes and suited her clear skin and vibrant hair.

As soon as they had gone, Chrissie turned to her husband.

'I reckon Megan is more than half in love with Steven. I do hope she doesn't do anything rash and give up her college course before she's qualified.'

'Don't worry, Chrissie. You worried she would never start at college, but things worked out. I suppose it's natural now she's all we have and she did look very pretty tonight, even if I am prejudiced,' he said, smiling. 'I expect she will get married some day, but I couldn't wish for a better lad than Steven for a son-in-law. It's a pity it might be years before he can afford to take a wife. His main ambition at present is proving he can make a success of that wee farm so I don't think you need worry.'

'Mmm, I know what you mean, but young love can be painful. Megan has been subdued since she came home. Maybe she's worried about her exam results. I'm sure it's more than the blisters on her feet that are troubling her, and I'd like to know how she got such bad ones.'

'I'm sure she'll tell us when it suits her,' John said easily, and drew out his pipe.

Megan was surprised to see Natalie Turner at the village dance. She had always given the impression she was too superior for any of the local entertainment. But Megan soon forgot about Natalie as Steven drew her into his arms for the first waltz. She was barely aware of her sore feet, but when a reel was announced for the next dance she elected to sit it out. Steven was surprised and disappointed. Megan was light as a feather and he enjoyed holding her in his arms. In fact, he didn't like the thought of her being held in the arms of the other men he had noticed eyeing her up, especially the good-looking young fellow who had been trying to catch her eye while he was dancing with Natalie Turner.

'You don't seem yourself tonight, Megan,' he said as they found chairs at the side of the floor. 'Didn't you feel like coming to the dance? Are you tired after your exams?'

'Oh, Steven, I was really looking forward to tonight. It's my feet. They're a bit sore. I've got a couple of blisters.'

'You should have told me. We could have gone to the pictures instead.'

She turned to him, her green eyes alight.

'Could we have, Steven? Would you have done that?'

'Of course I would if I'd known that's what you would have preferred, Meggie.'

She chewed her lower lip. Steven used to call her Meggie when he was trying to coax her or humour her when she was five or six years old. He had always been patient and kind, even when Sam told her she was a pest, as brothers do. Was she still a little girl in his eyes? They had always been such good friends, but did being friends make it impossible for Steven to see her as a woman? Would he never feel the longing which tugged at her own heart?

The next dance was a quickstep and before they could stand up together, Dr Lindsay Gray was there, asking her to dance. Steven frowned when Megan accepted. Natalie had followed him so Steven had little option but to ask her to dance.

This circumstance did not please Megan at all. She made sure she returned to Steven the moment the dance finished and when the compère announced a Gay Gordons she was determined to dance with him even if her feet dropped off. By the end she had to admit the blisters were very painful. It was Steven who suggested they should sit out the next dance.

'Only if you promise you'll not go off with Natalie and leave me here on my own.'

'Of course I shall not dance with Natalie again,' he said, putting an arm around her shoulders, drawing her close. 'You're my partner tonight. Don't you forget it.' He gave her shoulder a little squeeze.

Megan was happy again and she smiled.

'So who was the fellow who snatched you from under my nose?' Steven asked.

'Oh, that's Natalie's doctor friend Lint. I'm surprised he remembered me. I haven't seen him since the Christmas dance. He gave me a lift home because he was staying at Martinwold.'

'I see.' Out of the corner of his eye, Steven saw Rufus Anderson heading towards their end of the hall, and he cursed silently, remembering his mother telling him Anderson had a fancy for Megan. He was an only son and one day he would take over the farm.

'Oh, no,' Megan groaned. 'Here comes Maryanne and her brother.'

Steven was pleased she didn't seem to welcome their company any more than he did.

'I don't think I could face another dance yet,' she continued. 'It would have to be a slow one, even with you, Steven. I'm sorry I'm spoiling your evening.'

'Don't be a wee goose, Meggie, of course you're not. I've got you for company and it's a good band, isn't it?'

Before she could answer, Maryanne and Rufus Anderson joined them, sitting one on either side of them. Megan felt trapped and vaguely uneasy.

'Do you remember Steven, Maryanne?'

'No, I don't think so.' Maryanne frowned, then she smiled. 'But I'm pleased to meet you.'

'I remember Steven. You were a year older than me at school. You and Sam were great pals, weren't you?' Rufus said. He looked grave as he added, 'I was really sorry to hear he was killed.'

The two of them talked about farming for a little while, but during a lull in both conversation and music, Maryanne asked, 'Have you recovered from being out all night with Pauline's brother, Megan?' She giggled. 'I must say you look lovely tonight, but you looked terrible that morning coming down on the train.'

Megan felt Steven stiffen beside her and she said sharply, 'Don't exaggerate, Maryanne. I was not out all night.'

'Well, maybe not *all* night, but it was well after midnight. I met Pauline on my way to the bathroom and she was putting a hot-water bottle in your bed and worrying about you still being out with what's-his-name.'

Megan glanced at Steven. He was sitting straight-backed, watching her intently, but the laughter had gone, his blue eyes were shadowed with disappointment – and something else – sadness? But why should he feel sad? Maryanne was only teasing; she was never malicious, but it was obvious that Steven believed her. Megan's heart sank.

Rufus had heard Maryanne too. 'I thought you were supposed to be a model student, Megan. It seems you have hidden depths when you are away from home,' he said. 'Does my sister do anything naughty I should know about?'

'Of course not, and neither do I,' she said irritably.

Rufus raised his eyebrows knowingly, as if to say pull the other leg.

Megan rolled her eyes and grimaced in annoyance.

'Come and have this dance with me and tell me all about this exciting college life.'

'No, thanks, I'm sitting this one out.'

'I'm surprised you're here at all,' Maryanne said with genuine sympathy. 'Pauline said you had blisters on your feet by the time you got back. Are they still very sore?'

'A bit. I...' She looked unhappily at Steven. 'I think we're leaving soon.'

'Oh, but they're serving refreshments after the next dance. You must wait for the interval,' Maryanne urged.

'We will,' Steven said, then he looked at Megan. 'But I see you weren't exaggerating about having sore feet so we'll go home after that.'

As far as Megan was concerned the evening was ruined even before Natalie butted in. Having heard only the tail end, she demanded to know why they were leaving early. Rufus filled her in with a wildly exaggerated account of Megan's escapades at college.

Megan listened helplessly, knowing none of them would pay any attention to her denials. She had often heard that he who protests too much always convicts himself, so she sat tight-lipped and silent, miserable on account of her throbbing feet. She grew more upset as she sensed a growing constraint between her and Steven. How could he believe Maryanne's tale about her being out half the night with Derek Cameron? But she knew he had already drawn his own conclusions. She wanted to explain, but why should she feel guilty? She had done nothing wrong, except be too naive.

'Now we shall have a dreamy Scottish waltz until you've digested your fish paste sandwiches,' the compère announced in jocular tones after the interval. 'After that we'll liven up the rest of the evening with some of the new dances.'

'I'd like to stay for the waltz, Steven,' Megan said eagerly. She turned to him and he nodded and smiled down at her, taking her in his arms and drawing her close as the band began to play, but she had seen the shadows in his eyes. For the first time in their lives there was a barrier between them.

Fourteen

Natalie couldn't wait to tell her parents about Megan's escapades. She was tired of them thinking their herdsman's daughter was a paragon of virtue, as well as being clever and intelligent. She recounted Rufus Anderson's version about her staying out all night with the brother of a college friend.

Megan was neat and pretty with her ready smile and pleasant manner, though it was her hair which Natalie envied most. Natalie was also irked because she suspected Steven Caraford was more than a little in love with the girl, whether he realized it or not, and to make matters worse she knew Dr Lindsay Gray would have been dating Megan by now if she'd given him the slightest encouragement. At work he never missed an opportunity to enquire about her. So Natalie relished being able to inform them all that Megan Oliphant was not the perfect angel they had all believed.

Even so, Natalie would have been surprised if she had realized how seriously her parents would regard Megan's misdemeanours. They had a genuine liking for the Oliphants' girl, but they were also concerned for John and Chrissie, who clearly loved their children. The Turners knew how deeply the loss of their only son had affected them. The Oliphants had even contemplated giving up their work and emigrating to Australia when Sam was killed. Mr Turner had a healthy respect for his herdsman. John Oliphant had grown up with dairy cows; he had a wealth of experience as a herdsman and he and his wife made a good team, moreover they were honest and conscientious and almost impossible to replace.

Murdoch Turner didn't want Megan bringing them more heartbreak, or causing a scandal which might make them want to leave the area. As a parent himself, he decided John Oliphant should be warned about his daughter's escapades. The following morning, just before lunch, he proceeded to repeat Natalie's account of Megan's behaviour while she was away from home and their parental guidance.

John Oliphant stared at his boss in angry disbelief.

'I can't believe Megan would get herself a reputation for being one of those loose young females who stay out half the night with different men!' he exclaimed.

'Ah, but there's different standards since the war,' Murdoch Turner declared. 'Young people don't see things the way we did. They need more guidance, more discipline, if they're to keep on the right path through life.'

John Oliphant scowled at him. In his eyes it was Natalie who needed the discipline, but in his heart he knew there was something bothering Megan, and he didn't believe it was just sore feet, however bad they were. Was she in some kind of trouble? His heart sank at the possibility of Megan ruining her life with some man they had never even met.

'Thanks for the warning, Mr Turner,' he said stiffly. 'I shall have a word with Megan.' He strode grimly towards his house.

Megan was helping her mother prepare their midday meal.

'What's wrong, lassie?' Chrissie asked gently. 'You don't look your usual happy self. You were back early from the dance last night. Did you and Steven have a quarrel?'

'No. Oh, Mum, I almost wish we had. At least it might have cleared the air between us.' Her chin wobbled in an effort to hold back her tears.

'How do you mean, Meggie?'

Megan took a deep breath. 'He-he looked so disappointed in me, as though I'd let him down. Sam might have looked the same if he thought I'd been out half the night with a man when I was supposed to be in bed in a students' hostel. B-but Steven isn't my big brother, a-and he d-didn't say anything or ask questions like a brother would, so how could I explain? Anyway I haven't done anything I'm ashamed of. It was Rufus Anderson exaggerating everything for Natalie's benefit, but Steven was listening too.'

'What do you mean? What happened last night?'

'It wasn't last night, and it was only Maryanne having a bit of fun. But I could see Steven took it seriously. Then Rufus made things worse by exaggerating and teasing me even more and

208

giving Natalie a stupidly exaggerated account. You know the way she looks – all big eyes and then pretending to be shocked.'

'But what about? Start at the beginning, lassie. Has this something to do with the blisters?'

'Yes.' Megan gave a huge sigh. 'I wanted to give Dad and you a surprise. I wanted to show you how well I was doing with driving a car. Pauline Cameron's brother lives fairly near the college and he offered to teach both of us to drive. Pauline was too nervous and he lost patience with her, but I was really keen to learn and getting on all right. So when Derek said he would teach me, I seized the chance. I-I was getting on fine...'

'Until you crashed his car?' Chrissie said fearfully. 'Was he badly hurt?'

'No! No, nothing like that. You might have a bit of faith in me, Mum!' Megan said reproachfully. 'It was ... I thought Derek enjoyed teaching me to drive. I thought it gave him satisfaction. It never occurred to me he might think I was attractive or anything.'

'Oh.' Chrissie tensed, her mind leaping ahead to the blistered feet. 'What happened then?'

'We hadn't arranged a lesson for the last night of term. I hadn't expected him. When he arrived I was pleased so I grabbed my coat and went. I followed his directions, but I'd never been on the back roads before and when we were on this narrow road running through some woods I got nervous. Derek said he would drive until the road widened. When I got out he – he seized me a-and...'

'Oh dear Lord,' Chrissie whimpered.

'Don't be like that, Mum! Nothing happened. Honestly. B-but he wouldn't stop k-kissing me and I-I suppose I panicked. I screwed his nose really hard to make him let go and th-then I ran into the woods. I was scared to go back to the car. When he couldn't find me he drove off. I made my way out of the woods, but it was dark and I'd no idea where I was and it was coming on wet and – and it seemed to take me for ever to find my way back and it was so wet and c-cold and my feet were sore.'

Megan burst into tears and Chrissie took her in her arms, offering silent prayers that nothing more serious had happened to her precious bairn.

'Hush, hush, lassie. There's no harm done and your feet will get better soon. At least you don't seem to have suffered from getting wet.'

'No. Derek phoned Pauline. He said he was sorry he'd frightened me. He–he told Pauline he hadn't believed I was s-such an in-innocent. She was waiting up to let me in at the back door. She was so anxious and she's so kind and motherly. She'll make a lovely teacher if only she can pass her exams.'

'She's better than her brother then by the sound of him.'

'Yes, b-but I was so eager to learn to drive and to give you and Dad a surprise. It never entered my head that he wanted to go out with me or anything.'

'No, lassie, I don't suppose it did,' Chrissie said wryly, 'but you are a very attractive girl you

210

know.'

'Oh, Mum –' Megan gave a watery smile – 'you're not prejudiced of course.'

'Of course not.'

'Pauline said her brother was really worried and he wanted to apologize. She put her hot-water bottle in my bed as well as my own.'

'She does sound a nice lassie then...'

'Who is a nice lassie?' John demanded grimly, coming into the kitchen for his dinner.

Over Megan's head, his wife gave him a speaking glance.

'We were talking about one of Megan's college friends. Now, lassie, go and wash your face, and then we'll have our dinner.'

Megan was glad to escape.

Chrissie whispered to John, 'I'll tell you the whole story later, but I know now how she got the blisters.'

'The dinner can wait. What I want to know is why she was out half the night?' her husband said sternly.

Chrissie raised her eyebrows.

'I wonder where you heard that, but I'll explain that too,' she added hurriedly, 'and there's nothing to worry about, so take that look off your face, John Oliphant. We have a good and precious daughter and we should be proud and thankful. Her only concern is what Steven might think after Rufus Anderson told tall stories to Natalie Turner, just as a tease.'

John looked doubtful, but he held his peace until the meal was over.

* * *

211

Two days later John Oliphant suggested he and Megan should drive down to Steven's and help him sow some of his early potatoes and other vegetables in the garden. He regretted his lack of faith in Megan. He ought to have guessed Natalie had made the most of spreading rumours around. She had always been jealous of Megan. He wanted to make it up to her.

'I'll send a pan of soup and some sandwiches for all three of you,' Chrissie offered, 'then you don't need to hurry back.'

'We'll go as soon as I've finished the morning milking and cleaned up the byre,' her husband replied.

They had almost reached Schoirhead when he gave his verdict.

'Well, Megan, you're a lot better driver than your mother is so far. I'm impressed.'

'Thanks, Dad,' Megan mumbled uncomfortably, 'I suppose I have had a few more lessons than Mum. I really wanted to surprise you both. Now all I want is to get a driving licence and then I hope you'll lend me the car sometimes?' She gave him a wary smile.

'To come down to see Steven I suppose you mean?' he asked, suppressing a knowing smile.

'Sometimes, and to go other places too,' she said defensively.

'And are you going to be helping your mother and me in the dairy during the summer holidays? Ian will be leaving us by the first week in July. He's going to help his folks with the harvest before he goes to agricultural college. He's been a good lad, but we shall need to look for another helper so I need to know what your plans are.'

'I'll certainly be there to help all summer until I return to college in September.' She sighed. 'I wish I didn't have another whole year to do.'

'It'll be worth it, lassie. Look at the money you'll earn and the long holidays you'll get. Your mother will be real proud to be able to say "my daughter is a teacher". I can just hear her now,' he said.

'I suppose so.' Megan sighed.

'And look at it this way, since the war, even married women can go back and teach they tell me, not that I'd want my wife going away and leaving me every morning,' he added with a frown. 'Look on it as an insurance. We never know what lies ahead. If Steven's mother had been a teacher she could have gone back to work at a school instead of bringing up Fred, that idle scoundrel.'

Steven seemed pleased to see them, but Megan was conscious of a slight constraint. He was quieter than normal and his usual spark of humour was missing. Several times, as they worked side by side, she sensed his eyes on her. She helped him make the measuring lines with string, added the two big pegs he had made, then they marked out the plots together. They left her to plant the onions while Steven and her father rowed up and planted the early potatoes.

While Megan was clearing up after their dinner, Steven and her father went out to inspect the two fields which he had sown with oats.

Afterwards she planted some carrots and beet-root and a row of peas and one of beans while they finished earthing up the potato rows.

'Well, that looks neat and tidy now,' Steven said with satisfaction.

'We'll come back in a couple of weeks, or before Megan goes back to college anyway,' John Oliphant suggested. 'We'll bring some cabbage plants and put in more carrots and peas and some later onions.'

'That's only if you want us to,' Megan said diffidently.

Her father looked at her in surprise. 'Of course,' he said quietly.

Mrs McGuire shouted over the wall to Steven that she had baked some fresh scones and would he like some for his visitors. He winked at Mr Oliphant.

'She's curious to see who is here,' he said in a low voice. 'Will you go round and collect them, Megan? I suspect she wants to see you.'

'Of course,' she said. For the first time since she had arrived she saw a twinkle in his eyes and he seemed more like the old Steven.

Her father went to look at the dairy and the byre while she washed their tea things, but Steven stayed behind.

'It's not much of a house from a woman's point of view, is it?'

'It's much better than you led us to believe, Steven. In fact, there's nothing wrong with the house, it just needs the homely bits added.'

'The woman's touch,' he said with a grimace. 'Well, it will be a long time before it gets that.'

214

'So long as you're warm and comfortable...' Megan broke off when her father returned.

They didn't see Steven again until the day Megan and her father went back to finish the garden.

'I thought Steven might have been up to see us while you were at home, Megan, especially now he's got a motorbike,' Chrissie said.

'I suppose he visits his father when he has any spare time. He was ploughing another field ready to sow some turnips for next winter and his young chicks were being delivered the day after we were there last time.'

'Yes, I expect he keeps busy with only one pair of hands. Your father says he's thinking of getting a few feeding sheep to eat off his spare grass during the summer, until he gets his cow numbers built up and some young heifers to rear.'

Megan knew this was all true, but in her heart she had hoped he would visit too. She was sure he thought of her in a different light since the night of the dance. She went with her father to finish off the garden and Steven was as welcoming as ever to both of them, but there was no doubt he had plenty to keep him busy.

'Come and see my sow, Megan,' he said, just before they were going to leave. 'I call her Ella. She's due to farrow in three weeks.'

Shandy went with them and Megan bent to pat his silky head.

'This wee dog worships you, Steven. He never lets you out of his sight.'

215

'I know, I have a job getting away on the motorbike without him. I have to shut him in the house and sometimes he's a bit naughty. He chewed my slipper and a towel and often takes bits out of the chair legs.'

'I expect he's lonely without you.'

'I'd certainly be lonely without you, wouldn't I, Shandy, my old boy?' He bent down and hugged the little dog and Shandy responded, eagerly licking at his hands and face. 'Now, you lie down and wait there while we see Ella.'

Shandy did exactly as he was bid and Megan laughed with delight.

They went into the sty together and Ella allowed Steven to scratch her back. She grunted approvingly and he began to scratch her belly. She lay down and stretched out contentedly. Megan bent down beside him, giving the sow a gentle scratch. 'She loves this.'

'Yes, I want her to be tame and quiet. Hopefully she'll make a better mother when the piglets are born. Are your feet quite better now?' he asked unexpectedly.

Megan cursed herself for blushing so readily. 'Yes, of course. They didn't take long to heal.'

'I suppose I should stop writing letters to you now you have a boyfriend up there.' It was not a question and Megan frowned and didn't answer immediately.

'I don't have a boyfriend,' she said carefully, 'but you can stop writing the letters if you're too busy, or if you're fed up with writing,' she added stiffly.

'The way Maryanne and her brother talked it

sounded to me as if you had a serious relation-ship with someone.'

'He was giving me driving lessons. I've helped his sister a lot with her studying. I thought he was sort of repaying me, I suppose, b-but he-he wanted to be more than friends. We quarrelled. I walked back. It was a long way.'

'Hence the blisters, eh?' He raised one eye-brow the way he used to do when he only half believed her if she had been playing tricks. 'You always did have a bit of a temper when you were angry, I remember. He should have expected that with the colour of your hair.'

'My hair had nothing to do with it,' she said angrily and stood up.

He stood up too. They were very close. He looked down at her and shook his head slowly and she saw that oddly wistful look in his eyes again, or was it regret? Or disappointment? She didn't know, but she did know things were not the same between them.

'I expect you'll make it up when you get back to college and see him again.'

Megan turned away and didn't answer. She didn't want him to see the tears which had sprung to her eyes. Surely if he cared for her he would have trusted her.

Fifteen

At Willowburn Eddy Caraford's health continued to improve slowly and the weather grew warmer. On sunny days he was content to sit on the bench outside the kitchen door; when it was cooler he sat by the fire and watched Hannah as she cooked or did her housework or cleaned and packed her eggs ready for marketing. He could move around a little with his stick or with the furniture for support, but his right arm was almost useless and he had little strength in his affected leg. It was clear he would never be fit to work again as he used to do before the stroke, but he seemed to have developed a new serenity. Hannah was uncertain whether this was a good or a bad sign.

Steven visited every Sunday and sometimes during the week as well now the evenings were longer and light. He sensed the bond between his parents had strengthened rather that weakened since his father's illness. He watched his father's eyes following his wife with tender affection, and when she caught his eye they would exchange a smile. Steven almost envied them their rapport. This was not the grand passion of youth, the yearning desire Megan aroused in him now she had grown from mischievous child to desirable woman. The relationship between his parents was one of companionship and understanding. He knew it had grown over the years into deep and lasting friendship and it was a rare and valuable thing which he and Megan already shared. He realized now it was an acceptance of each other, their strengths and their weaknesses, a confiding of secret dreams and fears, the sharing of treasured memories. Whatever physical passion he might experience with another woman, he knew he would never feel the closeness of spirit he shared with Megan. It saddened and depressed him because he knew he must keep silent and allow Megan her freedom to form other relationships as he could not promise her any sort of future.

He felt a flare of resentment that he had sacrificed six good years of his life fighting a war neither he nor his fellow countrymen had wanted, while Fred had stayed at home. He could have built up the family's farm, made it more productive, knowing there was a market and decent prices for everything he could produce. The demand for food had never been greater. Demand still exceeded supply and the prices were guaranteed, but lack of capital held him back from expanding. The government had been compelled to ration staple foods as soon as war was declared. What greater incentive could any man want? Yet Fred had not only ignored a golden opportunity for himself, he had failed his family and his country, and he was still continuing in his idle ways. Willowburn still had only eight milking cows, no more than they had

219

kept before the war. Steven knew his mother and Edna were still doing the milking. The land girl had unintentionally mentioned that Fred only got out of bed in time to take the milk churns to the road end for the collecting lorry. Apparently, as soon as he returned he expected his breakfast to be ready, even though he knew Edna had the pigs to feed and his mother had her poultry to attend, as well as assisting his father to dress and shave and other daily routines, though she never complained. It made his blood boil to think of Fred being so arrogant and idle. He was glad he was no longer at Willowburn or he might have committed murder. It sickened him to see the increasing signs of neglect and untidiness about the neat little farm where he had grown up. Fortunately his father did not see how rapidly things were deteriorating since his stroke because he rarely managed to walk further than the garden or across the small yard at the back of the house. Unknown to any of them, other people were noticing and taking a serious view of Fred's haphazard management.

One Sunday afternoon towards the end of May Steven was surprised when his father beckoned him closer while his mother was upstairs changing her dress. His father's speech was still slow, but it was reasonably clear so long as he didn't get angry or excited, but sometimes he couldn't remember the words he wanted to use. Fred had no patience to listen or to help so the two rarely held a conversation, but Steven knew how much his father looked forward to hearing what was going on at Schoirhead and the other smallholdings. He was surprised to find it was not farming his father had in mind on this particular occasion.

'Ask Mr Kane to come to see me here.' Eddy Caraford enunciated his words carefully. 'On Friday afternoon.'

'The solicitor?' Steven was surprised, but his father nodded emphatically. 'But Mother takes her eggs to Annan on Fridays. She'll not—'

'I know.' Eddy Caraford nodded again. 'I want to ... to make things right – and tight – for her.'

'I see.' Steven frowned and chewed his lower lip.

His father watched him, then patted his knee.

'Hannah was always one o' the best. Ask him ... to come.'

'All right, if you're sure.'

'I am. Plenty time now ... to watch, to see things...'

'I'll telephone on Monday then and make an appointment for Mr Kane to call to see you here next Friday afternoon.' Steven repeated the arrangement carefully and watched his father nod with satisfaction.

The subject was never mentioned again so Steven had no idea what had transpired. He felt it was none of his business and it went out of his mind. In truth he had plenty of problems of his own. He was careful what he told the McGuires; he didn't want Annie passing on his problems to his mother, but he longed to have someone with whom he could safely share his concerns.

Megan went back to college with a heavy heart

after Easter, but in the middle of her second week she had a letter from Steven and her spirits rose. True, it was shorter than usual and not in his habitual chatty style. He kept away from personal topics, except to hope she was well. She had to restrain herself from replying the same day, but by the end of the week Steven had had the reply he had been hoping for.

He heaved a sigh of relief. Whatever friends Megan had made since she went to college there was no one yet who prevented her from writing to him as an old friend.

Megan was not too happy when she received Steven's next letter.

I have had some good luck and some bad. Ella farrowed twelve piglets and she is proving an excellent mother, calm and contented with plenty of milk so they are all thriving I have not needed a box by the Aga to nurse a wreckling as we feared. I have chosen two already which I hope to keep as gilts if all goes well with them, so you can give them names when you come home for the summer.

Megan's heart soared. Clearly Steven was expecting her to go down to Schoirhead again. She frowned as she read on.

I have not had the same success with one of the cows I bought. A few days ago, when I had finished the morning milking, I noticed a tiny fetus lying in the channel behind her.

She had aborted. I would not have noticed if she had been out in the fields. I hope it was a natural occurrence, but I fear it is more likely that my father was right and that it is contagious abortion following on from the trouble I had with Fred's heifers. I don't need to tell you the anxiety that causes me, but I scarcely know what to do. I need more cows, not to sell the ones I have.

I hear they are queuing for potatoes in London. I considered growing a few acres here as they would be a good crop and increase the fertility of the soil with all the manure I inherited from the previous tenant, but it would be impossible to gather them myself and I'm not sure where I could hire a squad or even whether I could afford to pay a gang of pickers. I may make more enquiries for next year. None of the other smallholders grow potatoes, except for their own use, but they all have at least a couple more cows than I have. Until I am sure mine are not infected with contagious abortion I am reluctant to spend any money on buying more in.

I am sorry if you are bored with this account of my failures, but I appreciate our long friendship more than I can say.

Ever your sincere friend,
Steven

PS I had a surprise visit from Natalie. This is the third time she has called in on her way home from her work in Carlisle. Twice I was working in the fields. Mrs McGuire refused to tell her where I was. She has not taken to Natalie since she overheard her calling Schoirhead a dump. I am invited to dinner with her parents next Tuesday evening at Martinwold. I can't imagine why they should invite me. I am not looking forward to it, but the food should be good! If it is not too late when I leave, I shall try to call on your parents.

'Oh, no!' Megan groaned aloud. 'Natalie means to get him. If only I was finished at college,' she wailed to Pauline, who was still her closest friend in spite of the unfortunate episode with Derek. Apparently he had been transferred to another branch of the bank some distance away. Whether the transfer was automatic or whether he had applied for it Megan didn't ask, but she was relieved to know he would not be calling at the college unexpectedly.

'It's not so very long until the summer vacation,' Pauline comforted her. 'I've got a job in a cafe, and I can't say I'm looking forward to all those weeks sweltering over teas and coffees. I need to earn some money, though, so it has to be done.'

'Yes, I suppose I'm lucky being able to work for my parents,' Megan said absently, her mind still on the Turners and their predatory daughter.

Steven discovered the invitation had been instigated by Mr Turner himself, but Natalie had insisted on delivering it in person. Mrs Turner was an excellent cook, and, judging by the three-course meal she served, they didn't seem greatly affected by rationing. Steven discovered they still had a live-in maid to help in the house. She came in to clear away the dishes, but Mrs Turner beckoned Natalie to help her with the coffee.

Steven guessed Mr Turner wished to speak to him alone.

'I feel I should keep an eye on your progress, Steven,' he began.

Steven felt himself stiffen at his patronizing manner.

'Natalie shows a lot of interest in your wee holding,' Mr Turner continued, 'and I did give you the reference to help you get your first tenancy.'

Steven squashed his irritation with an effort and answered his questions civilly. He didn't mention his anxieties about the possibility of his cattle being affected by contagious abortion, or his worries concerning his father and Willow-burn, but he was not surprised to learn Murdoch Turner kept his own ear to the ground, even on such matters.

'I believe your neighbour is elderly and in-firm?'

'Mr McGuire? I wouldn't say he's so old, but he is crippled with arthritis.'

'He has difficulty getting his own work done though? He'll not be fit to help you with hay-making then?'

'I wouldn't expect him to help me.' Steven frowned, wondering where this was leading.

'But you will need help. It's important to get good hay and to be ready for the weather, if and when it comes.'

'Yes, I know that.' Steven had wondered about the hay and harvest and he hoped Jimmy Kerr might lend a hand, but he was only available at weekends and in the evenings. Although the change in the clocks meant it was light almost until midnight in midsummer, it didn't prevent the dew falling. His father had always warned against building damp hay into the stacks.

'Take my advice,' Mr Turner went on. 'Make enquiries about getting a POW to help.'

'A prisoner of war?'

'Yes. You'll have to pay for the hours they work, but the camp attendants drop them off at your farm in the morning and collect them at five o'clock. Some of them are good workers. I've had one or two myself.'

'Thank you, I'll think about that. I imagine they'll all be going home soon.' He might mention the idea to the McGuires though.

'There's another thing...' Mr Turner broke into his thoughts. He sounded a little less assured now. 'I was at a meeting a week ago. I ran into Mr Griffiths. You know he's the agent for the estate?'

'Yes, of course. He's the agent for Willowburn.'

'I understand he's not happy with the way your brother is running the farm since your father had his stroke.'

'I'm not happy myself, but it's not my business so I keep quiet,' Steven said stiffly. He was beginning to wish he'd never come. 'If I criticized it would only make things unpleasant for my parents.'

'That's more or less what I said to Griffiths.'

Steven stared at him, his eyebrows raised in question. Willowburn had nothing to do with Mr Turner – not unless he was on one of the committees which inspected the farms to see if they were producing as much as they should. Mr Turner met his gaze.

'Griffiths was wondering whether your father was likely to get well enough to manage the farm again.'

'That's not very likely.' Steven frowned. 'He has made good progress, but not to that extent.'

'That's what he'd heard. He asked whether there was any chance of you retuning to Willowburn to take his place.'

'Why does he expect you to know that? Why doesn't he come and ask me himself?'

'Don't get angry, laddie. He knows I gave you a reference for the smallholding so Griffiths knows I'm taking an interest in you.'

Steven stared at him, then gave a hollow laugh. Oh, yes, Steven thought angrily, you'll have told half the county, no doubt.

'I'd never have left Willowburn in the first place if Fred and I could have worked together.'

Mr Turner nodded. 'I just thought I'd mention it. Griffiths will not let things go on as they are indefinitely. It puts his own job on the line if he doesn't see the farms are kept up to standard.' There was a warning note in his voice, but before either of them could say any more Natalie put her head round the door.

'Are you two going to sit at that table all night?

The coffee is getting cold. Do hurry up and come through to the lounge, Daddy.'

'We're coming now, sweetheart,' Mr Turner replied genially, and stood up, indicating Steven should precede him.

Afterwards Steven wished Natalie had not interrupted at that moment. Would Mr Turner have confided more of the agent's intentions? He would always wonder whether it would have made a difference if he had warned his father, or if he had dared to tell Fred he needed to pull up his socks and get on with farming instead of playing around with Edna.

Unknown to Steven, or his parents, Griffiths had already spoken to Fred, who had treated his warning with arrogant nonchalance.

At the beginning of the summer holidays Megan was over the moon when she got her driving licence.

'You'll remember petrol is still rationed, won't you, lassie? You'd better not plan too many visits to Steven's place.'

'Oh, Dad, I was not planning any,' Megan said, blushing because that had been her main aim in getting her driving licence.

She went off to bring in the cows for milking and Chrissie turned to her husband.

'You shouldn't encourage her to visit Steven, John. She might think you would approve of them getting serious.'

'So I would. I can't think of any lad I'd rather have for a son-in-law than Steven and they've always been good friends. I thought you liked him?'

'I do. He's a lovely lad.' Chrissie sighed heavily. 'But Megan has another year to do at college and then a year's teaching practice before she can call herself a qualified teacher. I don't want to see her throw away a good career to spend her life milking cows and looking after animals and having to scrape together every halfpenny before she can afford a new blouse. You said yourself Steven wouldn't be able to afford to keep a wife for years yet.'

'It was Steven who said that, I think. Anyway, it depends on the wife. If it was someone like Natalie Turner I don't think any ordinary farmer could afford to marry her. Megan's different altogether. You can tell she loves him and she'd do anything to help him.'

'I know that, John,' Chrissie said, 'but I do want her to finish her training at least. She would always have that to fall back on if things went wrong.'

'I'm not suggesting they should get married next week, or even next year,' John Oliphant defended himself, 'but money isn't everything. We've worked hard all our lives, but we've been together, working side by side and we've always looked after each other. I wouldn't swap that for the richest wife in the country.'

'Oh, John...' Chrissie blushed, her eyes bright. 'That's the nicest thing you've ever said.'

'Is it? Then maybe I should be taking a leaf out of Steven's book and practising my poetic skills, eh, lass?' he said, almost boyishly. 'Seriously, I've never fancied anybody else but you, love.

Do you regret getting married so young?'

'Of course not.' Chrissie's heart still beat faster at the look in her husband's eyes and she went readily into his embrace when he opened his arms. 'No,' she whispered, 'I've never regretted marrying you, John.'

Megan decided to pay Steven a surprise visit one evening to show him she had passed her driving test. When she arrived he had been haymaking and he was later than usual starting to milk his cows.

'How did you get here on your own?' he asked, his eyes lighting up in welcome.

'I came to show you I've passed my driving test.' She grinned. 'Now Dad says I can come anytime so long as I don't use up all his petrol ration.'

'I wish I'd known, although I suppose I'd still have been working late tonight. I took Mr Turner's advice and applied for a prisoner of war to help. The McGuires have got one too.'

'Are they good workers?'

'Yes, not bad. My man is called Johan. He's little more than a boy to look at him, but he's strong and he's enthusiastic.'

'Was he from a farm in Germany?'

'No, but he's eager to learn. He had been brought up in the country. He says he didn't want to fight in the war.'

'The same as you and Sam then,' Megan said wistfully. 'There must have been thousands of men and boys who felt the same on both sides.'

'Aye, I reckon so. The McGuires' man is called

Otto. He's an older man with dull, sad eyes. He makes me sad to look at him,' Steven added ruefully. 'Johan doesn't speak very good English yet, but I gather that Otto is missing his wife and his three wee boys – at least they were still schoolboys when he last saw them. He doesn't know whether they are alive or dead and it has been two years since the war ended.'

'That must be awful,' Megan said with sympathy. 'At least we know what happened to Sam, and we know he had you beside him, even though he did die in a foreign country.'

'Yes, I shall always be glad I was at his side. He knew he was not alone,' Steven said. 'But I know what you mean, it must be awful not to know whether your family are alive or dead or what has happened to them.'

'Can't the Red Cross people help? Or some other organization?'

'I think they're trying. The prisoners have to return to camp when the lorry comes for them at five o'clock,' he explained, 'so we worked at the hay as long as we could to make the most of their help. Then I finished unloading the two carts myself. Mr McGuire was building the stack, but he's finding it hard going. We're all working together to get my hay in and then his. I did the mowing for him too. He could never have managed it himself with his arthritis as bad as it is.'

'You're very good, Steven,' Megan said.

'Oh, they do a lot for me,' he said. 'Mrs McGuire is making dinner for all of us while we have the two men here, and even when I'm on

231

my own she often sends a meal round for me if she's been cooking or baking. Shandy keeps in with her too.'

The collie pricked up his velvety ears at the sound of his name and Megan crouched down to pat him affectionately.

'Their own dog died before I moved here so Mrs M sometimes gives him a bone when she's been making broth.'

'You've been lucky to get such friendly neighbours, Steven. If you've got a spare stool, I'll help you with the milking,' Megan offered.

'With my huge herd of four cows.' Steven grimaced wryly and shook his head. 'I'd rather you stay there and talk to me. You look so fresh and clean.'

Megan blushed slightly for there was no mistaking the admiration in his sparkling blue eyes.

'Anyway you've done your stint at milking already today, Megan. How many cows has your father at Martinwold now?'

'We have fifty-five milking and ten more waiting to calve.'

'Whew! I've a long way to go,' Steven groaned.

'We couldn't milk so many if we didn't have the milking machines.'

'No, I suppose not. Tell me all the news while I get on with these. How do you like being home from college? I expect it's hard to be back working in the byre after being away studying?'

'I enjoy it, especially getting the cows in early in the mornings. The scent of the honeysuckle in the hedgerows is heavenly and you know I always liked being out in the fresh air. I suppose that's why I enjoy gardening. I do hope I get a teaching post in a country school. It would be even better if I could get one near home.'

'I hope you do too,' Steven said. 'I miss you when you're not around.' He looked up at her from the flank of the cow he was milking and his smile made Megan's heart do a somersault.

'Shall I go inside and cook you some supper?' she asked when Steven started milking the last cow.

'That's the best offer I've had all day,' he said, 'but I don't think you'll find much in the pantry to cook with except eggs and more eggs,' he added ruefully.

'Sounds like omelette then.'

'The mushrooms are fresh. I picked them this morning when I was bringing Daisy in for work. Do you remember how Sam used to love look-ing for mushrooms?' he asked reminiscently.

'I do, and you would both get up extra early in the hope you could leave me behind,' she said with a pout, 'and the funny thing is that Sam never ate any mushrooms. I'll see if there's any-thing growing in the garden before I go in.'

There were plenty of new potatoes and spring onions, some young carrots and a few peas – plenty to make a tasty omelette, she decid-ed. Her efforts were more than rewarded by Steven's appreciation.

Later, as they cleared away and washed up together, he had to restrain himself several times from drawing her into his arms and kissing her, but he knew if he started he would never want to stop. He sighed.

'It's getting late and you have an early start too. I'll show you the pigs and you can choose their names the next time you come.'

As she drove home, Megan's heart soared. They had regained their old camaraderie. Only when she had been leaving had she seen the wistful shadows in Steven's eyes again. He had taken her hands in his and she thought he was going to kiss her goodnight, but in the end he had simply leaned forward and dropped a light, friendly kiss on her cheek.

'Come again soon, Meggie. You know how much I enjoy your company.'

The summer holidays seemed to be passing all too quickly. Megan visited Schoirhead at least once each week. She would have liked to go more often, but she was conscious she was using her father's car and his petrol ration so she agreed eagerly when Steven offered to come to her house one evening and take her for a run on the back of his motorbike. She enjoyed the feel of the wind in her hair and her arms around Steven's waist as she learned to move with him when they went round the curves in the twisting country roads, but he was always careful with her.

'I feel perfectly safe,' she said, laughing up into his face with delight. 'I really enjoyed it.'

'Would you like to come with me to Willow-burn, the next time I go then? I'm sure my mother and father would love to see you again. A cheerful face would brighten up their day.'

Megan was not so sure about that, but she wanted to go with Steven wherever he was going.

Hannah Caraford welcomed her warmly and Megan could see how pathetically pleased his father was to see Steven. She was shocked by her first sight of him. She remembered him as a strong, sturdy man who had walked tirelessly up and down the fields behind his horses. He had even let Sam have a go at ploughing once and he hadn't complained when Sam's furrow ended up like a dog's hind leg, as her brother had told her himself.

On the way home Steven drew the motorbike to a halt in a field gateway and they both climbed off.

'Shall we go for a bit of a walk?' Steven asked. 'It's a lovely evening, but I never stay late at Willowburn. Father tires easily and I avoid running into Fred if I can.'

'I'd like that,' Megan said, and Steven held open the gate into a grassy field. 'What did your mother mean when she mentioned moving away from Willowburn, Steven?'

'Moving? She's never mentioned that to me,' he said quickly.

'I got the impression she was mulling it over in her mind, but I was surprised you'd never mentioned it.'

'That's because I didn't realize Mother wanted to move,' Steven said, frowning thoughtfully.

He recalled Mr Turner's hints about Mr Griffiths' dissatisfaction with Fred's management of

Willowburn. He didn't blame the agent because his criticism was justified, but he wondered if his mother knew, or if she had heard rumours too. 'Maybe she is finding the work too much for her,' he said to Megan. 'She's not getting any younger and caring for my father must take up a lot of her time, especially when she still helps with the milking twice a day. I can't understand why Fred doesn't see he would be working for his own benefit; it's his own future at stake.'

'By the sound of things he only uses his brain to find ways of avoiding work,' Megan said. 'I hope I don't get any young pupils like that.'

'What else did Mother say? I wonder why she's never mentioned it to me,' Steven pondered, still frowning a little.

'We were just making conversation,' Megan said gently, 'so don't feel hurt, Steven. She must get lonely sometimes when your father can't hold a proper conversation any more, and if Fred is as sullen as you say. I'm surprised the land girl has stayed on this long, but she doesn't seem to be much company for your mother either.'

'I reckon Edna has stayed because she and Fred have a lot in common and they seem to have something going between them. Tell me exactly what Mother said,' he persisted.

'She only said she feels things are getting a bit too much for her at Willowburn,' Megan said slowly. 'I should think they are too, when she has so much to do outside, as well as cooking and washing for four adults, including an invalid.'

'You're very understanding, Megan,' Steven

said gratefully. 'Maybe Mother sensed you would be. She enjoys her poultry, but she wouldn't need to help with the milking if Fred would get himself out of bed in the mornings,' he added angrily, 'but if she relied on him they'd never have the churns ready in time for the milk lorry to collect them.'

'Well, don't go worrying about it yet. She thinks your father is not well enough to consider a move. Maybe I shouldn't have mentioned it, but she didn't say it was a secret. We were just talking in friendly fashion. In fact, I'd love to visit again if it's all right with you, Steven?'

'Of course it is. I thought my mother would enjoy your company, Meggie.' He took her hand and swung it as they walked. 'I certainly enjoy being with you. I'm going to miss you when you go back to college.'

'I shall miss you too, Steven,' Megan said softly. 'I wish I didn't have to go back, but I know how it would upset Mother if I gave up now.'

'Yes, it would. Anyway it would be silly to give up at this stage, and I wouldn't like your mother to blame me. It's not as though I've anything to offer you in place of a career,' he added bitterly, almost under his breath.

Megan heard. Did that mean he would have offered her marriage if he could have afforded a wife? she wondered hopefully.

'She won't blame you. You're my mother's blue-eyed boy since Sam died. Speaking of your mother though, you know it may not be such a bad thing if your parents did move from Willow-

237

burn and left Fred to get on with things, the way you have to do. Your mother fancies a cottage with a good-sized garden where she can keep her hens. I got the impression she had talked to Maryanne's mother about it, you know, Mrs Anderson.'

'Ah, yes, they meet at Annan on Fridays sometimes. She must be considering it then.' He wondered why his mother had confided in Megan and not in him, but he was glad the two of them had got on together.

Sixteen

Steven felt hay time had barely finished before it was time to harvest the corn. He still had only one horse, Daisy, and he did not possess a binder to cut the corn and deposit it in neatly tied sheaves, ready for setting up in stooks. Jimmy Kerr often popped into Schoirhead for a chat after work during the long summer evenings. The two young men got on well together. Although the other tenants were not as old as the McGuires, Jimmy considered they were all old-fashioned and stick-in-the-mud and he had welcomed a younger tenant, especially one as keen as Steven.

'I think I might be able to borrow a horse-drawn binder from Mr Turner,' Steven said, 'but it takes two horses so I should need to borrow the McGuires' gelding. I hate the idea of borrowing, especially from Mr Turner.'

'You could always marry that lass of his and then he'd give you the lot,' Jimmy teased. He had a strong suspicion he knew where Steven's affections lay and they were not with that stuck-up Turner girl. Steven gave him a sideways grin.

'Do you want me to sign my life away?'

'Aye, that's what you'd be doing with that family, I reckon. No, we canna have ye doing

239

that, mate.' Jimmy grinned back. 'Anyway, I've a better suggestion. I think I could arrange to hire a tractor and a binder from my boss's firm, like we did with the plough. He's hoping to make a sale to you eventually.'

'When I can afford a tractor I will certainly go to him first, tell him.'

'That's fair enough. He's a decent man. He wouldn't cheat you. Anyway, if we hire it would need to be over two weekends again. None of the smallholdings have big acreages of cereals, but they're all doing their bit.'

'Aye, Britain depends on the small farmers because there's so many of us. I read about Prime Minister Atlee issuing warnings of more austerity to come. He reckons Britain canna afford to buy imported produce. If the situation is that serious, we shall have to do our best to get the harvest in in good condition.'

'Aye, I'll ask Dad to talk to the other holders then, but I reckon they'll be glad to join in.'

Steven was happy to drive the tractor while Jimmy manipulated the binder and between them they cut the oats for all five of the Loaning smallholders. They all shared the cost of hiring the machines and the other three farmers were relieved to get theirs cut with the tractor and binder. They willingly paid Steven and Jimmy for their labour and Steven planned to put his extra money towards buying another milk cow.

There was still all the stooking and carting to do and Megan and her father both came down to help in the interval between the morning and evening milkings at Martinworld.

'I hope I shall not be in trouble with Mr Turner for stealing away his extra hands?' Steven asked with a grin. 'But I'm really glad to see you both.'

'Don't worry, laddie,' John Oliphant said. 'During the war I worked at Martinwold from five in the morning until ten or eleven at night during hay and harvest. This year Mr Turner has hired four POWs as extras. We prefer to help here, don't we, Megan?' He winked at his daughter.

'Yes, it's a lovely wee community down here,' she said, stripping off her sweater. She blushed a little when she looked up and saw the admiration in Steven's eyes. She rarely wore trousers, except in the byre, but she had donned a pair of fawn bib and brace overalls and a yellow shirt, thinking they would be more suitable if she was working with the other men. Although she was not tall, she had long legs and a narrow waist and Steven eyed her with approval.

'Megan said you were taking on some feeding sheep to eat off your extra grass, Steven. Did you get fixed up?' John Oliphant asked. He was genuinely interested in Steven's farming venture, more so since he had lost his own son. He still missed Sam's cheery company and he knew he always would.

'Aye, I got fixed up.' Steven sighed. 'They've come from a breeder up at Sanquhar, but the whole lot are as wild as the heather. I hadna bargained for that. If I lose a couple of them there'll be no profit in taking them. That's one lesson learned the hard way,' he added ruefully. 'Next year I shall make sure I'm better stocked with animals of my own to eat all the grass.'

'Aye, well, ye'll have had more time to plan and to build up by next season.'

'My main worry is wondering if any more cows will abort,' he said anxiously.

'I ken fine what a worry that must be,' John Oliphant sympathized. 'It's bad enough losing the calf, but the cows usually go right off their milk so you lose in every way, as well as spreading the disease to the rest. It's a dead loss all round. It would be best to get rid of them, but that's easier said than done for a young fellow starting up – or for an established farmer come to that. Most folks are inoculating now, but there's always some who would rather take a risk than spend the money.'

Stooking the sheaves was a laborious task, but it had to be done to allow the oats to ripen and harden and let the straw dry out. Mr McGuire found it almost beyond him and he could barely express his gratitude when Steven brought Megan and her father to help with his harvest as well. Mrs McGuire insisted on making their midday meal. She felt it was small repayment, but it was a token of their appreciation.

'We ought to bring you some of our rations now that the meat has been reduced again,' John Oliphant said.

'Aye, well, I can't do much with a shilling's worth a week, but they've increased the cheese and bread rations for farmers and fisherman, and I expect the miners deserve all the meat they can get.' The women had all learned to make a little go a long way.

'Aye, I wouldna like to work underground for all the tea in China, or all the beef in Britain,' John Oliphant said with a shiver. He looked at Megan, then winked at Mrs McGuire. 'They've even cut the petrol again – no more motoring for pleasure.'

'Och, the lassie works for her petrol whenever she comes down here,' Mrs McGuire declared. She was a staunch supporter of Megan. 'I'll bet some o' the gentry will not be so pleased now they've banned foreign holidays though. I expect they'll try to make out they're crossing the Channel on business.'

'Maybe they will, but that's limited to eight pounds a day for expenses now so that will clip their wings,' McGuire said with a note of satisfaction.

Annie McGuire thought it was a pity Megan was spending so much time at college training to be a teacher.

'She would make a fine wee wife for Steven,' she announced to McGuire. 'I would like a pleasant lassie like her for a neighbour.'

'Neighbour?' McGuire grunted. He'd had a long hard day and he was rarely free from pain now. 'I'm wondering how much longer we can go on here, Annie. I thought I'd be better with the summer weather, but I couldn't have managed without Steven's help. I reckon I'm no use. I'm finished. Useless I am,' he said dejectedly.

'Well, you know I don't mind moving if it's what you want,' Annie said doubtfully. She had fancied a wee bungalow near the shops for a long while, but she didn't want that if it was going to mean her Tom being miserable and having nothing to interest him. She knew farmers often went into a decline and died if they retired into the town. It was like trying to transplant a full-grown tree. They had waited a long time to get a wee place of their own and she knew Tom had hoped to live out his life at Number Two, The Loaning.

'If you want a wee hoose, Annie, that's what we'll have to do, for it's you and young Steven who do all the work here now. But, oh...' He shook his head. 'It's not how I expected to end ma life.'

'Don't talk like that!' Annie said in alarm. 'You're only fifty-eight.'

'I might as well be ninety-eight for all the good I am.' Mr McGuire sighed.

Annie McGuire lay awake most nights worrying and wondering what to do for the best. She hated to see Tom so depressed, but she knew they couldn't go on depending on Steven. He had his own way to make and he was ambitious. As soon as the harvest was over he was going to buy another cow, and a second one when he got the money for grazing the sheep.

Several times she teased Steven.

'Megan would make a fine wife for ye, laddie. She's not afraid of hard work or getting her hands dirty, for all she's blessed with a good brain. No air and graces about that one – not like the first hoity-toity young woman you brought.'

'If you mean Natalie, Mrs M, I didn't bring her,' Steven said. 'I think she was curious.'

'Curious she may be, but she fancies ye so

ye'd better watch out, ma lad.'

'Don't you worry. Natalie Turner wouldn't want a man like me. She has her sights set on one of these wealthy doctors, I reckon.'

'Well, I'm relieved to hear it. You'll not do any better than Megan.'

'I know that,' Steven said seriously. 'The trouble is Megan could take her pick of a dozen young men, all of them with more money and more time than I have, so there's no use dreaming the impossible.'

'Oh, laddie, I hear what you're saying, and I know it might be true, but Megan doesna strike me as the kind who would marry a man she didn't love for the sake o' his money.'

One morning, after Tom McGuire had suffered a worse week than usual, Annie announced, 'I've thought of a way we might be able to stay here, Tom, but it depends whether Steven would agree and we'd have to keep the arrangement a secret or we might both lose the tenancy.'

'That wouldna matter so much to us at our time o' life, but it would be the end o' the world to Steven so you'd better not be thinking up anything criminal, Annie.'

'Criminal! As though I would, Tom McGuire.' She explained her plan in detail. She knew Tom would agree to almost anything if he could stay where he was, but it all depended on Steven.

'There's only one thing to do and that's to ask him,' Mr McGuire said. 'We'll wait a while,' he decided. 'The prisoners are coming back today to help cart the corn in. We'll wait until we get that done.'

Once the last sheaf of corn was in the stack, Mr McGuire invited Steven to come round for supper and a drink of beer to celebrate.

'We'll expect you when you've finished milking.'

'That's kind of you both,' Steven said apologetically, 'but could we make it tomorrow night? I promised to take Megan to the Lyceum in Dumfries as soon as we finished the harvest. There's a film she wants to see.' He grinned. 'I don't want to miss an opportunity.'

'No, no, that ye don't, laddie. It's more important, taking out a fine young woman for the evening,' Mr McGuire's eyes twinkled wickedly. 'You know Annie would have the pair of you married if she had her way?'

'If I'd anything to offer a wife I'd agree with her.' Steven smiled ruefully.

'Ah, well, come round tomorrow night after milking then. There's something we'd like to talk over with ye in private.'

It was a long way to Dumfries on the back of Steven's wee motorbike, but Megan didn't mind so long as they could spend the time together. It was a lovely autumnal evening.

'I never thought I'd have much use for a motorbike, but it's been the handiest thing ever,' he said, 'especially for visiting Willowburn. I didn't expect I'd be lucky enough to have such a pretty passenger though.' He grinned and watched the colour deepen in Megan's cheeks. He was often surprised how easily Megan blushed and

246

how shy she still seemed with him, yet he knew she valued their friendship as much as he did. Did she ever think they could be more than friends? he wondered, enjoying the feel of her arms around him as she settled herself on the pillion.

He had saved his sweet ration for a month and had managed to get a tiny box of Rowntree's Dairybox chocolates from the grocer, or rather Mrs McGuire had got them for him, no doubt with a wee bit of bribery, he thought with a smile. He gave them to Megan as they went into the cinema.

'Oh, Steven, you shouldn't have spent your coupons on me,' Megan said, deeply touched by his thoughtfulness.

'There'll only be four or five chocolates altogether,' he said ruefully. 'Remind me to buy you the biggest box available when the rationing stops. I owe you a lot more than that, Megan,' he said seriously. 'I ought to pay you and your father for all the work you've done during the harvest.'

'We've enjoyed it, so we wouldn't have taken your money, even if you'd had any to spare. Dad was telling Mum what a lovely, friendly lot the smallholders are.'

'Yes, it makes a change from having Fred's sullen face for company,' he agreed wryly.

Steven reached for Megan's hand when the film started and she linked her fingers in his and seemed happy to stay that way. Each time there was an exciting bit in the film he felt her fingers tighten around his and he squeezed her hand reassuringly, earning a quick, shy smile before her attention was gripped again by the story.

Later, as they drew into Martinwold Farm, Steven switched off the engine and cruised silently down the slight incline to the shadow of the house wall. He turned to help Megan alight, but instead of letting her go he took her hands in his and drew her closer.

'I've really enjoyed this evening, Megan. I wish you didn't have go so far away to attend college.'

'So do I,' she said fervently. 'I wish I'd never started, but Mother believes they're giving me a great opportunity to have an easier life than they've had.'

'I thought your parents enjoyed the dairy and being able to work side by side?'

'They do. They admit they wouldn't want things any different for themselves, so I don't know why they think I want to be different.'

Steven was silent for a moment. Then he sighed. 'It must be wonderful to have the woman you love at your side all the time. Perhaps I should have settled for being a dairyman too.'

'Oh, no, Steven. You've always wanted to farm. We all know that. I'm certain you'll make a success of your wee holding and then the Department may offer you a bigger one.'

'Maybe, but I'm beginning to realize there are some things even more important than having a farm, Megan.'

Without waiting for a reply, he held her closer and gently traced the line of her mouth with his lips. Apart from an indrawn breath, Megan

248

offered no resistance and his arms tightened, his kisses deepened and grew more urgent. Instead of pushing him away as he had half expected, Megan slipped her arms around his neck, returning his kisses making his heart race with joy. It took all his self control to draw apart. Neither of them spoke. It was as though they were afraid words might shatter something precious. He held her hand tenderly as they moved closer to the back door of the house.

'It's been a wonderful evening, Megan,' he murmured gruffly. 'Do you think we might repeat it?' He was unaware of the wistful pleading in his voice.

'Dearest Steven, there's nothing I would like more...' The door opened, illuminating them and the pathway.

'Oh, hello, you two,' John Oliphant said awkwardly, seeing them standing close together, noticing their clasped hands. 'We didn't hear the motorbike. I'm just going to take a last look round the newly calved cows before I go to bed.'

'Yes, it's time I was on my way too,' Steven said. He bent his head and gave Megan a chaste kiss on her cheek. 'I hope you'll manage to come down to Schoirhead again soon?' he whispered and saw her nod.

'Not tomorrow evening, but I'll come the next if that's all right?'

'Anytime at all,' he answered with a wide smile. 'Good night, Meggie.' He raised his voice. 'Good night, Mr Oliphant.'

'G'night, son,' John Oliphant called cheerfully

over his shoulder as he whistled merrily on his way to the byre.

The following evening Steven shepherded his few cows back to their pasture, wishing he had twice as many and watching each of them for any more signs of infection. He led Daisy into the paddock at the back of the house, then washed and changed before he went round to the McGuires with Shandy at his heels. The dog lay down on the doorstep with his head on his paws, prepared to wait all night for him if necessary. Steven bent and patted the silky head and was rewarded by a wag of his tail. He was smiling as he chapped the door.

'Come in, laddie, no need to stand knocking. You know us well enough by now.'

Mrs McGuire was a good cook and generous too and Steven enjoyed his meal, but he sensed both the McGuires were tense and he wondered why.

'We don't know how to thank you for all you have done since you moved next door, Steven,' Mrs McGuire began.

'I'm sure there's no need to thank me for anything, Mrs M. You've almost kept me in food.'

'No more than you deserve and it's all I can offer. We were worried when Bob McKie became so ill. Although he was getting on a bit, he was a grand neighbour. We wondered who we'd get in his place, but we didn't expect to be needing so much help ourselves. We couldn't have got through the ploughing and sowing, nor

250

the hay and harvest without your help.'

'The thing is, laddie,' Mr McGuire broke in, 'I canna afford to employ a man all the time and I canna manage the farm any longer on my own...'

'But he doesna want to move out,' Mrs McGuire added hurriedly.

'I shall wither away if I've to move to the town.'

'I can understand that,' Steven sympathized. 'It's all I dreamed of during the war – getting back to the land and the animals.' He shuddered. 'What about a bit more help from one o' the POWs?' he asked.

Mr McGuire shook his head. 'There's not much profit on a place this size if you can't do most of the work yourself, and I should need to supervise a POW all the time. Anyway, I expect they'll be going home anytime now.'

'I suppose most of them will,' Steven agreed. 'Johan plans to stay, even after he's released, if they'll allow him.'

'Aye, he seemed a good laddie, but you organized them well, Steven, and we've noticed how you manage your own work, lad,' Mr Mc-Guire said. 'I can see why they made you a sergeant. We want to make a proposition. We'd like you to take over most of our holding—'

'We know our tenancy rules say we can't sublet the land,' Mrs McGuire broke in. She looked at him anxiously. 'But all the other holders know how much you've helped us this year. Surely nobody would know if you went on farming most of our land along with your own? If you paid the rent to us, we would pay it to the

Department as usual.' She looked at him hopefully.

Steven was reminded of Shandy when he longed for a tasty titbit.

'I don't understand...?'

'We'd like to stay in the house and keep the wee paddock at the back for our two sows and my hens so that we have a wee bit o' something to sell and to keep us interested,' Mrs McGuire went on persuasively. 'We daren't offer to sublet the land to anybody else because the Department are strict about maintaining the fences and the ditches. We know we could trust you to keep them in good order.'

'I see...' Steven said slowly, chewing his lower lip.

'We couldn't give you a proper lease, but you'd have the use o' the land for as long as we're here. It would give you chance to build up your stock for when you're ready to rent a bigger farm, and we all know you will one day, laddie,' Mr McGuire said. 'Of course the rent would be a bit less than yours because we'll still be in the house and grazing the paddock. You'd have about thirty acres extra...'

'We need to sell the cows of course,' Annie McGuire said. 'Maybe you could buy them from us if you'd like? At least ye'd know where they've come from and that they're healthy. We reared all o' them ourselves.'

'That would certainly be an advantage,' Steven said drily, 'if I could have afforded them.'

'You'd have more milk to sell and you can pay us when you're able,' Mrs McGuire pleaded.

'I'd like to think o' them still here.'

'I wouldn't like to be in debt,' Steven said quickly, but in spite of his habitual caution he could feel excitement rising in him. 'One thing for sure I wouldn't be taking sheep on for grazing again,' he said darkly, 'but the extra land would let me keep a wee flock of breeding ewes of my own.'

'Aye, a lowland breed maybe. Ewes with lambs would be more content,' Mr McGuire said. 'Yon hill sheep have certainly given ye a few headaches.'

'I could keep a few more cows as well. It might even be worth getting a milking machine when I can afford one,' Steven said, his eyes bright as his brain raced ahead. He sobered. 'The buildings wouldn't be very convenient for that though,' he mused aloud. 'There's one serious drawback as well.' He looked Mr McGuire in the eye. 'If yon man Wilson from the Department ever found out I was renting your land he'd probably throw both of us out.'

'He would if he knew,' McGuire said. 'Annie and me, we'd be no worse off because we can't carry on the way things are anyway, but it would be a terrible thing to happen to you, laddie, when you're starting out. Aye...' He frowned. 'Maybe we shouldna have asked ye.'

'But I don't see how he would find out,' Annie McGuire protested. 'It would be a private arrangement between us.'

'Can I think about it?' Steven said. 'I would like to discuss it with my father.'

'Aye, there's no hurry now the harvest is in,'

Mr McGuire said. 'Let us know before the end o' November though. We shall need to give six months' notice at the term if you don't take it on.'

'Give me time to do my sums and think about it, then I'll let you know,' Steven said.

'Be sure and keep it quiet,' Mr McGuire warned. 'Or we shall all be out on our necks.'

'Yes, of course,' Steven said, though his first thought had been to tell Megan when she visited him the following evening.

Seventeen

'I do wish the summer holidays could go on forever,' Megan said as she strolled across the newly harvested field with Steven. 'Did Dad mention that Mr Turner wondered whether you have any spare grass to keep ten to fifteen young heifers for him?'

'I haven't seen your father since we went to the pictures.'

'I thought he might have phoned you. Mr Turner is talking about extending the byre so that he can keep twenty more cows.'

'Twenty! My word, he is expanding.'

'Mmm ... he says there's never been a better time for farmers to expand and make progress. Dad's not sure whether to be pleased or not. He feels he and Mum and one boy can just about manage nicely with the number they have now, with two milking and one carrying to the dairy. Mum doesn't want two boys living in the house with extra washing and cooking.'

'No, I can see it would mean extra work all round for your mother.'

'I keep thinking they might take on a smaller dairy for the two of them if they had me off their hands. I wish I didn't have another year to do at college.'

'It will be worth it though. Just think of the

255

money you'll earn and the long summer holidays,' Steven said seriously.

Megan stopped walking and turned to face him.

'You sound like Mum. She knows, and you know, that money isn't everything in life, Steven. If it was, you would have made a career in the army and ended up with a good pension for your old age.'

'Mmm, maybe that's what I ought to have done,' Steven said morosely. He almost added, 'And then I could have asked you to marry me,' but he swallowed the words.

'You don't really mean that,' Megan said accusingly. 'Come on, I'll race you to the river.'

She was off, running fast down the gentle slope, but Steven had longer legs and he caught her up so that they fell together on to the grassy bank with the river flowing by a couple of feet below them.

'I'm putting the sheep in this field next week so they'll be in good condition for going back where they belong. I reckon I shall have earned my money for their keep. I'm not having any more like them.'

'I suppose that's one lesson learned. You'd be better with Mr Turner's heifers.'

'Probably, but I don't want him to think he's doing me any favours. I might be a poor small farmer, but I don't like being beholden to him.'

'Has Fred finished his harvest yet?'

'I hardly dare ask, but I did tell him how pleased I was with young Johan so if he's too mean to pay a POW to have extra labour it's his

256

own fault if the harvest is dragging on.' He stood up and held out a hand to pull Megan to her feet. She was light as a feather and before he realized it he had pulled her into his arms. He held her there, close against his chest, his heart beating rapidly. It seemed the most natural thing in the world and she offered no resistance when he kissed her upturned mouth, in fact she returned his kiss with enthusiasm. He lifted his head and looked down into her face.

'Ah, Megan,' he groaned softly, 'at times like this I wish I was a millionaire.' He released her, but he kept hold of her hand as they walked back along a more direct path to the farm.

'I don't want a millionaire,' Megan said softly.

'Maybe not, but I don't even have a fraction to offer, nothing like your other admirers. This is the McGuires' field we're walking through now,' he said. He was tempted to confide in her about their proposition and the plans going round and round in his head.

'I don't suppose they'll mind,' Megan said flatly, knowing Steven was deliberately changing the subject. He had never once said he loved her. Maybe he was already regretting the kisses which had set her heart pounding and her lips tingling. Maybe he only wanted a little light dalliance when she was available.

Even before they reached the front door they could hear the telephone ringing.

'I wonder who that can be,' Steven said as he ran to the house. 'I spoke to Mother last night...' He grabbed the receiver before it stopped ringing.

'Hello?'

'You're through now, caller,' the operator said. Before she had finished speaking Steven heard his mother's agitated voice.

'Where have you been, Steven? I've tried three times...'

'I'm here now, Mother. Is something wrong? Is it Dad?'

'Oh, Stevie. He-he's had another st-stroke.'

He could hear her voice trembling and knew she was near to tears. Hannah Caraford never gave in to tears. 'He-he ... It's bad, Stevie. Can you come? Doctor Burns doesn't think he'll last until morning.'

'Oh, Steven, how dreadful,' Megan said in distress when he relayed the news to her. 'Shall I drive you to Willowburn? You've had a shock and...'

'I'll be all right, Meggie. I'd better go on the motorbike so I can get back here,' he said. 'Whatever happens I shall need to return briefly to milk the cows and feed the pigs.'

'Go now then, but please be careful, dearest Steven,' Megan said softly. She put her arms around his middle and hugged him and for a moment he laid his cheek against her soft hair, wishing she could go with him, but his first priority now would be to comfort his mother.

'I will. I'm sorry to leave you here like this. Will you – will you tell the McGuires?'

'Of course. Telephone me if there's anything I can do,' Megan murmured. 'I'll fuel your Aga to keep it in for morning, and I'll feed Shandy before I leave. He senses you're upset.'

'Yes.' He bent and patted the dog's silky head. 'Will you ask the McGuires to keep an eye on him? I don't know when I shall be back.' He had a premonition his father would not recover this time.

'Ah, Steven, thank God you've come,' Hannah greeted him with heartfelt relief. 'Your father hasna regained consciousness.'

'What happened? Was it sudden?'

'We had a visit from Mr Griffiths, the agent for the estate.' Hannah looked up at him. 'If only he hadn't got so upset.'

'What did Mr Griffiths say to upset him, Mother?'

'They're terminating the tenancy at the end of November. Fred isna managing the farm to the standards they expect from their tenants.' She quoted Mr Griffiths' words. 'It seems he'd already given Fred a warning. It wasna Mr Griffiths' fault. He has a job to do, but when he realized Eddy was so upset he said we could stay on until the May term because your father had always been one if their best tenants. He even offered to let Fred stay on until the lease expires in another two years, if he would bring Willowburn back up to the standard of the other farms.'

'Surely Fred agreed to do that?'

'No. He swore at Mr Griffiths! He told him he could keep his farm. He stamped out of the house. That made Eddy worse...' Her voice shook and she pressed her hand to her mouth. 'I went with Mr Griffiths to the door to apologize. When I came back in Eddy was shaking. He asked me to help him upstairs. He collapsed before I could get him into bed. Doctor Burns doesn't hold out much hope.'

'I'll go up and see him,' Steven said.

'I'll come with you,' she whispered.

Steven put his arm around her shoulders and she leaned into him.

An hour later they heard Fred and Edna come in and go straight to their beds. Steven watched as his mother gently stroked his father's hand where it lay on the sheet.

'You should go home to bed too, Steven.'

'I'm staying,' he said firmly. 'I'll go home in time for the milking, but I'll come straight back afterwards.' They talked quietly together.

'I had been thinking we ought to move out,' Hannah said. 'Fred has been unbearable since Eddy has been unable to work. Mrs Anderson mentioned a grocer's shop to sell in her village. It has a house and a large garden and an orchard big enough to let us keep my hens and a pig. We could manage there, just the two of us, but I couldn't bring myself to mention moving in case I upset Eddy. Now I wish, oh how I wish, I had.'

Steven spoke soothingly and at last she dozed. It was very quiet and Steven found his own eyelids drooping. The sky was beginning to lighten when he opened them almost an hour later. He sat quietly, wondering what the future held. Eventually a bird began to sing in the garden and soon the other birds joined in. How full of joy they sounded. Through the window, he could see the sun was rising over the edge of the horizon, painting the sky in glorious colours of aqua-marine and gold and pink against the darker blue of the sky. His eyes moved back to his father.

'It seems terrible to think he may never see the wonder of another dawn,' he whispered softly. Almost as though he heard, his father gave a long sigh.

'Ah...' his mother breathed and clasped his hand. A moment later she murmured brokenly, 'He is at peace now. We don't know what glories he may see. We mustn't be s-sad, Steven.'

Before he left to milk his cows, Steven tapped on Fred's door to break the news of their father's death.

'Well, thank the lord for that,' he declared with satisfaction. 'He's run up enough bills for that old quack of a doctor.' Fred showed no trace of grief.

Steven closed the door, sickened by his callous response.

Megan and her parents were among the friends who attended the funeral and afterwards she and her mother helped to serve tea. Steven realized his mother was deeply affected by his father's death and she was struggling to keep her emotions under control so he was grateful for their help and support. The number of people surprised him, but he realized they were testimony to their liking and respect for his father. When most of the mourners had eaten their refreshments and left the house Mr Kane, the solicitor, drew Hannah aside.

'Would it be convenient for me to read the will

261

now, Mrs Caraford?'

'The will?' Hannah repeated vaguely.

'Yes, I would prefer to get it over today if you feel up to it.'

'There's no need for that,' Fred burst in rudely. 'I was a partner and a joint tenant with my father. Everything belongs to me now.' He looked smugly at Steven. He turned away, repelled by Fred's greed and lack of feeling. He prayed his father had managed to provide some small inheritance for his mother, but even if it meant giving up his holding he would repay the money she had given to him.

'Perhaps all three of you would come through to the front parlour?' Mr Kane said firmly. He eyed Fred with distaste. 'Even if your father had not made a will the law does not work like that.'

Steven gasped when he realized what his father had done. Belatedly he must have realized Fred would never improve his idle ways, nor would he care what happened to his stepmother. His cheating at the market had probably been the last straw.

'Mrs Caraford, when your husband first came to see me to make his son Frederick a partner, he informed me that he had made over a half share in the stock of Willowburn to you when you were married, although I understand the business continued to trade as WE Caraford and Son, as it had in his grandfather's time.'

'Y-yes, that's right. B-but I never thought of it as mine,' Hannah said brokenly. 'It was so that I could pay bills and write cheques. Eddy never liked doing that sort of thing...' Her voice shook

262

as she stared at the solicitor.

'Quite so. He transferred half of his own share in the farm to his son Frederick and at that time he assured me you would be willing to put half of your share into the name of his younger son, Steven Caraford, when he returned from the army to farm with you all at Willowburn. This would have made all four of you equal partners and...'

'What!' Fred bellowed. 'That's not right. He gave...'

'If you will let me finish,' Mr Kane interrupted coldly. 'I understood correctly Mr Steven Caraford did not return on account of Mr Frederick Caraford, and not because he did not wish to return to Willowburn.' He looked questioningly at Steven.

'Yes, that's correct. We, er ... we didn't get on.'

'That is what I understood your father to mean when I called to see him after his stroke. He was quite clear in his own mind what he wanted to do. So,' Mr Kane went on, looking sternly at Fred, 'when your father made you a partner he gave you half of his own share, which is a quarter of all the stock and implements at Willowburn, less any amounts owing by the business. The remainder of his share Mr Caraford left to his wife.'

'What? He can't have left the rest of it to her!' Fred shouted 'You've made a mistake. That would mean she owns three quarters of it. You misunderstood...'

'There is no mistake,' Mr Kane said firmly. 'He also mentioned that Mr Fred Caraford has

263

recently had fifty pounds in cash from the business. Since Mr Steven Caraford was not a partner it was his father's wish that he should receive the same amount, fifty pounds, in cash, along with the remaining horse, the two carts and any horse-drawn machinery which still remains at Willowburn. The vehicle belongs to Mrs Hannah Caraford, spouse of the deceased, along with any cash remaining in Mr Edward Caraford's personal bank account. I believe this will be only a small amount once the funeral expenses have been paid.'

'No!' Fred jumped to his feet and confronted Mr Kane. 'That's impossible. He wouldn't do this to me. He couldn't! I won't have it. I—'

'This is your father's last will and testament, Mr Caraford, and it is perfectly legal. I believe your father realized his wife would need a major share in the farm if she was to have any influence over its management. He also said she did more than her share of the work, while you – you never pulled your weight.'

'Why the – the...' Fred almost exploded, but Mr Kane went on calmly. 'From what I overheard today I believe you will not be carrying on the tenancy anyway?'

'No,' Fred muttered sullenly, 'but the money for the stock should belong to me, all of it.'

The solicitor ignored his outburst. 'So, Mrs Caraford, with your permission, I shall ask the auctioneer to call tomorrow to make a list of the stock and machinery as it stands at the time of your husband's death. This must be done without delay. He will also give an estimate of its value.'

'We don't need an auctioneer poking his nose into our affairs,' Fred growled angrily. His eyes narrowed slyly.

Steven knew that look and he didn't trust him. He guessed he was hatching some scheme or other to get more than his share.

'As the chief executor,' Mr Kane insisted, 'it is my duty to see that everything is valued fairly as it stands now. The auctioneer should make his valuation without delay.'

'Perhaps he could wait until after the week-end?' Hannah said with a placatory glance at Fred. She drew a weary hand across her brow.

'Very well, Mrs Caraford, I shall arrange it for Monday,' Mr Kane agreed.

Steven didn't usually discuss private business with Jimmy Kerr, but when that young man called to offer his condolences the following evening Steven was glad to chat for a while.

'The auctioneer is going to value everything on Monday morning, but Mother telephoned this morning to say Fred has announced he's emigrating to Canada as soon as he can get his share in cash. Mr Griffiths, the land agent, will terminate the tenancy at the November term. I expect there will have to be a farm sale. If the tractor doesn't make too much I might bid for it, now that you've proved how useful it would be around here. I'd like you to check it over for me first? Maybe we could go up to Willowburn one weekend?'

'Aye, I'll be glad to do that. I've served my

time so I'm supposed to be a proper mechanic.'
Jimmy grinned. 'Even if the boss does treat us
like tea boys.'

On Monday morning Jimmy recalled his conversation with Steven when he recognized the
land girl from Willowburn. She was driving a
Fordson tractor into the workshop area. Fred
Caraford drove in after her in a van. Jimmy
waylaid his boss on his way to attend to them.
'That's my neighbour Steven's half-brother.
The auctioneer is supposed to be valuing everything at Willowburn today. Why do you suppose
he's brought his tractor in here?'
A few minutes later he caught his boss's eye
and a jerk of his head summoning him to one
side of the workshop.
'Our Mr Caraford is wanting to sell the tractor.
He wants an immediate sale for cash in his
hand.'
'What? He can't do that, can he? I mean it's
not really his, is it?'
'Not if you've got your story right. The price
he's asking is too good to be true, even for cash
on the dot. I've told him I'll send a mechanic to
look over it. You go. Keep him as long as you
can while I make a couple of phone calls. Tell
him the brakes are not safe to drive it back home
and mention a few faults.'
Jimmy saw his opportunity to assess the
tractor on Steven's behalf and he set to work,
chatting to Edna as he made various checks. The
boss was longer than he had expected and he
was running short of things to check. Out of the

corner of his eye he recognized a couple of the local policemen heading to the corner behind a glass and wood partition which served as the office.

Fred was tapping impatiently on the roof of the van.

'Aren't you finished yet? D'ye ken what ye're doing?'

'Aye, I do. You'd sue the firm if we let you drive this away as it is.'

'It was safe enough to get here,' Fred snapped.

'You said I wouldn't need to drive it back,' Edna said in alarm. 'You said you'd take me back in the van.'

'Now, sir,' said one of the policemen, drawing Fred aside, 'can I have a word? I believe you're trying to sell stolen property.'

'What? You're crazy...'

'You're wanting to sell this tractor?'

'What if I am? It's mine to sell.'

'Is it? Are you sure about that?'

'Course I'm sure! I'm the owner.'

'Part owner, if my information is correct,' the policeman said. 'I understand you're from Willowburn and Mr Fraser, the auctioneer, is up there doing a valuation right at this moment?'

'So? What if he is?' Fred demanded sullenly.

'So I'm suggesting that you are trying to defraud the beneficiaries of your late father's estate out of this tractor by bringing it here this morning and trying to sell it for cash.' The policeman's tone was steely now and Fred look-ed at him warily.

'It's mine. It should all be mine! We don't need

an auctioneer!'

'Since you have just lost your father we'll let you off with a caution this time, Mr Caraford, but in my book you're stealing from his estate and depriving other beneficiaries. Now get this tractor back where it belongs or send the auctioneer here to value it. Any further attempts to defraud or steal and you will not get off so lightly.'

'I'm not driving it back!' Edna declared. 'He says it's not safe.'

'We'll get it repaired and let you know,' the boss said amiably, ignoring Fred's sullen scowl.

Megan's spirits sank every time she thought about going back to college. She had spent more time visiting Steven than she had dared to hope, partly due to having her driving licence and her father's generosity with the car, but also because Steven had welcomed her so warmly. If only she knew how he really felt.

Hannah Caraford had lost no time in dealing with Fred. He was unbearable to have in the house. She refused Steven's offer to repay her own money. Instead she had taken out a temporary bank loan herself and paid Fred his share of the valuation. So long as he got his money, he didn't care that both he and Edna were leaving her in the lurch with all the animals to care for. All he cared about was money and getting away from Willowburn for good. In spite of the work it was a relief to Hannah to see him go and she waved him and Edna off on the first leg of their journey. They planned to stay with Edna's aunt in Westmorland and then make arrangements to visit her cousin in Canada.

Steven was dismayed when he heard Fred and Edna had both left the minute Fred had had his share of the money.

'I think the authorities would allow Johan to lodge with you, Mother, if we vouched for him. He is keen to work and I'm thinking of taking him on myself if he wants to stay at Schoirhead now the other POWs are going home.'

'I've been wondering who I could get to help until the November term. The rent is paid until then and Mr Griffiths is quite willing to terminate the lease at short notice.'

'This is what I would like to do, Mother, and I think father would have approved. He was worried when he thought the cattle which Fred bought were diseased and there's a risk they have infected the two I had bought already. So I'm going to sell them all and disinfect all the buildings. As soon as I've done that I'll ask Tom Green, the haulier, to come and collect yours and move them to Schoirhead. I'll pay you the valuation price.'

'You don't need to do that, Steven. You couldn't afford it and anyway you will have your share to get once everything is sold.'

'I've worked it all out. I shall get the money for selling my own and I've a bit set aside to buy two more. Anyway I wouldn't miss the chance to have Father's cows.'

'He'd be pleased about that,' Hannah agreed slowly.

'If that house is still available that Mrs Anderson mentioned, I think you should go for it, then you can keep your hens and one of the sows if you want.'

'Yes, I'd like that, but I don't see how...'

'You leave the finances to me, but give me time to sell my own stock first. I shall feel a lot happier when I know I've got good, healthy stock.'

'Yes, I can understand that,' Hannah agreed. 'And it will be a relief if I don't have to milk them myself and attend to everything else until the end of November.'

Steven was dismayed when he realized his mother had taken out a bank loan to pay Fred his share. He sat down and worked out a plan of his own, then he made an appointment to see the bank manager. But he told neither the manager nor his mother that he was intending to rent the McGuires' land from them. He knew his mother would worry about the risk he was taking. He kept thinking about the young bus driver's philosophy and it was true he'd had to take far greater risks during the war. Even if he lost the tenancy of his land, it was nothing compared with a life.

The bank manger seemed pleased he had brought in his account book and worked out a plan for repaying the money each month when he received his milk cheque. He asked a great many questions, but in the end he agreed it was better that he should be the one with the loan rather than his mother, although his would be a much bigger sum.

Steven was glad when his mother did not

question him too closely about using the Mc-Guires' byre to house the dry cows and the three in-calf heifers. She seemed weary and he realized his father's illness and his death, plus the trouble with Fred, had all taken their toll on her. He sent his own cows to market, then he and Johan disinfected and scrubbed every inch of the byre and the sheds where the cattle had been housed. Megan came to lend a hand when she could get away. When they were finished and the buildings had been lime-washed he arranged for Tom Green, the haulier, to move the cows from Willowburn.

Megan promised to be at Schoirhead when they arrived so she could help Steven get them tied into their new stalls. The young haulier also stayed to help. Animals were always difficult in strange surroundings.

'I don't know how I would have managed without you, Megan,' Steven said when the cows were tied up and sniffing at the cake he had put in their troughs to tempt them into their new stalls.

'I know how much cows hate being moved to different stalls, but at least you knew which pairs stand together so that should help.' She chuckled. 'Even cows need friends.'

'Will you teach your young pupils about such things?' he asked with a grin.

'Oh, don't remind me,' she groaned. 'I wish I didn't need to study for another year.'

'Would you like to come and see over the shop that Mother is thinking of taking over when she moves out of Willowburn?'

'Would she mind?'

'Of course not. She was very grateful for your help at the funeral.' He grinned sideways at her and her heart leapt. 'She thinks the wee Meggie we used to know has grown up into a capable and sensible young woman.'

'Well, at least your mum has noticed I've grown up, but it does make me sound a bit boring – being capable and sensible.'

'Ah, Megan, you could never be boring, and don't think I haven't noticed you've grown up.' His eyes met hers and the wistful look was back in them.

She frowned. 'What's wrong, Steven?'

'I wish I could afford to compete with all your other admirers.'

'I don't have admirers.'

'That's the trouble, Megan Oliphant, you don't seem to know how attractive you are, but it's part of your charm and I hate these other men – men like Doctor Lindsay Gray and the one who taught you to drive.'

Megan's cheeks coloured. 'Oh, don't remind me,' she said. 'Tell me about the shop. Does it have living quarters?'

Steven eyed her speculatively. Why did she want to change the subject? Did she still see this man when she was at college?

'Yes, there's a house attached, behind the shop. It sounds ideal for Mother. She plans to keep on her hens and sell her own eggs, but she will have to stay at the farm until the end of November when the new tenants take over.'

'What about the pigs?'

'She says she can manage them until then. I try to go up every other day and I hope to buy the pigs from her in November. Ben has settled down in his new stable without any trouble. I expect he missed Daisy, especially when my father was not fit to work with him. He was a bit fresh and frisky, but he's a fine, fit horse and a bit faster than Daisy these days.'

Hannah was anxious about Steven taking on so much extra work and she wondered how he had managed to pay her so promptly, but she knew better than to question him too closely. After all, he was a man now and he had always been sensible. She was relieved to know she wouldn't have the cows to milk and muck out, especially with winter coming on. There was always more work when cattle were housed all the time and cleaning out the byres was heavy work. 'You're a good laddie, Steven. I hope you'll not be too overworked.'

'I hope to be able to afford Johan full time once everything is sorted out,' he said, but he was beginning to realize that taking over the McGuires' land and the upheaval at Willowburn meant he had too much to do. He hoped the increase in his monthly milk cheque would make it all worthwhile because he had decided if it was a good time for Mr Turner to expand, then it was a good time for him too. Even his hens were laying well and the income from them helped to pay for Johan's labour. Shawing the turnips and carting them in from the field was hard work and took up a great deal of time.

Johan hadn't understood he meant him to cut off the leaves and stalks of the turnips. Instead he had spent an hour setting them up in neat rows before Steven went to see how he was getting on.

'I show them off,' he said. 'Put best side up, yes?' Steven threw up his hands in dismay, but then he saw the funny side and grinned. He resolved to make doubly sure Johan understood him in future. It had been a waste of an hour's labour.

'I shall be glad when the owner collects the sheep I'm grazing for him,' he confided to Megan. 'The money will be useful, but I shall not take on any more like them. Thank goodness they've all survived so he can't quibble or dock the price we agreed. Have you time to help me move them on to the meadow? A fresh field will make sure they're in good condition when he comes to collect them in a week's time.'

'We'll move them now then, before I go home for the afternoon milking. Shandy is getting quite useful at rounding them up.'

'He is. I don't know what I'd do without him – or without you.'

A few days later Steven was running across the yard trying to avoid a soaking in the torrential rain. He heard Mrs McGuire calling to him over the dividing wall. 'Have you any leaks in your ceiling, Steven? It's dripping into our spare bedroom. There must be a tile off the roof.'

'I think my roof is all right so far,' Steven

called back. 'I didn't expect the rain would continue as heavy as this at the beginning of October. It's running like wee rivers between the turnip drills. It'll be a wonder if it doesn't wash my potatoes out o' the garden.'

'We often get floods when the tides are high, especially in March and late back end.'

'You go inside and keep dry. I'll have a look at your roof when it dries up,' Steven promised. But as the day wore on the rain became heavier than ever and, with the wind howling and gusting through every crack and corner, it was more like winter than autumn.

Steven was glad to get the cows into the byre, but they were wet and several times he had a wet tail swished around his neck during milking. All day the sky had been grey and leaden and by the time he had finished it was as dark as a December evening.

He was glad to make a dash for the house and strip off his wet clothes. Megan would be returning to college in a couple of days. He was going to miss her company and her lively conversation and more than that. There was no denying that he loved her. His body ached for her. She had arranged to come down this evening, but he didn't expect her to venture out in this weather. Some of the roads could be flooded and there would almost certainly be trees or branches down in places.

A gust and a howl of wind shrieked through the house. Steven shivered and huddled closer to the stove as he ate his supper. He turned on the radio to listen to the news on the Home Service.

Towards the end of the announcements there was a warning of high tides with flooding in places. He remembered the man from the government offices mentioning the high tides and occasional flooding in Schoirhead meadow, but...

'The sheep!' he yelled aloud. Surely the river wouldn't be in flood when it had been low all summer? But it was affected by the tides and they had already had a lot of rain. 'Dear God, I can't afford to lose the man's sheep now after grazing them all season,' he muttered, already pulling on his boots and raincoat again. He reached for his flat cap and pulled it well down against the buffeting wind. Shandy watched, his brown eyes alert, ears pricked. Steven bent and patted him.

'You don't like the rain either old boy, but I might need you to help me round them up if the river is rising.' They hurried through the orchard, knocking on the McGuires' door as they passed. He opened the door and called in, 'I'm going to check the sheep. There are warnings of floods. Your field is the nearest higher ground. Can I put them in there for tonight?'

'Aye, they'd be safer there anyway and it's as good as yours now, lad,' Mr McGuire said.

'Be careful, Steven. We've had a lot of rain already and the river can be dangerous. It will be high tide in an hour or so. Come in when you come back and I'll have a hot drink ready,' Mrs McGuire called.

'Will do. Thanks.' Steven smiled in spite of the wild weather. He'd been lucky to get such kindly

276

neighbours. Shandy followed at his heels, head down, tail between his legs.

Steven was relieved to see the sheep huddled together midway down the meadow. He sent Shandy to bring them towards the McGuires' pasture while he opened the gate. Shandy brought them along the line of the fence towards him. The sheep came willingly and he counted them as they passed. It was getting darker now. Could he have made a mistake? But he knew he hadn't. 'Three short!' he muttered. He peered through the driving rain, but it was impossible to see to the far end of the field. He sighed. He had to make sure. If he lost three there would be no profit left. Long before they reached the river-bank he was wading. He could hear the roar and surge of the water. He was dismayed to see it spreading over the meadow like a lake. Surely there wouldn't be any sheep down here? He was about to turn away when Shandy barked and began to wade towards the willow tree which grew on the bank of the river.

'Come back here, boy!' Steven called urgently. Then he saw them: three sheep huddled together amidst the swirling water. There was a ridge of higher ground where the water usually divided and washed around it. Less than a fortnight ago it had been possible to cross from one side to the other via the gravely bank, but it was not even visible now. Steven knew the three sheep must be standing on it, but the water was already up to their bellies and it was rising further with the tide.

Cautiously he waded towards the willow tree.

It was impossible to see where the riverbank and the field merged, but he knew the tree grew at the edge. Shandy began to bark in agitation. He sensed the danger too and he tried to go backwards and forwards along the edge of the river. Alarmed, as much by the barking dog as by the water, two of the sheep leapt towards the bank, but their fleeces were thick and heavy. Steven was afraid they would submerge. He hung on to an overhanging branch of the tree and hauled one of them to firmer ground. It paddled until it reached higher ground then trotted off towards the rest of the flock. He glimpsed the gleaming eyes of the second one and grabbed blindly. The sheep was a dead weight with his soggy fleece, but he was desperate to survive and to join his mates. Steven heaved and he sprang. Steven fell backwards on to the flooded field and the sheep made another desperate leap, using Steven's chest as a springboard, before running off to join the rest. For a moment or two Steven lay winded and bruised, submerged except for his head. He was thoroughly wet to his skin now with little to lose and he hated the thought of leaving the lone sheep to be swept away by the fiercely flowing torrent. It was dark now, but he could make out the darker shape of it and see two eyes shining. It was bleating pitifully for the rest. Shandy barked frenziedly.

'One more try to get this one to jump, old boy,' Steven muttered.

Shandy seemed to understand and for a few moments the dog was quiet. Steven edged forward, then with one hand clinging to a low branch of the willow tree he leaned forward and waved his free arm wildly, giving an almighty bellow. As he intended the startled sheep lunged into the water. Steven grabbed at him and missed. He was being swept downstream now, but his fingers fastened on the thick wool as he made a last frantic grab. It was enough to slow him and turn him sideways. Without warning he seemed to leap. Steven lost his grip on the branch and fell head first into the swirling river. He felt the sheep's small sharp feet on his back and then the weight was gone, but he was left flailing helplessly. He could swim but he was not a strong swimmer and he was fully clothed. He felt himself being carried away.

Even during the war, even that dreadful night when he and Sam had lain side by side waiting for darkness, he had never felt so terrified as he did now. He couldn't see. He didn't know where the edge of the riverbank was, he was completely disorientated. The words of the army padre came back to him reciting from some poet or other... 'In the darkest hour even an atheist half believes in God.' He could hear Shandy's bark growing fainter. He thought of Megan and fought again to keep his head up, gulping for air in rasping gasps, but the current was strong and he was being swept along like a matchbox.

Eighteen

Megan would not have ventured out on such a night, but she would be back at college in two days and her heart was heavy at the thought of not seeing Steven again until Christmas. She was surprised to find Schoirhead in darkness. Few people bothered to lock their doors and she dashed to Steven's door and pushed it open. The house was empty with no sign of Shandy either. Her heart beat faster. She switched on the lights. They flickered with the gusting wind. She hoped Steven would see the light and come in. The wind was frightening the way it whined and moaned around the corners of the house and through every crack. It seemed worse here than it had at home. She peered out of the windows but the buildings were still in darkness.

She paced about, unable to settle. Where could Steven be? She made up her mind, belted up her raincoat again and knotted a scarf around her head. Outside she listened intently, peering out into the stormy night. There was nothing and no one to be seen. In desperation she ran through the orchard and knocked on the McGuires' door. It opened at once.

'Steven! Thank the good Lord you're back...' Annie McGuire's words trailed away. 'It's not

Steven.' Her voice trembled. 'Come in, come in, lassie.'

'Where is Steven, Mrs McGuire? D-do you know? Please...?

'He should have been back ages ago.' Mrs McGuire was wringing her hands in distress. Mr McGuire had risen from his chair and his face looked pale and drawn.

'He went to move the sheep out of the meadow in case the river floods. He's been gone too long. Far too long.' His voice shook.

Megan stared at them, her eyes wide and frightened now.

'Then I must go search for him,' she said, her voice low and intense.

'Aye.' Mr McGuire didn't try to stop her and she knew then they were even more frightened and anxious than she was. He was pulling on his cap and coat, taking up his stick, but he was so slow. He would hold her back. 'Please...' She put out her hand as though to keep him away. He ignored her.

'Steven was using one o' the horses today. He's still in the stable. Take him, lass. I'll help you harness him.'

Megan wanted to run to the meadow, but outside Mr McGuire shouted against the wind. 'Ye must take a rope in case he's in trouble. The horse will go faster than you can. The river must be over. The horse is taller and stronger than you, lassie.' He was doing his best to hurry.

'Megan!' Mrs McGuire called her back.

Megan wanted to ignore her. She wanted to run to the field, but they knew this area better than either herself or Steven. She ran back to the house.

'Take this bicycle torch, lassie. It might be useful. He might see it. I've threaded a string through the back. Put it round your neck, then ye'll not drop it. Hang on tight to the horse, ma bairn. Promise ye'll not let go.'

Mrs McGuire was near to sobbing and Megan's alarm grew.

'Yes. Right.' Megan ran. She passed Mr McGuire and by the time he arrived at the stable she had the collar over Ben's head and the bridle in place, but she was shaking with terror.

'I'll fix the rest and buckle the girth strap. You might need him to pull ... or something,' he said anxiously. 'Can't think what's keeping the laddie. Must be in some sort o' trouble. His life is worth more'n all the sheep in Scotland,' he said as he reached for a coil of rope and tied one end firmly to the hooks on the horse's collar, then coiled it in a loop round the hames.

'Keep that end tied to the horse,' he warned. 'You can throw the rope if ye need to. For God's sake, lassie, dinnae go near the riverbank and dinnae take any risks. I've seen it wash away a horse and cart once, and claim a young life. Promise? Please God it takes none tonight.'

'I-I promise.'

'Here then...' He set his stick aside and cupped his hands. 'Get on his back and I'll lead him frae the stable.'

'On his back? I-I can't r-ride him...'

'Ye can. He'll be quicker than you. He has four legs. He's solid against this wind. Come on, up

282

with ye and hang on tight. I'd go myself, but I'd be more hindrance than help. Steven wouldna want anything to happen to you though, lassie. You're too precious to him. He told me he'd ask ye to be his wife if he'd anything to offer ye.'

The words rang in Megan's ears, over and over, as she guided the horse through the deepening gloom. She was terrified perched so high on top of Ben, but her knees clung tightly and she crouched low. So far Ben was behaving beautifully in spite of the wail of the wind and the thrashing branches of the trees. Then they were on the track and she urged him to go faster, clinging on as best she could.

'Please God, keep Steven safe,' she murmured aloud. As they drew nearer the McGuires' field she saw the sheep huddled together in the gateway. Hope flared and she tried to guide Ben towards them, but he stopped dead, almost causing her to slide off. His back was broad and she had no saddle. His ears were pricked.

'Come on, old boy,' she urged desperately. 'A wee bit further. He must be with the sheep.'

Ben refused to budge, his ears twitching. Megan listened intently, but she could hear nothing except the wind and rain. Was that the roar of the river she could hear? She shuddered. Should she allow the horse to follow his instincts? He walked on more slowly now as though testing the ground as he put one foot in front of the other, sloshing through the water. He didn't like it and it was already well up his legs. She was sure they were heading towards the river, away from the huddled sheep. It was like being in the middle of a lake and Megan began to shake with fright. She turned on the torch and shone it around, but there was nothing but the swirl of the dark water all around her. She was terrified, but she was even more afraid for Steven.

'Please, God, don't let him die,' she whispered.

It was impossible to judge where the edge of the river might be. She had to trust Ben and at least he had four feet and he seemed to be going cautiously. He stopped and pricked his ears again and this time she heard it, the distant barking of a dog.

'Shandy...?' she breathed. She urged Ben forward, but he seemed to have changed direction. She couldn't get her bearings. And then she saw the willow tree. She knew that was at the river-bank and Shandy's barking was clearer now. She wished she could whistle like Steven. Instead she cupped her hands to her mouth and called. The wind seemed to blow her voice back to her and Ben set off again with a jerk, almost tipping her into the water. She prayed fervently as they splashed towards the willow tree. Then, out of the gloom, she saw Shandy doing his best to wade or swim towards them. He stopped, tried to bark, then turned and swam away from them.

He was not going near the willow tree. Megan could only guess he was heading further down the river. They could only be a few hundred yards from the boundary fence and neither she nor Ben could go further than that, even if they could see anything in the darkness with the deepening water all around them. She uttered a silent thank you to Mr McGuire for insisting she ride on Ben's back. Shandy came towards them again, and again he turned and swam away as though urging them to follow. She drew Ben to a halt and shouted as loud as she could above the wind and the roar of the water, but the thunder of the river in flood was deafening.

'Ste-even! Hall-ooo ... Stee-v-en.' The only reply was Shandy barking and Ben moved forward of his own will – slowly, carefully, his ears twitching nervously. Megan could feel the rain trickling down her back; her thighs and shoulders were soaked through, but fear rendered her immune to the cold. Her heart was filled with dread. She called again. She thought she heard a faint 'halloo'. Ben kept moving. She could see the tops of the fence posts now. They were almost at the boundary and her heart sank. She called again. This time she heard the words.

'Water gate!'

Megan knew that every water course had a swinging barrier across it where there was a boundary between farms. It was usually a wooden frame with vertical spars which allowed the water to flow on its way unimpeded but when the water was low it prevented the cattle from paddling along the river bed and climbing out on to a neighbour's land. She guessed it must be in line with the boundary fence, but where was the edge of the river? They were close judging by the noise of the rushing torrents. Mr McGuire had warned her it was powerful enough to sweep away both her and her powerful steed. She shuddered. What chance could Steven have against such a force?

'Steven? Steven...? It's me – Megan. I'm beside the boundary fence. I'm on Ben.'

'Here...' Steven called weakly. He knew he couldn't hold on much longer. The water gate had long since washed away. All that remained was one of the poles set in the riverbank. He couldn't cling on much longer and he doubted if it would hold firm either.

'I-I can't see you.' She edged Ben very slowly alongside the fence, knowing that any minute he might find there was no ground beneath his feet, only the treacherous river. 'I've got a rope...'

A rope! Steven uttered several swift prayers. Hope brought a burst of strength. 'Throw into ... river. Far as you can.'

Megan threw but the rope stayed slack and her heart sank. She urged Ben further along the side of the fence. Then she saw Shandy, standing on his hind legs, his head only just above the water, but it was enough to let her know she could take Ben so far. He seemed reluctant to move now. He sensed the danger. She coiled in the rope and threw again. For a moment it tightened. Then it went slack and her heart sank. Steven had tried to reach it with one hand, but had almost lost his grip of the post altogether.

'Loop the end.' He had neither breath nor strength for more.

Again Megan hauled in the rope. Her cold fingers fumbled and she struggled to tie a loop firmly enough to stand Steven's weight and the pull of the river. She threw again. This time

Steven grasped it and managed to get it over his shoulder. He was not sure whether he had the strength to hold on to it.

'Steven?' The rope was not slackening this time, but there was no reply. Shandy barked twice. Megan gave a little tug.

'Tie to fence.'

'It's tied to Ben. Shall we pull?' Steven took his courage in both hands and let go of the pole. He sank beneath the rushing water. He felt it sweeping him away. But he still had hold of the rope with one hand. He could feel the circle and managed to push his other arm through before blackness swamped him.

'Steven?' Megan heard herself scream.

It startled Ben and he jerked back. The rope was taut. Steven must be holding on. He must! He must! Megan knew the tears were running down her cheeks as fast as the rain.

'Steady boy,' she coaxed, her voice trembling. She tried to urge Ben to back slowly away from the river and then to turn so that the weight would be on his shoulders and the collar. The rope stayed tight and she could feel the pressure on it, but why didn't Steven call to her? Ben moved again, and then another step, and another. He was so obedient, almost as though he understood. Then Shandy was barking frenziedly, swimming now towards the rope.

'Steven! Oh dear God please don't let him die now,' she sobbed and slid down from the horse's back. It was a shock to find herself in water up to her chest. It was icy cold, but she could see Steven with the rope around his shoulder and one arm. She clung to the fence as she waded towards him. She cupped his head in her hands, holding it above the water. Shandy swam closer and tried to lick his face. 'Steven, oh, Steven, please don't die,' Megan whimpered. 'I love you so much. Pl-please don't die.' She was rubbing his cold cheeks instinctively. She had to get him on the horse, but how? Shandy swam beside the fence. Again he stood on his hind legs to keep his head above the water. Holding the rope and Steven, she urged Ben closer. He obeyed. Now if only she could hoist Steven on to his back. She knew it was a forlorn hope, but she had to try and at least it was something to hold on to, for she could feel her own limbs trembling and her arms felt as though they had been pulled from their sockets. Ben moved forward and the rope tightened again, but it helped. Moments later Megan was panting against the fence as she hauled Steven half over it. She rubbed his back and pummelled his shoulders.

'Open your eyes, Stevie, please open your eyes.'

He began to cough up water. Shandy had pulled himself along the fence to them and he barked ecstatically, trying to lick Steven's face. Megan continued rubbing his back, crying and praying at the same time. Shandy nuzzled against him, as though willing him to speak. He opened his eyes. He coughed again, bringing up the river water.

'Megan...?' he gasped.

'Yes, I'm here. Oh, Stevie.'

'Not dreaming?' He screwed his eyes tight

shut and coughed up more water as she rubbed and pummelled. Once he had caught his breath he twisted his head to look at Megan and the torch which was shining in every direction as she moved. He could see her small, even teeth gleaming whitely as she gnawed her lower lip.

'Are we safe?' he croaked.

'We need to get you home and warmed up,' she said. 'Do you think Ben can carry both of us?'

'Of course he can.' He coughed and tried to get his breath. He felt wretched.

'But how shall we get on to his back?'

Steven tugged the rope from around his shoulders and hauled himself slowly to the horse's shoulder. Megan sensed he hadn't much strength left, but he patted Ben's neck and spoke to him, then he pulled him parallel to the fence. Megan felt trapped he was so close and so big.

'Put one foot on the fence and jump. I'll steady you, Megan.'

'But you, Steven...'

'Don't worry about me.'

Megan clung to Ben's harness and did as Steven told her, springing away from the fence and hauling herself over his broad back. She was no sooner straightened up, than Steven put his foot on the fence post and she was pulling him up behind her. For a moment he sagged against her, breathing hard and coughing.

'Wrap the rope around both of us and tie it fast to his collar,' he gasped, and Megan knew he was uncertain whether or not he had the strength left to hold on until they got home. She did as he instructed but before she could take hold of the rein Shandy gave one joyous bark and sprang up, wedging himself in front of her and currying down on Ben's broad back. In spite of the trauma, and shivering with cold, they both burst out laughing.

'If we hadn't been soaked already we'd certainly be very wet now,' Megan said with a chuckle. 'But he deserves a ride. He saved your life, Steven. I wouldn't have known where you were but for Shandy.' She felt Steven's arms tighten around her and he leaned forward to press his icy lips to her cheek.

'You saved my life, Megan,' he said hoarsely. 'I can never repay you for what you've done tonight, my darling girl.' His voice was hoarse from coughing, but when he recovered his breath he continued. 'I thought I was going to die and I'd never told you how dear you are to me.' He coughed and gasped to get his breath, but he managed to say softly, 'It was my greatest regret. You would never know how much I love you.'

'You do?' Megan twisted round to see his face and almost tipped the three of them into the water as Ben plodded steadily on.

'Steady, sweetheart! We've had enough bathing for one night.' His arms tightened and he fell silent, gathering his strength.

She could feel his head against her shoulder. She urged Ben on as fast as he could go through the water. She knew Steven urgently needed warmth and rest, but she also knew this was a time for truth.

'I think I've loved you all my life, Steven, but I hardly dared hope you would ever love me – n-not as a woman anyway.'

'What a place to say such things,' Steven croaked.

His voice was husky and Megan didn't know whether it was with emotion or coughing up river water.

'I've nothing to offer you except my life,' Steven told her.

'Oh, Steven, your life is the most precious thing in the world to me. I thought I was going to lose you tonight and I *know* now you're all I'll ever want.'

'Dearest Megan, how can that be when you have so much choice?'

'Choice? You must know there is only one choice for me and that's to share my life with you. Don't you know how afraid I am that you might choose someone else to be your wife before I can even finish at college?'

'No, no. I'd wait for you forever if I believed you wanted to marry me.'

They were both silent, shivering with cold in the icy wind, but then Megan half turned towards Steven and stroked his cold cheek with equally icy fingers. 'I don't want you to wait any longer than we must, but I hate to let Mum down when she has set her heart on me qualifying to be a teacher.'

'I understand that, Meggie, and I agree. It is one of the things I love about you – the way you consider people, so tender and generous. There will never be anyone else but you, Meggie, however long I have to wait. Only promise me you will marry me when the time is right, my love.'

'I promise a thousand times over,' Megan called, laughing in spite of her chattering teeth and shivering limbs. 'Steven, this has been the worst and the best night of my life.' She caught her breath on a little sob.

'The water's getting shallower,' Steven said with relief. 'Ben has carried us through.'

'Yes, you're a fine fellow,' Megan breathed with relief as she leaned forward to pat the horse's neck.

Ben seemed to understand. He was already clear of the water now and moving faster up the incline towards home.

'There are lights ahead,' Steven said. 'I almost despaired of seeing any of this again.' His arms were locked around her as Ben carried them home. He leaned closer and gently turned her face to his. Their skin was so cold, but as their lips met heat flared between them.

'We'll soon be home now. We must get dried and warm again, Meggie,' Steven said huskily.

'And you ... What was that?' Ben also pricked his ears and Shandy stirred.

'It sounded like voices.' They saw the flickering light of a torch and as they drew nearer they could make out the figures of men making their way towards the river. Megan switched on the bicycle lamp and flashed it ahead.

'We're here! We're safe...' Steven tried to call and ended up coughing while his chest heaved in protest. Shandy jumped to the ground barking joyously as he ran towards the men.

'Megan? Steven?'

'That's my father!' Megan said in astonishment. 'Whatever can he be doing here. How...? Dad, we're here! We're both all right.'

As they drew nearer Steven recognized Jimmy Kerr and his father with their collie dog at their heels, and the taller, slimmer figure of John Oliphant.

As soon as they drew near enough for speech John said, 'Thank God you're both safe.' His voice shook.

Megan was unsure whether it was rain or tears running down her father's face. The men walked the rest of the way home beside them.

'What are all the lights?' Steven asked.

'The McGuires were worried sick about you. We all were,' John Oliphant said. 'They telephoned your mother, Steven. She came round via Martinwold and brought us with her. We've just arrived. We were coming to search.'

'Shandy showed me the way,' Megan said, her voice wobbling now as she began to feel the reaction.

'Good boy!' Mr Kerr said warmly. 'I knew he'd be a good friend to ye, lad.'

'He is – one of the very best a man could have,' Steven agreed fervently. 'Megan saved my life.'

'Only with Shandy's guidance, and thanks to Ben, and to Mr McGuire's advice,' Megan said tremulously.

'Run ahead, Jimmy. Tell them they're both safe, even if they do look like drowned rats,' Mr

Kerr said. 'Steven, your mother and Mrs Mc-Guire will probably strip the clothes off your back and bathe ye like a bairn.' He grinned.

When Steven drew Ben to a halt Megan almost fell into her father's arms. Now they were safe she couldn't stop her teeth chattering with nerves and cold and her legs felt like jelly. She thought she might never be warm again.

'I'll take your horse to his stable, Steven,' Mr Kerr said. 'I'll rub him down well and give him some feed. He'll be all right with me.'

'Thanks,' Steven said croakily. 'Thank you all.'

'Get inside and into a hot bath, lad. It'll be a wonder if ye dinnae get pneumonia. You've had a lucky escape.' But Steven clung to Ben. He knew his legs were shaking so badly they would not hold him up.

John Oliphant relinquished his daughter to Chrissie and came back. He hugged Steven tightly.

'Thank God you're alive, lad. I couldn't bear to lose you as well as Sam,' he said and half-carried Steven towards the house.

Chrissie was weeping silently as she hugged Megan tightly in her relief.

'I'll never, never pester you again, lassie, about finishing college. I'm so thankful you're safe. We both are.'

'You're getting wet, Mum,' Megan said softly, 'and I'm all right, really I am.'

'Mrs McGuire is running a hot bath for ye and I brought dry clothes, but we must get ye home and into bed.'

She turned away to follow Mrs McGuire, but Hannah took Megan in her arms and held her gently.

'You saved his life, lassie. I'll never be able to repay you for that as long as I live,' she said with quiet sincerity, 'and neither will Steven.'

A little while later Steven lay in a hot bath in his own tiny bathroom while Megan bathed at the McGuires, each wondering whether the other had really meant the words of love they had uttered in the midst of their relief, and, if they did, where could they lead? What did their future hold?

Nineteen

Steven longed to speak to Megan again before she went home, but he knew his mother was right. She needed to get home and into bed, and so did he.

'I've put an oven shelf in your bed to warm it up. I'll bring you a hot drink,' Hannah told him firmly. 'Mr McGuire gave me a tot of whisky. He reckons it will ward off the chills and help you sleep.'

'I suppose you're right,' he agreed wearily. He ached all over and he knew he would have plenty of bruises by morning.

'I'll stay tonight and go home early in the morning,' Hannah said. 'Don't argue. I want to be sure you don't develop pneumonia.'

Hannah not only stayed overnight, she also helped Steven milk his cows and cooked him a hot breakfast before she went home to attend to her own pigs and poultry.

'If you're wise you'll go back to bed, Steven. You look exhausted and you're going to have a nasty bruise on the side of your face.'

'That's the least of my worries,' Steven said. 'I must check the sheep and make sure they're all there. The owner is taking them back next week.'

'And good riddance I should say,' Hannah said with feeling.

'Then I must see Megan, Mother. She will be going back to college tomorrow if she is well enough. I owe her my life and I never thanked her properly.'

Hannah studied him in silence. 'You really love Megan, don't you, son?'

'Yes, I do...' He twirled a teaspoon round and round until it fell on the floor with a clatter. 'I love her with all my heart. I'd like to marry her, but what do I have to offer a wife? And Megan has another year of studying to do, and she will have a good career when she finishes. I'd be selfish to ask her to give that up to marry me and slave away here.'

'I do understand how you feel, laddie, but if I were Megan I'd like to be given the opportunity to decide what I wanted to do with my life. You owe her that at least. I think she must love you very much to risk her own life as she did last night. The McGuires were convinced you must have both been drowned and washed away with the tide. They were in a terrible state when they phoned. That's why I went to get Chrissie and John and brought them with me in the van.'

'Yes, I must see them all as soon as I've finished here,' Steven said.

'I understand, laddie,' Hannah said. 'If you insist on going today, will you call in at Willowburn before you go to Martinwold? There's something I'd like to give you for Megan.'

'Today? Is it urgent?'

'Not urgent, but important I think.'

297

It was early afternoon by the time Steven arrived at Martinwold and Chrissie Oliphant watched Megan's face light up at the sound of his motorbike.

'I told you he'd come, lassie,' she said softly. 'I believe he loves you as much as you love him.'

'You guessed, Mum?'

'Your dad and I have known for some time. Anyway, we couldn't miss the way you look at each other, even if you hadn't risked your life for Steven last night. When I thought you might both have drowned, and never known what it was to love each other, I knew then that nothing else mattered. I vowed I would never badger you again to go back to college or to have a career unless it was what you wanted.'

John Oliphant had seen Steven arrive and he crossed the yard to ask how he felt after his ordeal.

'I'm fine, but how is Megan?' he asked anxiously. 'She saved my life, you know. I never got the chance to thank her properly last night, and I know she goes back to college tomorrow.'

'If she saved your life, Steven, it's because it's as precious to her as her own, and to us. Chrissie and me ... well, we both realized that when we thought we might have lost you both.'

'I know,' Steven said quietly. He looked John Oliphant in the eye. 'I love Megan more than anything on earth, but I've nothing to offer her as things are. She has the prospects of a good career and a well-paid job. I'm seriously considering giving up my farm and getting a job myself.'

'Eh, laddie, don't do that! You wouldn't be the same without your wee farm. Anyway, Megan is as keen as you are. At least discuss it with her and give her a choice.'

'That's what my mother said!' Steven exclaimed, looking at Megan's father in surprise.

'She's a wise woman, your mother. Let's go in or Megan will be rushing out to rescue you again.'

'Maybe we should go for a walk so we can talk things over...'

'If I were you, laddie, I'd get her on the back of that motorbike and take her back to your place. We'll come down with the car to fetch her back after milking.'

'You would? And what will Mrs Oliphant say to that? This is Megan's last day at home.'

'We'll soon see.' They went together into the house and it was John Oliphant who told Megan to get wrapped up for a ride on the motorbike and informed his wife of the arrangements.

'That's a splendid idea,' Chrissie said. 'And we'll bring the supper with us and all eat together at your house, Steven. I would like to thank the McGuires properly. They were so kind and Mrs McGuire insisted on wrapping Megan in one of her best blankets to bring her home last night.'

Steven and Megan scarcely talked as they made the journey back to Schoirhead. They were

299

content to feel each other close and safe. As soon as they entered the kitchen, Shandy came to greet them, wagging his tail in approval as Steven drew Megan into his arms.

'Did you really mean it when you said you loved me, Meggie?' Steven asked softly.

'You must know I mean it, Steven, and you?'

'I love you with all my heart, even if I didn't owe you my life. I love you so much that I've decided to give up the holding and get a job so that I can offer you some security.'

'No! Oh, no, Steven, you can't do that. It wouldn't be the same and you would always regret not having your wee farm. I'll help you. We could do so much more with two of us. I'll keep lots of hens like your mother does, and we don't need more acres for more pigs. I love you as you are, Steven. I don't want you to change or to make sacrifices for me. Anyway, Mum wishes she had never insisted I should go to college and she even realizes I may want to give it up.'

'And what do you want, Megan?'

'I want to be with you, but I feel I'm letting my parents down if I give up now.'

'I agree, but I would like the world to know you have promised to marry me, however long it takes.' He felt in his pocket and drew out a shabby leather box. He opened it to reveal a ring with delicate gold filigree set with three small diamonds.

'My mother gave me this, but it would make her happy if you would be happy to accept it. It belonged to her grandmother. One day I would like to buy you whatever ring your heart desires, but right now I would be proud and honoured if you would wear this as a symbol of my love for you. As an engagement ring to tell the world that we belong to each other.'

'Oh, Steven ... It's a beautiful ring,' Megan whispered huskily, 'I would be proud to wear it. I want everyone to know you love me.'

It was some time before either of them could speak again and Megan's cheeks were flushed when Steven drew away at last.

'Do you think we might manage to last a year before we marry, Meggie?' Steven asked with a smile. 'I think we both owe it to your parents to wait until you finish college?'

'You are willing to wait?' Megan asked, her eyes shining.

'Until the end of time if need be, so long as I know you love me and we belong together.'

'Oh, Steven, you're so good, so kind and patient. You always were.'

'Not so patient as all that,' he said gruffly, drawing her into his arms again.

'I shall be home for Christmas and Easter, and then we could arrange to be married at the beginning of the summer holidays so I would be here to help you with the hay and harvest.'

'I think your mother would prefer it if you completed your teacher training with the year's teaching you're supposed to do,' Steven said seriously. 'But I think they accept married women as teachers since the war, so if you're lucky enough to get a school near here I reckon we could be married and you could still do it.' He looked at her intently. 'So long as we're careful and don't get any babies before you're finished.' He chuckled, seeing Megan's ready blush. He hugged her tight and swung her off her feet. 'I do love it when you blush so prettily, Meggie,' Steven said.

'Would you mind if I telephone my mother? I can't wait to tell her we're engaged, and I know she'll be pleased that you're willing to wait until I finish college.'

'Yes, you do that, and then I have a something else to tell you, if you're sure you want to be the wife of a struggling farmer.'

'I want to be your wife, Steven Caraford, whatever you are, but I think I shall enjoy being a struggling farmer's wife,' Megan said.

Chrissie was delighted with the news. As soon as she had put the telephone down she picked it up again and dialled the operator to speak to Hannah Caraford.

'I expect you've already guessed their news,' she said jubilantly. 'Will you come with us if we call round for you tonight? I thought we could make it a wee celebration supper.'

'That would be lovely, Chrissie,' Hannah said warmly. 'I am glad they have agreed Megan should finish college, but I'm sure they will be happy together.'

'Do you think we should ask the McGuires to join us?' Chrissie asked diffidently. 'I don't know them very well, but they were so kind last night and they seem to care deeply for Steven.'

'That's a splendid idea. They have no family of their own and I know they will be delighted about this engagement. They like Megan.'

'We'll keep it as a surprise for Megan and Steven, shall we?'

'Yes, and I'll bring the bottle of wine I've been hoarding for a special occasion.'

'What was it you were going to tell me, Steven?' Megan asked sometime later. 'You said it was a secret?'

'It is ... well, confidential really.' He grinned widely because he was so happy. 'I shall not have any secrets from my wife so I may as well start now.' He told her about the McGuires' proposal to sublet their land to him.

'It is a bit of a risk, the subletting, but it will allow me to keep the eight cows from Willow-burn as well as the four which belonged to the McGuires.' His face grew serious. 'I have taken out a bank loan, so you see, Meggie, you really are getting a very poor deal.'

'Oh, Steven, I love you, not your money. It will be soon enough to worry if things don't work out as you plan.'

'I sincerely hope they will. I have arranged to pay back a sum each month from my extra milk cheque. One thing you may not approve of though ... I'm arranging to have Johan to live here in the house and to work with me full-time. I was astonished at how pleased he seemed when I suggested it, even though he knows he will have to survive my cooking and maybe do some himself.'

'Well, obviously he doesn't want to go back and the poor boy will have no where else to go in this country.'

'Will you mind, having a live-in man?'

'No, he seems a pleasant fellow and my parents usually have a boy living with us to help them in the byre so I'm used to it.'

'You're so good, Meggie, so practical, and understanding.' He began to laugh. 'Can you imagine what Natalie Turner would have said?'

'Natalie would have got Daddy to intervene and find a solution,' Megan said darkly.

'Yes and the Caraford pride would not have suffered that.' He pulled her into his arms again and lifted her off her feet. 'My wee Meggie, I shall never want to stop kissing you.'

It was later than usual by the time Steven and Megan started the milking and later than they realized when they returned to the house with their arms around each other. They were surprised when they went indoors to find the table laid with a pretty cloth, wine glasses and a vase of flowers. Hannah had lit the fire in the front room and the McGuires were also there, talking with her and Megan's parents as though they had all known each other all their lives. They beamed as they offered their congratulations.

'Why did it take two of you longer to milk those few cows than it takes Steven on his own, I wonder,' John Oliphant asked innocently with a wicked glint in his eye.

Steven and Megan glanced at each other.

'Ach, I know all about it,' John went on. 'I remember the days when I used to snatch a wee kiss and cuddle during the milking.'

'Don't tease them, John,' Chrissie admonished, seeing Megan blush. 'I guessed you'd be outside helping Steven, lassie, so I brought you some clean clothes to change into. We thought we could all have a wee celebration. Hannah has made a lovely chocolate cake and brought a bottle of wine and Mrs McGuire has brought us an apple pie and shortbread. I'm afraid all I could make is a ham and leek casserole at such short notice and with the meat rationing and all.'

'Oh, Mum.' Megan flung her arms around her mother's neck. 'It will all be delicious and I'm so happy I don't need food.'

'Ah, we'll soon see about that, lass,' Mr McGuire teased. 'When you've been working outside you'll find your appetite.'

Much later they all gave a cheer as Steven gave Megan a lingering kiss goodnight before her parents drove her home.

A year seemed such a long time to wait, but it was Megan's final year of studying and teaching sessions and she was kept very busy. Steven was fully occupied with his additional cows to milk and the McGuires' land to manage. The other three holdings were all about sixty acres each, so he knew he had only a few more acres than they had to manage and he was determined to make a good job. Johan had moved into the spare bedroom at Schoirhead and his help was invaluable now that he no longer needed to hurry away at five o' clock in the afternoon. The McGuires had renamed him Joe and gradually taken him into their hearts, recognizing his lonely state, his shy smile and obliging manner.

As soon as he was sure he could rely on his young helper, Steven left him to do the afternoon milking and set off on his motorbike straight after breakfast one Saturday morning. He planned to spend the day with Megan and his heart sang as the miles sped by.

'I know you'll soon be home for Christmas,' he said, noticing her look of astonishment, 'but I couldn't wait so long to see you again.'

'Oh, Steven! How wonderful.' She launched herself into his arms, oblivious to some of her fellow students cheering and grinning from the library windows.

'What news do you know of everyone?' Megan asked as they sat over lunch in a small tea room.

'Joe has settled wonderfully and he seems pleased that I trust him enough to milk the cows himself while I'm away today. Jimmy Kerr has had an upheaval in his life though. He was very worried for a while. His boss retired and his business was taken over by one of the agricultural suppliers in Annan. His boss started off as a country blacksmith before he set up in the town, repairing machinery, so Jimmy thought he might have difficulty finding work. He must be good at his job though because Bradleys, the firm who has bought the business, have offered him a job in charge of the machinery repair side and they're sending him to Yorkshire for two weeks training in the factory which supplies their tractors.'

'That's a wonderful opportunity!' Megan exclaimed. 'I remember Jimmy complaining about

306

all the smallholders being stick-in-the-muds and not wanting to move away from horses. This will suit him well.'

'Yes, it's a great opportunity. Though I must say I still like my horses, even now I've got the old tractor from Willowburn.'

'Did you ask Jimmy if he will be best man at our wedding, Steven?'

'I did, and he said he would so long as he could kiss the bride.' Steven chuckled as he watched the colour rise in Megan's cheeks.

'I'm sure he never said that,' she declared. 'What other news? How is your mother?'

'She has moved most of her stuff out of Willowburn, including one sow, and all of her poultry. I have the other two sows at Schoirhead and one of them is due to farrow soon. Mother has plenty of space and I think it will be ideal once she gets settled. Mr Griffiths, the land agent, gave his approval for her to move out early. He says the new tenant will move in straight away. I went up to Willowburn and took Joe with me a few times so we have left everything clean and tidy and the sheds all cleaned out. Mother said he was pleased about that.' Steven flushed, but he went on. 'He said it was a pity I hadn't been the one to take over Willowburn and if ever I'm looking for another farm I'm to let him know. He'll see what he can do, even if it is only to give me a reference.'

'That's wonderful, especially when you have so much to do at Schoirhead. I'm glad he appreciates you – almost as much as I do.'

'It's a pity we're in such a public place, Megan

Oliphant,' Steven growled in a low voice, 'because I badly want to kiss your cheeky dimples.'

Steven went to see Megan during the Easter and summer terms whenever he could spare the time, but he longed to have her closer.

Joe took pride in his work and was always pleased to be left in charge. The McGuires kept an eye on him and told Steven how hard he worked during his absences. The most welcome news came when Megan was given a placement for her year's teaching practice at a small village school only four miles up the main road from Schoirhead.

'Now we can fix our wedding,' she told him jubilantly.

They arranged it for the second week in July.

'We have no plans for a honeymoon,' Megan told her mother. 'It might be the middle of hay time and so long as we're together that's all we want.'

'I know it is, lassie. Sam would have been so happy for you both.'

'I think he would too,' Megan said.

'And he would have been as proud as we were to see our wee Megan winning the award for the best student of the year,' Chrissie said, her voice choked with tears. 'I'm glad you finished your course. Even Mr Turner is proud of you.'

'Yes, and hasn't he been generous with a wedding present!'

'He has that. He told your father he wouldn't offer money or the pair of you might buy another cow so he ordered the electric washing machine.

He suggested to the other workers they should buy you the electric iron and he organized it for them. Aren't you lucky?'

'I think I'm the luckiest girl in the world. I thought Princess Elizabeth was so lovely at her wedding last November, but I'm sure she will not be any happier than Steven and me.'

'No, I'm sure she will have her problems, even though she is a royal princess.' Chrissie sighed. She had made a rare visit to the cinema to see the royal wedding in colour. It had been wonderful. Exactly the happy celebration the country wanted to see after all the years of bombing and destruction. The rationing continued with even more severity.

'I wish we could have more rations to make a better wedding reception,' Chrissie said, voicing her thoughts aloud as her mind returned to their own plans.

'Don't worry about it, Mum.' Megan hugged her. 'I shall be too excited, or too nervous, to eat and everyone will be pleased to have a free meal.'

They had arranged to hold it in the village hall, and Chrissie, Hannah and Mrs McGuire had all been saving as many coupons as they could, or hoarding any offer of tinned fruit and table jellies. Hannah had managed to get enough dried fruit to make a single tier wedding cake.

Once again the Turners had surprised them with their generosity; promising Chrissie a whole ham from their own stock, and as many tomatoes as they required from their green-house. John had grown plenty of new potatoes and salad vegetables in his own garden so there would be no shortage there and Hannah had offered to supply chutneys and pickles and make some of the trifles. The butcher had promised to set aside a piece of pickled brisket to the value of three weeks' meat ration from all three households.

'It will still be small, but it will add a bit of variety and I have three capons to pluck and dress,' Chrissie listed her plans anxiously.

'Don't worry,' Hannah said when they discussed the final arrangements. 'Everybody knows the rationing is as bad as it ever was. I think you have organized everything splendidly and the Turners have been surprisingly generous. Is Natalie coming to the wedding with her parents?'

'No.' Chrissie smiled knowingly. 'She happens to be going away for a weekend and of course it has to be then. I'm sure she would have married Steven if he had looked in her direction.'

'I'm very glad he didn't,' Hannah said with feeling. 'I think he has always had tender feelings for Megan. I know how much he values her friendship and now that it has blossomed into love I'm sure it will prove a firm foundation for a happy marriage.'

'I expect you know John and I regard Steven as a second son. We couldn't be happier.'

'I can't believe what an excellent job Miss Gillies has made out of a parcel of parachute silk and curtain lace,' Megan said as she pirouetted in front of the mirror in her wedding dress. She was to wear her mother's veil and Chrissie pinned it on carefully. She blinked rapidly to hide her tears. It was hard to believe her little girl would soon be a married woman.

'You look beautiful, Meggie,' she said huskily.

'You're not prejudiced of course?' Megan said with a chuckle. 'I think Maryanne might need help fixing her head dress if we're to get to the Kirk on time.'

'I'll see to it,' Chrissie promised with a last wee tweak at the bridal dress. 'I'm glad you will have one night away on your own. It was a good idea of Hannah's and generous of her to pay for it and to offer to stay at Schoirhead overnight to look after Joe and help him with the milking.'

'Yes, we really appreciate it,' Megan said eagerly. 'But we feel bad about Dad lending us his car and letting us have his petrol ration.'

'We all want you to be very happy, lassie,' Chrissie said. 'You both deserve it.'

Twenty

The summer seemed to pass on a cloud of bliss for Steven and Megan, in spite of the work of finishing the haymaking and bringing in the harvest, and having twelve cows to milk as well as three sows all with litters of young pigs. Steven had been pleased with the two lots of store pigs he had sold so far and he was planning to take his two young gilts to the boar.

It had been a relief to make the final payment to the bank at the end of July and clear the bank loan.

'I was determined to start our life together without any debts hanging over us,' he told Megan. 'If you change your mind and want to keep on teaching after this year I shall understand, Meggie, and we can sell two of the sows to make less work.'

'I'm sure I shall not change my mind,' Megan said firmly. 'I can't tell you how much I'm dreading the thought of being away at school all day and leaving you here on your own.'

'I shall not be on my own. Joe will be here.'

'You know very well what I mean!' Megan said, her green eyes sparkling. 'You'll surely not be creeping up on Joe to steel a kiss...?

Steven threw back his head and laughed. 'I

think he might run away if I did that. Seriously, Megan, I am going to miss you, but I know the sensible thing is to finish off your teaching qualification. At least you will get the school holidays. It's a pity you'll have a two-mile cycle ride to catch the bus at the main road.'

'It would have been worse if I'd been forty miles away and we'd had to wait another year to be married,' Megan reminded him.

Steven drew her to him and his arms tightened around her slender waist. He bent to kiss her ear and her neck, and then her lips. 'I don't think I could have waited so long,' he said gruffly. 'As it is we shall have to be careful not to make any mistakes and get a baby before you're ready. You're such a temptation, sweetheart.'

'I know,' Megan said breathlessly. 'At least we shall not have to pay for a nurse and all that sort of thing now that the government have brought in free health care for everybody. Mother says some women really needed to see a doctor, but if they couldn't afford to pay they risked their own lives as well as that of the baby.'

'Well, we shall never take that risk, whether we have to pay or not,' Steven assured her firmly. 'I realize now how dreadful it must have been for people like my mother and my father to lose the love of their lives after so short a time.' He kissed her passionately. 'Let's not even think about it.'

As the days grew shorter and colder Steven worried about Megan cycling to the main road to wait for the bus. He knew she was a lot tougher than she looked, but he loved her to distraction. It was Jimmy Kerr who came up with a solution. The firm of Bradleys had a garage as well as the agricultural engineering side and an ironmonger's shop.

'They have a decent second-hand car for sale. You wouldn't get much for your motorbike, but you could trade it in.'

'I'll think about it,' Steven said. He hadn't planned to buy a car for a long while.

'They have a little van to sell as well,' Jimmy said. 'That would be more useful and it's cheaper, but it depends whether Megan would want to be seen driving a van to school.'

Megan was insistent that her bicycle was perfectly adequate, but ten days later she was drenched after cycling home in a thunderstorm and Steven decided they must have the van.

'What use would the money be if you got ill, Meggie? And I couldn't bear it if anything happened to you.'

So Megan was often seen driving to and from work in her wee van and she frequently found herself bringing messages for one or other of the smallholders. She loved teaching her class of six- and seven-year-olds and her headmistress was kind and understanding, a willing listener to any anxieties she might have. However, she was constantly aware of all the help the other smallholders' wives gave their husbands and she longed to help Steven and work at his side. Some days when he was working late she went to work before he came in for breakfast and she only saw him when they ate their evening meal together; even then Joe was always there. They never seemed to have time alone together when they could indulge in idle chatter or gentle flirting. They were beginning to feel the strain.

One evening in May Steven had been sowing turnips all day and he was hot and tired and they still had the cows to milk. Jimmy Kerr called in at the house as Megan was making their evening meal.

'I know Steven and Joe are busy with the turnips, but they must be nearly finished. I wondered whether they would come out with me for a drink tonight.'

'I could ask them,' Megan said, her heart sinking. When did Steven ever have time for an evening of leisure in her company these days? Or, if he did, it always seemed to be when she had lessons to prepare for the following day. They were both too conscientious about their work. She looked at Jimmy. 'Is it some sort of celebration?'

'Well, sort of.' He gave her a shy smile. 'I've been promoted and it just happens to be my birthday as well.'

'Congratulations, Jimmy,' Megan said warmly. 'Why don't you pop into the byre and tell Steven your news. I'm sure he'll be delighted for you, and he can tell you if he's free tonight.'

So Steven and Joe joined some of Jimmy's friends from work for a night of revelry. Megan was in bed and half asleep by the time they came home, singing merrily and rather drunk. It was the first time she had seen Steven intoxicated. He didn't seem the least bit tired as he sat on the edge of the bed and gently stroked her face while singing a popular love song to her. Eventually he stripped off his clothes, tossing them around the room in gay abandon, totally unlike his usual self. He rolled into bed beside her and proceeded to make wild and passionate love. His happiness and carefree state were infectious and neither of them remembered the little packages which Steven kept in the bedside cupboard.

Steven was worse for wear the following morning and both he and Joe slept through their alarms. Megan had a struggle to waken them. She brewed a large pot of strong tea and persuaded them to drink it. Eventually they crawled to the byre to get on with the milking. She knew they were both feeling wretched and they were running late if the milk was to be cooled and into the churns in time for the milk lorry to collect it. She decided to milk some of the cows herself. They couldn't afford to miss the lorry. Consequently she was late for work herself. She knew that would be a black mark against her in whatever reports her headmistress had to write about her at the end of her year.

She needed to discuss her situation with Steven. He had insisted she should save the money she earned and put it in a separate bank account to be kept for a rainy day, or to buy herself something she needed, but they couldn't go on like this indefinitely. Although she enjoyed teaching she also wanted to be at home so they could work side by side, and she wanted to help Steven build up his wee farm. She knew it was his ambition to move to a larger farm some day when they had enough stock and more machinery and enough income to afford a bigger rent.

As things turned out the decision was made for her. By the end of June she knew she was expecting a child. She also knew it was not what Steven had planned or intended and she was nervous about telling him.

She waited until she knew Joe would be out for the evening. Before she had chance to say anything, Steven had a suggestion of his own. 'It's a lovely evening,' he said as she cleared away the dishes after their meal. 'It's Friday too. Do you feel like a walk, Meggie? It seems ages since we had time to go for a stroll and a chat.'

'I'd love to come.' She responded eagerly, pleased to see the old Steven she knew and loved. As they walked beside the river they both remembered the night of the flood.

'Shall we sit for a while beneath the willow tree?' Steven suggested. 'It's hard to believe the water ever came over the banks when you see it now.'

Megan shuddered at the memory and he drew her close. She leaned her head against his shoulder.

'I love you so much, Megan. I never seem to get the time, or the opportunity, to tell you these days. Perhaps I shouldn't have invited Joe to lodge in the house with us. It makes extra work for you and I know how busy you are.'

'He's no trouble really, and you couldn't have managed everything without help, especially when I've been working.'

'I suppose you're right.' He ran his fingers up and down her bare arm. 'But it's good to be on our own for once.'

'Yes, it's lovely.' She sighed happily. 'It will soon be the summer holidays and the end of my year's teaching practice.'

'I know. You enjoy teaching your young pupils, don't you, Meggie?'

'I do, but, Steven, I'd enjoy working beside you every day even more.'

'Would you? Do you mean that Meggie? Teaching must be so much easier. I didn't think you would want to give it up now you've started, especially when I see how much you enjoy it.'

'I'd give it up any day so long as I know you want me here beside you.'

'Oh, Meggie, you must know how much I miss you when you're away all day, but I know that's selfish of me, especially when you're so good at your work and so interested in what you do.'

'It would be even better being beside you and having children of our own.' She sat up and looked into his face. 'What would you say to us having a baby, Steven?'

'It would be wonderful, our very own child and you at home all day looking after her instead of being at school.'

'It might be a "him", a wee boy, just like you were,' Megan said softly.

'Maybe we could have one of each then?'

'Starting now?'

'You mean right here and now? Underneath the willow tree?'

'Of course.' She laughed up at him, her green eyes sparkling.

'Oh, you wanton woman, Megan Caraford, I love you more than I can say.'

It was quite a while before they sat up and Megan confessed.

'We're already expecting our first child, Steven,' she said gently.

'We are?' He looked startled. 'How ever could that happen?'

Megan began to laugh. 'How do you suppose such things happen?'

'B-but you know what I mean ... I- I thought ... Are you sure, Megan? Do you feel all right?'

'Yes, and yes, so don't start fussing. My mother carried on helping with the milking almost until Sam and I were born. Are you pleased?'

'Am I pleased indeed! I'm the luckiest man on earth.' He drew her into his arms and kissed her tenderly.